The Language of Dreams

MARION EHRENBERG

◆ FriesenPress

One Printers Way
Altona, MB R0G 0B0
Canada

www.friesenpress.com

Copyright © 2022 by Marion Felix Ehrenberg
First Edition — 2022

The Language of Dreams

Contact:
Email: marion.ehrenberg.author@gmail.com
Website: https://marionehrenberg.com

All rights reserved.

This is a work of fiction. Names, characters, businesses, places, events, locales, and incidents are either the products of the author's imagination or used in a fictitious manner. Any resemblance to actual persons, living or dead, or actual events is purely coincidental.

No part of this publication may be reproduced in any form, or by any means, electronic or mechanical, including photocopying, recording, or any information browsing, storage, or retrieval system, without permission in writing from FriesenPress.

ISBN
978-1-03-914348-7 (Hardcover)
978-1-03-914347-0 (Paperback)
978-1-03-914349-4 (eBook)

1. Fiction, Psychological

Distributed to the trade by The Ingram Book Company

Marion Ehrenberg's novel will resonate with those who also love Irv Yalom's great fiction. It is a psychological portrait of two intriguing women who are thrown together in a therapy room and emerge transformed. This is a story worthy of television series. We want to stay in the world of our protagonist, the therapist, and see what she does next.

—Wendy Goldman Rohm, NYT Best Selling Author
& Internationally Recognized Journalist

Ehrenberg's handling of the psychoanalysis process ... is expert and delicate ... this is a strong character study about how people react when backed into a corner ... A complex ... engaging novel about temptation and ethical quandaries.

—*Kirkus Reviews*

The Language of Dreams is a unique story, artfully told ... a page-turner ... a psychological thriller ... breathtaking ...

—Aliss Terrell, American writer, musician, filmmaker, Paris, France

The characters were vivid, the plot was twisty and engaging, and there were no dull moments. The clinical part was dead-on and will ring true with many psychotherapy practitioners, who will find themselves struggling with the same issues as the protagonist.

—Dr. James Marcia, Professor & Master Psychotherapist

PART I:
Summer's End

ONE

*N*othing *in this room will change my mind.* Clare repeated this thought like a mantra as she scanned the room. It was irksome to find such unexpected beauty in a place Clare had dreaded ever since that cranky old judge ordered her to see a shrink. There was a rug in her favourite palette of crimson and cerulean blues on the shiny wood floor. Clare slipped her tanned feet out of her flip-flops and ran them over its rugged texture, leaving traces of sand to mark her disrespect. She recognized the print of Raeburn's *Little Girl* from her art history class, a child smiling innocently and holding a bouquet of wildflowers in her chubby arms. Naïve kid: she was up for disappointment. Clare's meanness backfired, as it often did; when she looked again into the child's imploring eyes, she saw a sadness that stung in her own.

Under other circumstances, Clare would have enjoyed a room filled with beautiful old stuff that smelled like her grandmother's house. Not today. Dimmed lights, Zen music, none of it would trick her into letting down her guard and spilling her guts to a complete stranger. Much too scary. Clare's eyes settled on the fancy nameplate fastened to the door at the far end of the waiting room. Dr. Avery Frontiera, Psychologist. The antique clock on the coffee table said two fifty-six; four minutes until the appointment time.

A wave of breathlessness and nausea suddenly overwhelmed Clare. She swallowed hard and reminded herself that she was here by choice, to avoid even more unattractive options. Two fifty-eight.

CHAPTER ONE

She had this under control and told herself she was nothing like the other pathetic people who chose to come here. She was here only to go through the motions.

At the periphery of her vision, Clare noticed a collection of figurines on the cherry wood bookcase beside her. She reached for one, her eyes never leaving the closed door, and slipped it into the pocket of her roomy skirt. Two fifty-nine. The wave of nerves reached its crest, now feeling more like excitement, and then ebbed away, leaving a flood of soft wetness between her legs. Her fingertips traced the precise, naked features of the young man carved from white Italian marble resting in the folds of her pocket. The weight of the new possession on her thigh was cool and strangely comforting.

Clare was now ready for the door to open.

Avery Frontiera sat in her antique armchair, head bent over the referral letter describing her new client. Her name was Clare Thomas Lane. She was a twenty-two-year-old fine arts student, adopted at age five following the death of her biological mother; biological father unknown; normal development; good student; no history of mental health problems. A psychiatric assessment report had been completed at the request of Clare's lawyer.

With time running short, Avery skimmed through the documents. The judge had endorsed the psychiatrist's recommendation for "four to six months of intensive psychotherapy at the treating psychologist's discretion so that this otherwise talented young woman can overcome the disturbing pattern of shoplifting and petty theft that has repeatedly brought her to the attention of the courts." Avery sighed. She'd accepted the referral because she knew Clare's lawyer; he'd caught her off guard on the telephone and left her with a more positive impression of the circumstances than what she now saw in the paperwork. She should have just said no, as she taught her clients, but it was too late for that now. Avery took a deep breath and resigned herself to a therapy relationship that, at best, would be challenging, and, at worst, would fail.

This afternoon, however, her new client Clare was the least of Avery's worries. Her real anguish lay buried by paper towel at the bottom of the trash can in her office bathroom. She was only one day late, but against her better judgment had rushed out on her lunch hour to buy a package of pregnancy tests. Once again, no pink lines, no signs of life—not on the first test or the second one she'd used in desperation—just clear-cut negatives on the disappointing pieces of plastic.

How had her life come to a point where she'd rush around for a pregnancy test in the middle of the day? Avery felt so steady, so confident in most ways. She still loved her job and was good at it; many of her therapist friends had lost their passion and complained about feeling burnt out. Tonight, she'd talk to Roland about starting the adoption process while they kept trying for pregnancy; that seemed like a better plan and she was pretty sure that, as a couple, they'd be solid candidates for adoption.

Her new client, Clare, was going to be a challenge, but she was up for it. Avery smoothed her skirt as she stood up, then opened the door to her waiting room. A slim, young woman slouched in the armchair, her wavy long hair a half-curtain over her face as she bent over a book on her lap. Eventually, her chin tilted upward and the curtain parted to reveal unblinking, grey-green eyes and a mouth set in defiance. For a split second, Avery saw a strangely familiar sadness flash in the young woman's eyes.

"Please, come in."

Clare looked up at her court-appointed psychologist. Just as Clare had anticipated: boring, middle-aged, annoying shrink smile, with her right hand *so caringly* outstretched. Did she think she was inviting a child to come in from the playground for milk and

CHAPTER ONE

cookies? This doctor was so predictable, so condescending. She had this completely under control, Clare told herself. She stood up from the armchair with ostentatious effort, grabbed her keys in one hand, and kept her other hand entertained with the little, white Italian man in her pocket.

Clare offered a half-hearted smile, but ignored the extended hand as she made her way into the inner office and flopped down on the love seat. Its spicy leather scent brought back a sickening memory of the last time she had sat on a similar style of sofa, unfortunately, with the pudgy arm of a middle-aged art dealer around her. His hand had edged toward her breast before he signed off on buying the first painting Clare had ever sold. Clare dismissed the uncomfortable feelings pooling in her gut and told herself he was just another disgusting man she'd used for her own purposes. She tossed her book onto the coffee table. Satisfied with her entrance, she sat back with arms crossed to study the doctor.

Frontiera didn't appear offended. She was just sitting there, appearing calm, even kind, but much too passive for Clare's liking. The shrink started to speak, something about some form that had to be signed, but Clare muted the sound of the doctor's voice and continued to watch her. *Screenshot*: Marginally attractive woman in her forties. Lines around her eyes and mouth, shapeless teal blouse, uninteresting tan-coloured skirt falling midway down her calves. Her forelegs were more defined than expected, like those of a ballet dancer, an aging ballerina past her prime. Married? Yes, there's the ring. Adventurous in bed? she mused. Hardly, Clare determined, and put on a full smirk. Did she have children? Not sure, there were no give-away framed photographs. It felt unfair and unnerving that the doctor had read a file of information about her, but Clare knew nothing about the doctor. In her head, she knew that it had to be this way, but the looming mistrust that came over her felt overwhelming. Suddenly fragments of the doctor's annoying monologue were breaking through: … I'll send a progress report to the court … the sessions will be billed to your lawyer …

This mention of court and her lawyer annoyed Clare.

"How much do you charge?" *In it for the money?* Why else would the doctor agree to see someone who didn't want to be there?

"I charge two hundred dollars for each one-hour session, Clare," the middle-aged shrink responded. She didn't look the least bit guilty.

"How'd you decide that?" Clare barked. Maybe one more insulting question would get under the *good doctor's* skin. Clare didn't care about the money at all, as her adoptive parents were willing to pay whatever cost. They were only too eager to help their beloved daughter whose *little problem* with kleptomania just had to be the result of being an adopted child.

The do-gooder just sat there, saying nothing. Without reading a word, Clare signed the consent form that Frontiera had placed on the coffee table in front of her.

"Clare, I've read the report the court psychiatrist wrote and I see why the judge thought you should come to see me. What I'd like to hear about is your understanding of why you're here. What do you think about all this?"

Clare crossed her arms over her chest before she spoke.

"I'm here because I'm a thief. But the judge thinks I can be redeemed by you. Supposedly that's worth doing because of *the potential of my artistic talent.*" She placed the dramatic emphasis of two-fingered quotation marks around the last two words. "Oh yes, and what do I think about all this? Hmm, let's see. I don't buy any of it. But since I'd rather not see the inside of a jail cell, here I am, chatting with you."

Clare leaned back on the couch, feeling quite satisfied as she put on her best sarcastic smile. What would the shrink do next? *Screenshot Number Two*: The doctor was leaning forward, her eyes appearing genuinely interested, her arms resting in her lap. Clare

5

CHAPTER ONE

scanned for signs of irritation, aversion, or rejection. None detected. Confused, Clare reached inside her pocket for the figurine.

"A thief. What do you steal?"

"I usually steal ... I don't know ... just, kind of beautiful stuff. It's too hard to explain," Clare stumbled. She thought about the shimmer of the antique emerald earrings; the shiny charcoal slip with the deep purple lace and satiny feel; gold leaf stencils and other expensive art supplies; figurines like the one in her pocket.

"What is it you feel about these beautiful things?"

They move me, Clare thought, *they make me hungry and weak and sad. I don't know; I just need them. Somehow ... they take the edge off of all that longing ... for her.*

"I don't feel anything about them. I just want them," Clare said, bracing for another possibly disturbing question.

"Perhaps the next time you're drawn to some beautiful object, notice the sensations you experience," the doctor suggested with an encouraging smile.

Four thirty-eight. Twenty more minutes of this doctor trying to screw with her head. Clare felt her eyelids fluttering as she rolled her eyes up to somewhere close to the ceiling. She realized at this moment that eye rolls were gestures she'd left behind with her teens, and it suddenly bothered her that her presentation was anything less than the savvy young woman she wished to portray.

"Ok, I guess that's worth considering," the savvy one said.

"In the time we've left together today, Clare, I'd like to hear more about you and your life. I understand you're studying fine arts, but I know little else about you."

She had no idea why, but Clare suddenly felt a softening within herself, a feeling somewhere between relief and gratitude, as if she'd just been let off the hook. She dismissed this confusing feeling and went on to sketch herself as a confident young woman. She reassured herself that she knew exactly who she was and wouldn't bend to the doctor's annoying attempts to make a dent in her personality. Clare explained that she was a third-year student interested in multi-media abstract realism paintings, sculpture, and photography. By choice, and *not* because she doesn't get along with other people, she lived by herself in a studio apartment overlooking a coffee shop not far from the campus. *Of course,* as a feminist, she preferred to be on her own and saw men casually.

And what about your family? Dr. Frontiera prompted.

Her parents—"adoptive," she emphasized, "not real parents; don't have any of those"—visited her about once a month for lunch or dinner, but Clare was too busy these days to go and see them because it involved a two-hour bus ride—well, except for at Christmas and, you know, other commercialized, *family* holidays.

At this moment, an image of her adoptive parents, Molly and Jim, hugging Clare and her new teddy bear on that Christmas morning when she was seven filtered through her mind and caught in her throat. How coldly she had described her parents. What was wrong with her? They'd been there for her no matter what. She did love them, but she also saw them as weak for letting her get away with everything.

What else did she want to say about herself? She ate whatever she pleased, unworried about her weight. Clare pointed to her feminist book on the doctor's coffee table and took a heady spin into the importance of showing *real* women's bodies in her art. *Even those of amateur dancers past their prime,* Clare thought, surprising even herself with the depth of her nastiness. Health habits, including smoking, were on the doctor's typical list of shrink questions. No, not cigarettes, but a joint at a party or sitting on her balcony; she could always get into that. She loved drinking wine, especially smooth, Spanish red. Just to be clear, that wasn't something she was considering giving up or would even be willing to talk about again. She liked whatever gave her pleasure and had no interest in social conventions or rules of any kind.

CHAPTER ONE

Dr. Frontiera listened, nodding and taking notes. The doctor appeared satisfied to have extracted, come to think of it, much more information than Clare had expected to release. It was four forty-seven, but Frontiera wasn't quite done with her yet.

"And when do you feel happiest, Clare?" she asked.

Didn't therapists only ask about misery and mistakes?

"Making art, on a good day when it's just kind of flowing out of me," Clare said truthfully. Four fifty. "And, of course, when I'm stealing *objects of beauty*," she added, proud of her boldness.

The doctor smiled ever so slightly. "We're coming to the end of our time together. Do you have any more classes today?"

"Actually, my sculpting class is on Friday evenings," Clare said, wondering why, at this very moment, she was almost liking this doctor.

"I hope you enjoy your class, Clare. Let me take a quick look in my appointment book," the doctor said, flipping through its pages. "Now that we've met for the first time, I see that I have a weekly session available ... not on a Friday, like today, but on ... Wednesdays at four. Can we make that our regular time?"

Regular time? How did this happen when she was against regular anything? The fleeting feeling of connection with the doctor drowned in Clare's irritation.

"I suppose that'll work, but sometimes stuff will come up and I won't be able to make it," Clare snapped.

She stood up abruptly and, with a moment's hesitation, plucked her appointment card from the doctor's outstretched hand and put it in her pocket. Suddenly, another wave of nausea like she had felt in the waiting room overcame her. Clare covered her mouth with her hand and caught sight of a door standing ajar near the back of the therapy room.

"I'm just going to use your washroom before I go," Clare said, as she rushed in that direction.

"There's a public washroom …" Clare heard the doctor saying as she closed the private washroom door behind her.

Clare turned on the water, pressed her hands onto the countertop, and leaned over the sink to catch her breath. When the panic gave way, Clare washed her face and gulped water from her cupped hands. She pulled a paper towel from the dispenser and blotted her face dry in front of the mirror. The mirror was mounted on the front of what looked like a medicine cabinet. *Hmm.* What might the good doctor keep in her medicine cabinet? Maybe she was on medication to handle her own mental health? Yes, she was a thief *and* a snoop, Clare thought, as she watched a smirk coming over her face in the mirror's reflection.

Clare flushed the toilet to create a sound barrier and opened the medicine cabinet as quietly as possible. Lipstick, hand lotion, a disappointing bottle of Aspirin, some extra toilet paper rolls … *But look at this*, she thought triumphantly: a package of pregnancy tests, same brand as she kept in her bathroom drawer at home. The toilet had finished flushing and Clare turned on the water again. Dr. Frontiera would think her new client very conscientious about washing her hands, she chuckled to herself. Clare carefully opened the pregnancy test package to find two of the three tests missing. She reclosed the package, placed it exactly where she found it on the shelf, and shut the medicine cabinet door. Her violation of the doctor's privacy was almost complete.

Clare sat down on the toilet seat and pulled the trash can onto her lap. She shook the container until the paper towels fell to one side and the familiar shapes of the two plastic tabs were revealed on the bottom. She's not pregnant, times two—the result Clare was always relieved to find with a single test—but judging from the doctor's age, probably not the result she was looking for. Checking for pregnancy during the workday, not once, but twice, after the first test didn't give her the answer she wanted, must mean she's desperate

9

CHAPTER ONE

for a baby. *Maybe Frontiera's one of those professional women who looks like she has everything, but is missing what she really wants?*

It felt satisfying, reassuring even, to have some personal scoop about this psychologist who was going to report to the judge after she was finished screwing with Clare. The anger about this unfairness flared up again. Clare took some tissues from the Kleenex box and used these to pull the two pregnancy tests from the trash can and place them neatly side by side beside the sink; the doctor would be sure to find them on her next visit to her *private* washroom. Frontiera should know what she was up against.

Clare threw out the Kleenex, hurriedly washed her hands, and opened the door to find Dr. Frontiera standing in front of it, looking alarmed.

"Clare, are you alright? I was about to knock and ask if you're ok."

"I'm *so* much better now, *thank you, Doctor*," Clare said, feeling that smirk spreading over her face again. "But I'd better hurry on out of here and get to my sculpting."

Clare grabbed her things and rushed to the door of the waiting room, where she saw a sad-looking man sitting in the armchair. Clare glanced at the washroom key hanging from the hook near the door with a sign pointing to the public washrooms down the hall outside the office suites. These were exactly the kind of instructions Clare tended to overlook—or, truth be told, to happily ignore.

Clare's unusually long stay in the washroom set into motion a string of worries for Avery as the slow minutes passed. Perhaps she was throwing up because of a panic attack and running the water to hide the sound; or maybe she'd fainted because of some medical condition that Avery didn't know about yet? At what point should she knock on the door and offer to call for help? When Clare finally stepped out of the bathroom, an indelible smirk on her face, Avery's concerns evaporated and left her with an uneasy feeling that she'd been had. Without another word, Clare turned her back and hurried out of the office, leaving the door to the waiting room wide open. Avery's next client was already sitting there.

"I'll be with you shortly, Paul," Avery said, managing a weak smile before retreating to her office and closing the door to the waiting room.

Avery pressed her back against the door and took a deep breath. Gone was the sense of accomplishment she'd felt about the first session with Clare unfolding much better than anticipated. Avery's cheeks warmed and a sick feeling rose up from her stomach as she crossed the room and pushed open the bathroom door. The light was still on. Avery gasped when she saw the two plastic tabs sitting on the countertop. She felt outside her body as she slammed the door and locked it. As if in a trance, Avery smoothed her skirt one more time as she crossed the room and opened the door to the waiting room to see her last client of the day.

TWO

Forty-eight-year-old Roland Frontiera stood in the kitchen pouring himself a generous Jameson's on ice. He caught his reflection in the window. That was all the encouragement he needed to lift an eyebrow and break out his winning smile. "*Slainté!*" he said out loud as he raised his glass. He'd resurrected this local expression of cheers in the old-world pubs he'd finally come back to in County Clare. Before this trip, Irish pubbing had been a faint memory left from his years abroad as a university student. Roland had become a little more convincing at saying *slainté* each time he used the expression.

He'd pretty well nailed it by the time he said *slainté* to the attractive Irish cashier at Shannon Airport's duty-free store, where he bought his take-home bottle of the good stuff. "J. Jameson & Sons, Triple Distilled Irish Whiskey since 1790," he'd read out from the label like the clever professor he thought might appeal to her. "Who are we to argue with that, *Annalivia?*" Roland had leaned in closely to where the blushing young woman was trapped in the cashier's booth to read the embroidered writing on the pocket of her pretty white blouse. In the meantime, Avery was sitting at the gate, wrapped up in her book. Harmless flirting was a natural part of the Irish culture, he'd told himself, especially when his wife wasn't looking.

The arrangement with Avery busy at her conference in Ennis had been ideal, allowing him to do his own kind of exploration during the day; he zigzagged from pub to pub and other old haunts from his

CHAPTER TWO

university days at the National University of Ireland in Galway. The horizontal rains and traffic stopped by sheep crossing the road only made him feel more at home.

Roland swallowed another mouthful of whiskey as he pictured Avery sitting across from him at Poet's Corner Bar in the evenings with her intelligent eyes and natural elegance, telling him what she had learned about *Jungian dream analysis*, whatever that was. With this pleasant image of his perfect wife before him, Roland uttered another *slainté*, drank down what was left of the good Irish stuff, and placed his glass in the dishwasher. He uncorked the bottle of merlot, a favourite of Avery's that he had picked up on his way home, and set it and two glasses on the countertop. *Just let it breathe*, he thought. He swept up a dishcloth hanging from the sink and opened the stained-glass French doors leading from the kitchen out onto the terrace, where he wiped down the wrought-iron table and chairs. He arranged a casual setting for two on the patio table. The assortment of sushi, seaweed salad, and tempura he'd picked up at Kyota Korners next door to his office, Frontiera and Sons Financial, was perfect for a Friday evening.

Roland was the master of easy, skating on the surface and organizing all aspects of his life to simulate a confident baseball player's slow, comfortable slide into home base with the sounds of the cheering audience in his mind.

THREE

"Ave? Up here, Honey," she heard Roland calling down the stairs as she opened the front door. "I've got dinner going on for you."

The Frontieras' home, a classic in the coastline community of La Jolla, was layered up and down the side of a cliff overlooking the beach. Avery set her soft-sided briefcase on the mahogany bench in the front hall, realizing only now that she hadn't eaten since breakfast. *That's what happens when you spend your lunch hour buying pregnancy tests and upsetting yourself before seeing a full afternoon of patients*, she chastised herself. Glancing up the Mediterranean staircase to the landing, she saw the gentle swing of the grandfather clock's pendulum; it was seven thirty. Her legs felt leaden by the time she reached the landing.

"Hi," was all she managed before tears filled her eyes.

"What's wrong?"

She pulled out the pregnancy tests and showed him.

"Avey baby, come here." He wrapped her in his arms. "We've been through this so many times. We don't have to do this anymore; we're good just the two of us."

"I know it's hard on both of us, but I really do want us to have the baby we always wanted. So I was thinking … maybe we should get started on adoption while we keep trying?" As Avery nuzzled her damp face into Roland's shoulder, she felt his body tensing. He gave

CHAPTER THREE

her one more perfunctory squeeze before he extracted himself and turned to walk away.

"Time to eat" were his only words, as she saw his back disappearing into the kitchen.

Avery stood frozen, then hugged her shoulders for warmth.

The night unfolded in a series of smudged images: Roland's larger-than-life face, his exaggerated expressions as he told her about his financial manoeuvres of the day in an attempt to cover silence. They poured red wine into glasses and gulped in desperation. Finally, they dropped their clothes to the floor and sank into opposite sides of their king-sized bed. Roland rolled over to face his wife and cup her cheeks in his hands. With the bedroom illuminated only faintly by the nightlight, it was difficult for Avery to make out the expression on his face. She felt somewhere between hopeful and scared.

"Avey, I'm sorry, I love you, but I don't want a baby. I could see how upset you were earlier, so I didn't want to say anything more right then. I've been thinking about it a lot, and I just don't want to keep trying. I like things the way they are, and I don't want someone else's kid, either. I've tried to wrap my mind around this, but it's not working."

"What are you talking about, Roland? I can't believe you're saying this to me," Avery said, imploring the shadowy face of her husband.

"Listen, I never really wanted a baby in the same way that you do—I think you're just naturally much more cut out to be a parent than I am—but I kind of tried to go along with it to make you happy. I really did try. Look, we're both getting older, right? Just you and me; it's perfect. No more pregnancy tests and sad eyes. Think about it: the life that we have doesn't get better."

Roland's words toppled over Avery like a cascade of boulders in a rockslide. Avery felt she had no choice but to dive for cover somewhere deep inside of herself. No more words. She used her last bit of energy to remove Roland's hands from her face and roll away from him. He offered no resistance and no support; he just let her go. She wrapped herself around her body pillow and allowed the swell of red wine to transport her.

Avery felt herself unfolding from the tense, crumpled figure on her bed and ... *drifting into lightness and calm ... floating weightless in pale yellow and cottony soft summer dress; a silent hovercraft just over the cool grass underneath the apple tree at her grandmother's farm. Arms outstretched, warmed by an August sun in turquoise skies, she spirals in slow circles until she lands softly on her back on a bed of grass and mossy softness. She hears a woman's voice singing to the strum of her guitar. The apple tree's leaves are falling, encircling each other in a slow and whimsical dance as they near the ground; some land on her gently. Dazed by warmth and comfort, Avery is enveloped in a sense of abundance, her belly protruding as she touches it. Elated with the discovery of her pregnancy, she looks up, and up further still, to the turquoise skies painted with cottony clouds. She squints at the figure of a young woman sitting on a high branch of the tree, outlined against the backdrop of the sun. As Avery's eyes adjust to the light, she's shocked to see beautiful Clare, singing softly as she flicks another leaf into the air. The leaf twirls in slow motion, morphing from summer's sweet green to plastic white tab of a pregnancy test to white bullet accelerating straight toward Avery's belly. Immobilized by terror, Avery can't move or scream the words inside her head*: Don't kill my baby!

Avery awoke as if an electric shock had snapped her into a sitting position. Her heart thudded against her breastbone. Was she having a heart attack? Bathed in perspiration, she looked down to see her fingers digging into her flat abdomen. Roland snored beside her, a bystander who didn't share her dreams. He was not the kind of husband she could wake up and tell her crazy dreams, who would let her fall back asleep in the safety of his arms.

FOUR

Here I go again, Avery thought as she walked down the hall of the Mercy Medical Building. It had been years since she was here. *Dr. Samuel Mahler, Psychoanalyst.* She took a seat on the charcoal-coloured couch. On the wall, a certificate showed a Ph.D. in Clinical Psychology from New York's Stony Brook University. Framed in black, it had yellowed so much she struggled to make out the date. Some month in 1975? Dr. Mahler had told her about his two years as a psychology resident, learning psychodynamic therapy at the Karl Menninger Clinic in Topeka, Kansas, of all places. He had a habit of veering off topic, especially once he was no longer just her therapist but also a mentor, during her years of training as a psychologist. Today, she needed every second of his attention.

Beside the tall, grey filing cabinet, its paint worn around the handles by countless openings of drawers, Avery noticed a handwritten sign taped above the water dispenser (new since her last appointment three years ago): "Please *[underlined twice]* put your empty cups in the trash below *[arrow pointing downward].* Thank you." The rug beneath Avery's feet was worn thin from many years of restless feet. The room smelled of English breakfast tea, leather shoes, and a hint of Dr. Mahler's Old Spice aftershave.

This comforting aroma relaxed Avery's body into the couch, but a sudden punch of anxiety hit her in the gut: how could she explain the absolute mess she had created by the end of her first session with

CHAPTER FOUR

Clare? With Clare's second appointment tomorrow, she was grateful Dr. Mahler had agreed to see her on such short notice. But Clare wasn't the only reason. Avery felt tears welling up in her eyes. *I don't want to sit alone in my pain. Thank God for Dr. Mahler.* It occurred to her that Roland had no idea where she was, and she felt equally disconnected from his life.

At exactly two o'clock, Dr. Mahler opened the door of his office. He stood there, as always, with his white shirt sleeves rolled up to just above the elbows, revealing crepey, fine-freckled skin on his arms. His milk-white hair was mussed from his habit of running his hands through it, and outdated round silver spectacles perched on his nose. Dr. Mahler stood with one hand on his hip, narrowing his eyes as if to make out the current emotional state of his patient. His face melted into a warm compassionate smile; Avery probably didn't look like she was doing so well.

"Avery, come … come inside and sit down." He beckoned her to the worn leather couch, sat down across from her, and leaned forward with his elbows on his knees, arms loosely crossed, and weathered old hands dangling. "Go ahead: just tell me the whole story."

And she did. In the only place where this was possible, Avery released the latch of her well-contained, finely edited self. It all poured out of her. She spoke freely, quickly, not just about what happened in her session with her defiant new client, Clare, but also of her pregnancy tests, and then the dream, which left no question in Avery's mind that she needed help.

"There it is, the whole big mess, Dr. Mahler, so here I am." Avery saw him nod ever so slightly.

"And there's more?" Dr. Mahler raised his thick white eyebrows above the silver-rimmed spectacles.

This recognition that there was more to the story—and of course there was—left Avery feeling understood at last. She confessed her intense disappointment about Roland's reaction to yet another missed pregnancy, her rage at his breaking the promise that they would have a baby together—"naturally, or with help, or through adoption, somehow—you know what I mean, Dr. Mahler; where there's a will there's a way." And Roland's admission that he had never even wanted a baby and still didn't!

"And what am I left with, Dr. Mahler?" Tears welled up in her eyes, blurring her view of Dr. Mahler's face.

"And what *are* you left with now, Avery?" Dr. Mahler asked.

"Just this cold distance between me and Roland. We both walk on eggshells around each other. I feel I can't talk to him anymore. I'm in pain all the time. I feel alone … alone all over again." It was such a relief to speak the truth out loud.

"Again?" Dr. Mahler asked.

She felt herself smiling knowingly. She would've asked the exact same question if she were sitting in his chair. Dr. Mahler didn't return her smile. He waited, still leaning forward, his body language encouraging Avery to stay with her deeper thoughts and not wiggle away.

Avery shed the momentary foothold she'd found in her professional self. Instead, she was six, wearing her favourite yellow sundress with tiny pink polka dots; she stood on the beach outside her parents' home, holding her sand pail tightly in one hand, her other hand cupped over her eyes, as she watched her brother Sebastian and his ten-year-old friend tunnel out the moat for their sandcastle. Avery felt her mouth turn downward with disappointment: her brother was playing with someone else. She'd felt completely alone, too frozen by sadness to turn around and go back into the house. But just then, Sebastian looked up from his moat and smiled at her. She could see his summer-brown face. He yelled out, so that Avery could hear him, "Hey! Finn, look, it's Avery coming out of the house. Perfect, she's got her pail and her shovel. We're gonna need all the help we can get, and my little sis is an expert at finding the shells and sticks we need."

CHAPTER FOUR

She remembered her brother's words exactly. She'd run the fastest run her little body could manage, losing both flip-flops along the way to get to where the big boys were at work. She fought to hold on to the image of her brother, but instead, sadness began to pool, drowning the last of her memories.

"Avery, I think I know where you are right now," Dr. Mahler said, "Please, try to tell me if your marriage is now that unbearable loneliness you felt in your childhood, all over again?"

Avery's mind returned to a vicious fight her parents had when she was sixteen. They argued over whose fault it had been that Sebastian had taken his life. Dr. Mahler knew this story, of course, but despite all the work they'd done together on these memories and what they meant now, Avery was still physically startled as she remembered her father slamming the front door so hard that the mirror in the front hall shattered on the floor. *Seven more years of bad luck*, she'd thought to herself that day, as she hugged her knees on Sebastian's empty bed. On that day, her mother had slammed the door in her own way, retreating into impenetrable grief and depression, busying herself with studying Sebastian's letters for clues. She examined his clothes, the pictures he chose to frame, anything at all, but never noticed that Avery was grieving, too, and that she probably knew her brother better than anyone.

Avery looked up at Dr. Mahler before she spoke.

"I do feel the same loneliness I felt when Sebastian died, and I guess my parents kind of died, too. But I think with Roland, it's been building up for a long time. What happened on the weekend was just so crystal clear, I couldn't ignore it anymore. I so want the family I lost when Sebastian died and my mother disappeared. I wanted all that with Roland."

"Avery, I'm very sorry for all that pain coming from your childhood and showing up again with Roland. I feel for you, dear Avery."

Dr. Mahler paused, looked into her eyes, his head nodding ever so slightly. "But we aren't going to figure all of that out overnight, are we?"

Avery noticed that he pushed his shirtsleeves just a little higher up his arms before he continued.

"We have twenty-four minutes left together today. You see your fiery client, Clare, tomorrow. So, let's analyze together. You're having a classic countertransference reaction to your new client, at the very least because she's touching the nerve of your unfulfilled desire to have a baby. It was foolish to bring these plastic things, whatever you like to call them, into your office, much too emotional for your workday, but what's done is done and I'm sure you won't be doing that again. We know you'll never leave your private bathroom unlocked, so that's not something we need to go over."

Avery shook her head, feeling a bit like an obedient school child. She saw the familiar glint in Dr. Mahler's eyes, and she knew where they were going next.

"Now, the dream you had was actually *exquisite*. We can use this material. We see the obvious symbolization of fertility in the fruit tree where Clare's sitting—in your case, a conflicted fertility. Even an apple tree; it's really quite perfect." Dr. Mahler was excited now; a strand of white hair had sprung out of place over his forehead. Avery began to wonder whether she would be permitted to participate in the dream analysis, but she also knew that Dr. Mahler was in time-efficiency mode. So far, he was right on.

"So, the apple tree. The original apple tree, we'd have to locate in Adam and Eve's garden." Avery felt sceptical about relocating her grandmother's tree, but ok, he was the guru of dream interpretation.

"I think in this case, it may be more about good and evil, rather than original sin. So we see Clare up in the tree; you can't quite make her out, but she's singing and playing her guitar; it's all really lovely at first. You're floating ... and pregnant and safe. Then it changes when Clare sends you a nasty bullet that kills the baby you hoped for. Is she good or evil? Friend or foe?" Dr. Mahler opened his hands in unspoken question.

Avery's furrowed brow didn't stop Dr. Mahler.

"That's what your dream is about, Avery. Because you were unexpectedly exposed to, let's face it, a very challenging, young, *probably fertile* client, in a place that's so tender in your heart. And you're even more vulnerable and alone because your husband doesn't want to have a baby with you; we'll get to this in later sessions. So you're trying to decide, is this person who has come into your professional life, snooped around in your bathroom, and unearthed a vulnerable topic for you, is she a good person or a bad person?"

As always, Dr. Mahler's insights were helpful. A *normal* psychoanalyst would let her do about ninety-five percent of the talking, but that would mean it would take at least another year for Avery to figure out what to do with Clare. *Better this way*, she thought, as she prepared to speak.

"Neither, Dr. Mahler," Avery said, "Clare's neither good nor bad, not friend or foe, to me personally. You're right, of course: she's just a client who acted out her issues in my bathroom … Oh God, I still can't believe I had such poor judgment …" Avery started her next tirade of self-recrimination. Dr. Mahler waved his hand: there was no time to spare for self-indulgent reproach. She guessed he thought she could do that later at home if she still felt the urge.

"Exactly, Avery. You have your personal problems about whether you're going to be able to save your marriage and what you'll do about having a baby. This has absolutely nothing to do with Clare. Now, what do you think you need to do to correct this situation in your next session?" He glanced at the clock, possibly of 1970s vintage, on the shelf above her.

"Now that I better understand what happened," Avery said, feeling a surge of confidence rise up in her chest. "I have to deal with the situation head-on. I need to be honest with Clare about what happened, admitting it was my mistake to leave my bathroom door unlocked but not offering any further information about my personal life. Just because I erred by bringing my personal business to my office, doesn't mean my life is now open for discussion. This will be the best way to repair the therapist-client boundary. Then I need to move on to assist Clare to the best of my abilities, keeping the boundaries clear and predictable for her. If that's not possible for some reason, for me or for Clare, then I need to help her to find another qualified psychologist." Avery felt her professional self resurfacing; the little girl standing on the beach disappeared deep into her psyche.

Dr. Mahler looked satisfied with her response. It was two forty-seven. There was no doubt her analyst would use the remaining three minutes of the classic fifty-minute hour.

"Yes, that's about right, I think, for now. But I think you also need to take care of the personal business that's come up *again*—but, in fairness, also in a different way at this phase in your life—with Roland and the baby you want. I can see your pain and I am here to help you."

All true, she thought, but before she could respond, he spoke again.

"Let's make this our regular time. We could beat around the bush with our schedules, but this is the only spot I have available. This is my thinking time, but I will think instead while I'm eating my sandwich."

"Thank you so much, Dr. Mahler. I'll see you next week."

Avery got up to leave. It was two forty-nine, but Dr. Mahler stood up to express one final thought.

"It was actually an excellent, rich dream you brought in today. So much material for us to work with."

For us, or for you, Dr. Mahler? she wondered. He was right that the dream had meaning and helped them move forward. She felt much better, come to think of it.

"And Avery, other than the unfortunate pregnancy test incident, it sounded like a very good start with your new client. In any case, it's two fifty, so we'd better say good-bye. I hope you're sticking to the fifty-minute hour. It all starts to go downhill when we don't preserve our boundaries and keep that space for our notes and thinking time."

Dr. Mahler had now wandered out to the waiting room to pull a file from the cabinet.

"I try, Dr. Mahler. See you next week. Wish me luck for tomorrow."

"Luck has very little to do with it, my dear Avery. Coincidence? Maybe a little more." He walked back into his office and closed the door.

FIVE

"*Cinq, six, sept, huit* ... and uu-up and turn ... *encore un fois, les rondes-des-jambes,*" Madame Paloma dictated. She was perfectly poised in first position, facing the dutiful adult ballet disciples assembled before her. Clad in Lulelemon and other expensive dancewear, they moved precisely in unison. All seemed perfectly content, even enthusiastic, to pay good money for being bossed, criticized, and, on the rare occasion, praised. The mirrored wall to which the ballet barre was attached wasn't just there for dancers to self-correct their physical form; it served as a side-view, rear-view, and 360-degree tool for Madame Paloma's scrutiny. She stood with one hand resting on her hip, an invisible baton in the other, delicately balanced between manicured thumb and index finger to emphasize the graceful but regimented tempo of each movement.

Avery was still thinking about her afternoon appointment with Dr. Mahler. She inhaled deeply, closed her eyes, and exhaled as she *pliéd*. It was all about letting everything else go and just focusing on the here and now of thighs melting into a perfectly articulated, diamond-shaped form. From a deep thigh bend, her muscles found the exact electric moment at which to shoot upward; Avery rose onto her toes in one tall motion, arms raised in fifth position above her head. Upstretched, she gracefully pivoted to face in the other direction. Her left hand reached for the security of the barre and found it. *Brossez les pieds,* she thought to herself, as her right foot brushed forward, extended *en pointe,* then traced the invisible semi-circle on the smooth surface of the wooden floor. Avery made a mental note of how good this moment felt at the end of a long day. She'd try to call up this memory the next time her weaker, exhausted self told her to keep driving home and skip class—especially now, when being home filled her with loneliness.

Following the pivot, Billie, who'd been in the class with her for six months, was now positioned directly in front of Avery, his trendy ponytail thrust back as he exaggerated the movements prescribed by Madame Paloma to create a dance more like the hip ballet jazz he claimed was the cutting edge on the East Coast. He'd been brought to San Diego as a marketing executive for an up-and-coming advertising firm.

Madame Paloma, now with both hands on her hips, was walking the line when she stopped beside Billie. She didn't look impressed.

"*Monsieur Billie*, please extinguish your teenager hip *thrusters* to join my classical ballet class. You'll see that great dignity comes from this." Madame Paloma's words rolled from her pursed lips.

Billie's face reddened, and he straightened his posture while staring straight ahead. *A thirty-eight-year-old man has been reduced to a thirteen-year-old teenager*, Avery thought to herself, as Madame Paloma sailed down the line. Suddenly she reappeared beside Avery.

"*A-verry*, your hand should be light as a feather on the barre … You're not squeezing the last of the day's milk from the cow's udder."

Embarrassed, Avery looked down at her right hand gripping the ballet barre, her knuckles white. "Sorry; you're right, I'm holding on too tight."

Madame Paloma nodded her head once and was about to turn away from Avery when she hesitated. Her face warmed into a smile as she looked directly into Avery's eyes.

"But I saw you make me a gorgeous, diamond-shape *plié* and a very brave and tall pivot. *Bon courage.*"

After class Madame Paloma sometimes invited her students for a glass of red wine at the nearby Osteria Romantica Bistro. By the second or third glass, she liked to tell the story of defecting to Paris from her native Czechoslovakia in 1968, just after the Prague Spring. Despite the bravery of artists and progressives, she always said, the Soviets crushed the bid for liberalization. Paloma's dancer parents were among the leaders of the Prague Spring, and they disappeared not long after it was shut down.

Czechoslovakian bureaucracy issued a permit for seventeen-year-old Paloma to audition for a part in *Swan Lake* at the Paris Opera, expecting she'd return because her beloved grandmother still lived in Prague. Paloma performed for a whole season. But following the closing show, after a deep-kneed curtsy and a dutiful kiss blown in thanks to the Czechoslovakian Republic, Paloma left through the back door and ran through the alleys to join three others and a shadowy figure who provided them with the necessary forged paperwork. They had to pay every franc they had saved, plus several more instalments. It was not until the summer of 1993 that Paloma returned to the newly sovereign Czech Republic to stand before her grandmother's and parents' graves. She curtsied, kissed her fingers before touching the family gravestone, and set down a bouquet of wild pink roses. *My wild pink rose,* that's what her grandmother had called Paloma as a little girl, *hermůj divoký růžové růže,* "*Růže*" for short.

As much as Madame Paloma liked to tell her story to her students, this last part where she demonstrated how she kissed her fingers always seemed to catch her off guard. She would cover her eyes with her hands and start to cry, reverting to her Czech mother tongue. With her students' support and another glass of wine, Madame Paloma would resume her story. After many years in Paris as a prima ballerina and reputable choreographer, Paloma was hired by the San Diego School of Creative and Performing Arts, which allowed her to emigrate to the U.S. There, she taught *the beautiful*

CHAPTER FIVE

talented childrens—she never had her own children—everything she knew about ballet, dignity, and the essential roles of music, dance, and theatre as the guardians of the human spirit. Paloma carried her history with mesmerizing grace and dignity, sprinkling her discipline and wisdom here and there amongst her students, like an antidote to fast-paced living in modern America.

Avery, who'd not taken ballet lessons since Sebastian fell ill with schizophrenia, discovered Paloma's studio eight years ago after she had a dream of dancing with him. She told Dr. Mahler that this dream left her searching once again for her beloved brother, the reasons he took his own life, and the parts of herself she'd given up as a teenager. The year after her brother died, Avery's high school guidance counsellor, seeing that the downcast young girl was losing the battle against a household steeped in grief, had told Avery about an after-school ballet group. That faint breeze of hope carried Avery's feet up the driveway after school to ask about the dance class. It was as if she'd woken her mother from a coma; her eyes opened wide and lit up in an anger Avery had never seen. "How dare you even think about dancing on your brother's grave?" Avery's mother spat back at her daughter before she raged from the room.

Telling Dr. Mahler about this incident was the only time Avery had ever seen her kind psychoanalyst cry. His silver spectacles dangling from one hand, the other freckle-sprinkled hand wiping tears from his soft brown eyes, he told her that an innocent young girl being struck down by this horrible image of dancing on her brother's grave—her only *crime* being that she chose life and wanted to dance—made him unspeakably sad. Avery had watched, feeling horrified and cared for all at the same time, as he'd pulled out a checkered cotton handkerchief to dry his eyes and blow his nose. "I think your dream is telling you that you must dance again," he said, once he'd regained his composure. Sebastian would dance in the heavens if he saw his little sister releasing herself from these chains of disapproval. Dr. Mahler was certain of this, and then Avery was, too.

A week or two after that session, Avery went to Madame Paloma's dance school for the first time to enquire about adult classes.

And here she was, eight years later, standing at the barre, warming up, focusing on bringing a soft weightlessness to her hands, while Madame Paloma continued to walk her line, conducting and correcting. Several times that evening, Avery felt Madame Paloma's eyes on her, observant and concerned.

Framed by floor-to-ceiling windows at the back of the studio, the dusty rose sunset transformed as night fell: purple waves blanketed the La Jolla hills until blackness had absorbed the last traces of violet outside the window. With the essential barre workout completed, Madame Paloma commanded students to move across the floor diagonally from one corner to the other in groups of three, organized in a V-formation, *like beautiful flocks of birds spirited away from the winter storms, la migration maintenant!* Pachelbel's Canon sounded from the studio speakers as the first two groups of three side-stepped, then pirouetted, more or less elegantly, to what seemed like a very far away corner.

Avery stood ready at the head of the third V-formation with a still-humbled Billie, who appeared to have found the dignity of the perfectly upright classical ballet dancer, to the left behind her, and Lauren, who worked as a speech therapist at La Jolla Elementary School, at Avery's right hand.

"And now *Ah-verry's* peoples … Five, six, seven, *go* … Step, step, step, *pi-rou-ette,* land it with *confi-danse* and, step, step, step, *pi-rou-ette* …"

Forever the attentive student, Avery set her eyes on the marble white look-alike statue of ancient Greek goddess Persephone, holding a bird in hand, positioned in the far corner of the room. Using the bird as her visual focus, Avery attempted her first pirouette of the sequence, remembering to let go of her eye-lock on the bird at the last possible second (*head turns last,* she remembered from her childhood). Having spun her head around, she resumed her

CHAPTER FIVE

focus on the bird, bringing her body back into alignment. It worked perfectly. Avery smiled to herself, and Madame Paloma noticed and was nodding.

Encouraged, Avery set out to lead her flock further across the room: step, step, step, prepare, and turn. Avery was about to break into a smile at landing her second pirouette successfully, but as she reset her focus on the bird, she stopped dead and squinted in disbelief. The white marble bird on Persephone's hand was metamorphosizing into a large black raven, its feathers lifting slightly as it looked directly at Avery with its glistening, metallic eyes. Then the raven swooped toward her, talons and claws exposed beneath outspread shiny black wings. Avery fell to the floor in a child's pose and covered her head. She felt the movement of air as the raven dived toward her, only to graze her hands, head, arms and back with its wings with surprising gentleness.

Avery uncurled and looked up to see Madame Paloma crouched beside her, the other students standing by with concerned expressions on their faces. Avery looked up cautiously at the statue of Persephone's white marble bird, still perched motionless on her hand. Avery shook her head in disbelief as she struggled to her feet, Madame Paloma holding her arm for support. Was it happening? Were her brother's genes finally catching up with her? Was that her first hallucination triggered by the stressful encounter with Roland? Madame Paloma looked into Avery's eyes and addressed the rest of the class.

"*Ah-verry* has lost her balance; this can *'appen* when we set up for a very *tall and proud pirouette.* Ok, next group of three prepare to cross the room. *Ah-verry,* perhaps you'd like to get a cup of water from the cooler and sit on the side to recover from your fall."

Avery nodded gratefully as the rest of the class obediently regrouped. Sipping her water, she glanced at the statue several more times. As she remembered the raven brushing over her body, she felt strangely calm. *Wait until Dr. Mahler heard about a statue coming to life during ballet class.* Would he think it was high time for medication? And why wasn't she more freaked out about what just happened?

After the class was over, Madame Paloma walked over to Avery and extended her hand; she held a key.

"*Ah-verry,* my dear, I think you experienced something important this evening. I know you're a very smart person and you like to think about things in your head, but whatever is going on is also showing up in your body. I could feel it all evening. You need your ballet right now more than ever, not just on Tuesday nights. I'll trust you with the studio key. You know the schedule when the studio is empty. You can come and go as you please. Remember, dance and movement always tell some kind of a story, maybe the truth."

"Thank you, Madame Paloma. You're very kind. I'll try not to break anything!" They grinned at each other to release the intimate moment.

The second Avery drove through the wrought iron gates of Rockland Estates after her ballet class and saw Roland's Jeep there, a surge of anger charged through her. The past few days were a storm of disturbing dreams and visions, instant replays of things said, splashes of emotion, all swirling together in a mad collage. *What did Roland mean, I never* really *wanted a baby and I still don't?* Avery thought of that Christmas Eve fourteen years earlier, when Roland, drunk on champagne, took her hands and asked her to marry him. He promised her anything and everything she wanted. He told her he'd fill her belly with a beautiful little baby who would be the apple of their eyes. And now? He was five years older than she, and maybe it was too late for him now. Had he never really wanted a baby, only telling her what he thought she wanted to hear? This thought enraged her. She stepped harder on the gas pedal, her tires spitting gravel. She slammed on the brakes as a wave of nausea came over

CHAPTER FIVE

her. *What are* you *doing?* Anger always reminded her of her father's rage when she was a child. It knew no boundaries. Some nights, too many, Avery awoke to doors slamming and things breaking. She would get up and tiptoe to Sebastian's room to hide under the covers with him. God, she missed him.

Unsettled by her anger and the memories it evoked, Avery called upon her well-honed talents of conciliation, borne of a lifetime of walking on eggshells in a volatile household. No matter how disappointing, Roland's promises were irrelevant now. She simply needed to accept that she wouldn't get the baby she wanted.

But then, something changed; her own reasonableness infuriated her. She stepped harder on the gas and sped toward the garage door, then slammed on the brakes to avoid a collision.

SIX

*R*oland sat with his friends around a tall pub table at the La Jolla Country Club House Bar; he was in the middle of telling a joke when he checked his watch. It was ten after eight. Oh good: lots of time before he'd be missed at home. It was Tuesday night, and Avery was at her ballet class. Roland had come off the golf course with three of his cronies just after sunset, affable and liquored up enough to push from consciousness the images of Avery's despondence after their big weekend talk. Instead, he lingered with pleasing images of his elegant wife in perfect ballet positions. He remembered some years ago when she came home, over-the-top excited after her first ballet class at a studio run by some old Czech diva. Roland had asked her for a little demo of what she'd learned that day, and she offered him a few pretty moves. What he remembered most vividly were the graceful movements of her hands and the sparkle of her wedding band, and how lucky he felt to have such a beautiful wife, finally that perfect wife who was so completely accepted by his family.

Roland's mind wandered further to the day of his wedding, when his father pulled him aside to give him a painfully firm handshake that drained the last few drops of rebel blood from him. "Son, you've finally done it right with Avery," he'd said. "Now we can be that family, that dynasty, I've always envisioned. I see nothing standing in the way of you becoming a full partner with me and your brother at the firm."

CHAPTER SIX

Roland remembered his father had slapped his back so vigorously that his left shoulder blade still burned in pain when he saw Avery walking toward him on her father's arm a few minutes later. That slap still stung. *Enough of rehashing my past with my father*, Roland thought, as he returned to the lovely memory of Avery's ballet demonstration. Yes, there she was again in his mind's eye, moving into a series of *pliés* that left him desiring an encore in their bedroom. Roland closed his eyes as he sat back in his club chair; his friends' conversation faded into the distance.

Just as he was relaxing into remembering Avery move into the deep thigh bend of a *grand plié*, her stomach flat and hips perfectly poised, a rush of bodily heat overcame him: he saw a younger version of himself promising to fill that sensual belly with a baby. Roland felt uncomfortable pools of guilt and something a little too close to self-hatred circulating in his sickened gut. He wiped the sweat off his brow with the arm of his golf shirt.

"Hey, mate!" his buddy Matt called. "You look like you just saw a ghost. You sick or something? You know you had a lot of decent swings today, but you can't always come in first. You have to let old Brad over here win once in a while, or he'll stop hangin' around with us."

The group exploded into laughter.

"I think I just had a bit too much sun," Roland said.

"We can take care of that for you, buddy," Brad said, still laughing. "Marcie, can you mix a Tequila Sunset for my friend over here? He needs something to recover from the sunstroke that *supposedly* caused him to lose his golf game."

More laughter, now including Roland's characteristic guffaws, rolled over the table. Marcie winked as she set down a perfectly layered Tequila Sunset in front of him.

Roland took a swig of his drink. "Much better, thanks, Brad. If it wasn't getting dark out there, I would say let's have a rematch right now!"

Roland hesitated and cleared his throat before he went on.

"Lads, my wife wants to have a baby. Things are kind of stressful at my house right now, because she's big into it and it's kind of hanging in the air all the time. Have you guys come across this?"

"Isn't it a bit too late for that?" Matt asked. "I'm just a few years older than you, Rol, but my kids are almost all grown up now. I couldn't imagine doing it all again at this age. It takes a huge amount of energy, and your life isn't your own once you start that whole business. Forget about golf games and drinks with your mates."

"My wife wanted to have another one a few years ago. She was about forty or so then. I think it was just the *change* talking. She got all emotional," Brad added.

The men were looking deeply into their drinks now as if searching for some kind of a map to get them out of this talk about *the change*. But Brad had connected with a newfound sensitivity and wasn't quite finished yet.

"It's very important to be extra caring when they're emotional like this, you know—when they're running out of time, Rol." Matt hid his face by leaning it on his outspread left hand, while his right hand signalled Marcie for another drink.

"I know all about this," Brad continued. "What you have to do is give her lots of affection and compliments." Brad leaned in closer to the table and lowered his voice: "Then, you surprise her with some kind of a romantic trip; you know, the kind you could never do with little kids. That's the clincher. Then they just kind of forget about it."

"Alrighty, so it's settled then," said never-married Sam, who had stayed rather quiet. "Cheers men! Here's to golf and best friends. Where would we be without that?" A few *here-here's* were uttered with sighs of relief that the uncomfortable issue had been solved.

Much later that same night, his buddies deposited Roland onto his doorstep.

CHAPTER SIX

"Let's put him in the lounge chair on the patio. We don't want to wake up the wife," Matt said, and the group laughed one more time. Those were the last words Roland heard before he drifted off into a hazy sleep, hoping that the complicated feelings he'd had earlier that evening would evaporate by the morning.

The next morning, Avery awoke to the classical guitar sounds of her iPhone alarm. She rolled over to see the opposite side of the bed was untouched; without her glasses, it looked to her like a sea of white linens still smooth from the touch of her hands and puffy white clouds of pillows gathering at the headboard. Roland's alarm – the grating sound of a revving motorbike that he said reminded him of college – suddenly sounded from somewhere else, possibly outside her window. "Turn that damned annoying thing off!" she shouted out the window.

Avery grabbed her housecoat and tracked Roland to a lounge chair on their front patio, his arms and legs grotesquely sprawled over the dignified piece of garden furniture. He kept snoring even when she shut off the alarm on his iPhone and tossed it onto his belly after reading the texts on the screen. *Hey bud, you better grab some Tylenol. Marcie's ready to pour you another Tequila Sunset if you're up for it, my man.* Then, *Rol, she's gonna be mighty pissed when she finds you on the patio!* Yup, even more pissed than she already was. Looked like the handiwork of fellow man-children Matt, Brad, and Sam.

An hour later, after her shower and coffee, Avery walked past him a second time enroute to her car. She revved her engine and grimaced. From the rear-view window, she could see Roland's head lifting from the lounge chair. She stepped hard on the gas, spitting gravel in his direction, and dismissed the impulse to text Roland and tell him she hoped he was feeling all right.

SEVEN

*A*very stood on her balcony, closed her eyes, and inhaled deeply. It was two forty-five p.m. and it was best, she thought, to take a few minutes to relax before Clare was due to arrive for her second appointment.

Avery opened her eyes to the beach view on the other side of the boulevard where she parked her car. The rippled sand and palm trees had been a deciding factor when she fell in love with her office suite almost thirteen years ago. Roland had been tickled to buy this perfect piece of real estate and, in those days, he liked to brag about the important work his wife did there. Even Roland's father had given Avery a little pat on her back after she graduated with her doctorate and started her practice. *I'm rather glad, dear, that you're helping those who are not strong enough to manage life's problems,* was George Frontiera's take on Avery's profession.

Avery made out the figure of an elderly man in a Henry Fonda hat walking slowly on the water's edge. An exuberant dog with large, puppy feet was running ahead and then back to his human, carving playful ellipses in the sand. Avery noticed a young family spread out on a blanket with all the paraphernalia necessary for taking young children to the beach. *I would like to take* my *children to the beach,* Avery thought, before she veered away from this dangerous topic.

She checked her watch; it was two forty-nine, still plenty of time. Another figure stepped from the far left end of the landscape into Avery's visual field. Avery squinted into the sunlight to see this

CHAPTER SEVEN

person stop every few feet to kick sand, debris, and water, rather futilely, back into the ocean. As the shape came closer, Avery saw long, ginger curls and realized it was a female figure. Could it be Clare walking towards her appointment?

Avery marched back inside her office and took out of the cabinet her binoculars, a gift from Roland to observe the many interesting species of birds that frequented the shoreline. She stood just inside her open balcony doors like a spy and focused the lenses: it *was* Clare, her red curls catching the sunlight and moving with the breeze. She stopped again, picked up a handful of pebbles and heaved them far out into the ocean. The dog registered some interest in the beach newcomer with a cock of his head, but then his dog sense sent him scampering back to his owner. Now Clare was getting something out of her bag; it was a bright red towel that she lay out, then sat upon. *What?* In disbelief, Avery checked her watch to see it was two fifty-five. *There's no time for sitting on the beach.* Avery refocused her binoculars: Clare reached for her iPhone, glanced at it, threw it back in her bag. Then she lay down on her towel and crossed one leg over the other, her left foot swinging freely. *How leisurely of her.* When Avery felt herself wanting to stomp her feet in frustration, her higher self finally gained the upper hand. She realized how much her disrespectful young client was pushing her buttons. She needed to get on top of it.

Avery went inside and put her binoculars away. Then she closed her balcony doors and turned on the air conditioning. She pulled Clare's file from the filing cabinet to review her notes and give serious thought into Clare's defiance and ambivalence. Why was Clare regressing to such petulant adolescent behaviour? It was provocative and irritating on the outside, but on the inside, arrested development almost always suggested trauma and unresolved childhood loss. Avery felt herself softening as she sat like a proper psychotherapist, spending the allotted session time focused on her client—whether or not Clare chose to be present in the room. Avery left the door from her office to the waiting room wide open.

At four twenty-one, Avery heard the waiting room door open. She turned around to find Clare standing in the doorway of her office.

"I was kind of delayed, but I'm here now."

"Please come in, Clare."

Clare arranged herself on the couch. She shook out her curls before she spoke. Avery noticed a few granules of sand landing like salt from a saltshaker on the couch with each swing of the curls.

"So. Are you going to try for a baby again next month? Being a smart doctor like yourself, you must know that at your age you need to get right on it ... You know what they say about women in their forties only having a handful of good eggs left! *If* that." Avery thought Clare looked pleased to have delivered a flawlessly provocative opening statement, likely rehearsed while sunbathing on the beach.

"Clare, it was a mistake to leave personal items like that in my office bathroom. I also forgot to lock my private bathroom and I should've mentioned where to find the public washroom at the beginning of our time together." She paused briefly to ensure that her apology could settle into the room before continuing. "That being said, I felt it intrusive that you took pregnancy tests back out of the garbage and set them out on the counter." The slightest blush rose into Clare's cheeks. "But here we are. Therapy has to be focused on you, not me. It won't work any other way. So, I can't talk to you about my personal life, including any hopes I might have about having a baby."

"Hopes you *might* have? This is where all you shrinks fail." Clare shook her head in disgust.

"What do you mean, *this is how we fail?*"

CHAPTER SEVEN

"You people just pretend to be so perfect. You're completely unreachable, acting like *you* don't sweat about being pregnant, just like everybody else." Clare rummaged through her bag to pull out a nail file, which she swiped roughly back and forth. "Whatever. Do what you want. I don't really care."

"Clare, you sure *look* like you care just a little, like you're going through something. I'd appreciate if you'd try to tell me how you're feeling. I want to understand how it feels from where you're sitting."

Avery's words appeared to catch Clare off guard. She looked up from her nails and tossed the file back into her bag.

"I feel like you've put yourself in this separate class ... that you think I'm beneath you, like I'm not even worthy of talking with you about what actually happened here last week." Clare's expression hovered between angry and hurt.

"You feel like I'm implying that you're not important enough for a personal conversation about my pregnancy tests at the bottom of the trash can?"

"Exactly. I might be younger than you, but I know a lot. Like that you've waited too long to have a baby and now it's not going so well. And you have regrets."

Clare was dead right.

"I *do* know you're intelligent. Although I've only met with you for a very short time, I can see you know a lot. I don't feel you aren't worth talking to about my private life. But I do know it wouldn't be right if I used our time together to talk about me. And you're very much right that I'm a human being with feelings, with hopes and regrets and vulnerabilities, just like you, no better, no worse than any other person. But my job is to concentrate on *your* feelings, your history, your hopes, and your regrets ... even if you don't like how you got here to see me, which I can understand. But here we both are together. We could consider just making the best of it."

Avery saw the tiniest hint of a nod in the slight movement through the spirals of Clare's long curls. Avery waited in silence. Finally, Clare spoke.

"I have a few regrets, even about what happened in your bathroom last week. I'm not going to talk to you about them right now. Not today, but maybe one day. We'll have to see. I can't promise anything."

Avery recognized this minute seed of potential trust and smiled at Clare.

"If that day comes, I'll be ready to listen. And when you're ready, *I would* like to hear what was happening for you when you went through the trash can and placed the pregnancy tests on the countertop. But there's no rush."

Clare rolled her eyes, then moved to a new topic.

"I'm still trying to finish my painting."

"Which painting is that?"

"It's about the shackles of the supremacist white patriarchy. I said I'd do it after San Diego's Second Women's March in January. There'll be an art exhibit at the Museum of Contemporary Art showing works inspired by that day. And then we'll march again. If the world's still standing, that is."

Avery thought this was a great idea, but she didn't say so. "How do you feel about your painting so far, Clare?"

"It's absolutely horrible. There's this Black woman shackled to a tree, surrounded by ominous, white, middle-aged dudes whose faces are partly hidden by hoods. They're wearing cloaks with logos that tell you exactly who they are. Like their greedy corporations and the KKK, you know. In the upper branches, I painted the tree's face with an expression of complete panic as it looks down at the woman and the men around her. So the image is about environmental issues, too. It's my biggest canvas yet, and it's in my apartment."

Avery felt sickened by the grotesque image. She experienced a distinct rush of worry for the woman in the painting, and something

CHAPTER SEVEN

close to rage at the figures surrounding her. Even without seeing the painting, Clare's artwork was evoking precisely the emotions the artist intended.

"What's left for you to do on the painting, Clare?" Avery asked.

"Well, obviously, I've got a huge problem I haven't quite solved yet." Clare folded her arms across her chest and looked at Avery as if the answer would be self-evident to any intelligent onlooker.

"What's the problem you're trying to solve?"

"Well, of course, I want people to feel the sickening terror, the rage, the helplessness, all of it—like what you're probably feeling right now, with me just talking about it, though of course we aren't going to talk about your feelings. But I can't just leave the woman there like that to be swallowed up by those evil, sick-fuck men. So I'm trying to figure out a way of saving her or raising her up, hopefully while blowing up all those bastards around her—but without hurting the tree, of course—but I don't want people to not feel the terror first. Otherwise they won't experience what's so screwed up in our world right now."

Avery felt a respect for her young client. How ironic that Clare worked so hard to present herself as that entitled someone who couldn't care less, when underneath her cloak of anger and defiance, she obviously cared so much. A vision of revolving canvases cascaded through Avery's mind.

"That's a difficult problem, Clare, I can see that. I wonder if one canvas isn't enough for all you want to say. Perhaps two or three canvases could tell the story as you envision it, and on the day of the Women's March next January, those images could be moving over a large screen at the museum, or they could be attached to different sides of a pillar so people could walk around it."

Clare stared at Avery, looking dumbfounded. She opened her mouth several times, then closed it again. Looking uncertain about what to do next, Clare did what many young people would do in this instance. She reached for her iPhone.

"It's four forty-nine. I think we're done here, and I gotta go." Clare gathered her things as noisily as possible, perhaps to create a sound wall to stop Avery from speaking.

"You know, Clare," Avery said as, her client walked toward the door, "I can't help but think that the tree could empower the victim out of her terrifying situation, that nature would somehow help to release her."

"That actually isn't the worst idea I've ever heard," Clare muttered, just loud enough for Avery to hear, as she crossed the waiting room.

I shall take that as a compliment. Avery smiled to herself before she sat down to write her progress note. *Don't get too high on yourself just yet though; we're still coming down from spying on clients with binoculars.*

EIGHT

Why does this always happen to me? Clare had felt immense satisfaction when she unleashed her anger and all that bad behaviour on Frontiera. She wouldn't be pushed around. No one could make her do anything; not the judge, not the shrink. They could make her show up, on her own sweet time, but they couldn't make her buy in. At moments when she felt enraged like this, *anything* she could do to release all that built-up resentment and make herself feel better seemed completely acceptable to her. Clare felt entitled to her entitlement; it was her right, given all she'd been through. But that's not the place where she landed at the end.

Clare poured herself a drink, sat down on her couch, and gulped down most of her red wine before setting down the glass on the coffee table. It was starting to get dark, but she left the lights off. No one needed to see this, especially not her. Clare pulled out a jumbo paper clip from her pocket and unbent it into the shape of a metallic spike. She'd behaved like a spoiled child. Again. The shame of it disgusted her.

Clare winced as she scratched hard across her stomach with the sharp end of the paper clip. The wound across her belly stung and, for a second, the sirens of bodily pain drowned out the shame and feeling of unworthiness. No one really wanted her; not Frontiera who was paid to talk to her, not even the playful puppy at the beach who ran in the other direction when he saw her sour face. And certainly not her real father. She felt tears rolling over her cheeks. Clare

CHAPTER EIGHT

made a fist around the top of the paper clip, about to dig in deeper. She stopped herself. No: she wouldn't let him do that to her tonight.

"Siri, call Molly," Clare said into the darkness.

"Clare?" Molly's gentle voice made Clare cry a little harder.

"Clare, it's alright, honey, Jim and I are right here for you. We're on the speaker phone, dear, so we can both talk to you."

"I'm not feeling very good right now," Clare said softly. "I need your help. Tell me again what you know about what happened to me ... before I came to you. I need to hear it."

"Of course, dear. Anything at all we can do to help you feel better. Your real mother died of breast cancer, the poor angel. Your grandmother tried to care for you, but she was too frail. Your birth certificate said you were born in L.A. Your father couldn't raise you for some reason, we don't know why, but he did provide for you financially. He didn't want to be known to us; his name wasn't even on your birth certificate. Jim and I reckoned he might have been ashamed of himself, and so he should be. That's all we know about your biological family. We're so sorry, darling, I wish we had more to tell you."

"So my father didn't want me, but you did?"

Molly's steady voice felt like a salve on the painful scratch on Clare's belly. It took the edge off of the self-doubt and the unrelenting self-blame that lived deep in her insides. Clare unclenched her fist and let the ugly shape of jagged wire drop to the floor.

"Molly and me? We wanted you desperately," Jim said in his reassuringly thick Scottish accent. "We'd been waitin' for a child for years. We were thrilled when the adoption agency called us. 'Please, bring her right over,' we said."

"We didn't even need to discuss it," Molly chimed in.

"What was I like when ... I came to you? Tell me that part; I want to picture it."

Clare closed her eyes and took a deep breath.

"I remember running out to the car to meet you," Molly said. "Beautiful red curls, intelligent eyes. But you looked sad, like you'd been through a lot. The adoption lady tried to take your hand to go up the walk to the front door. But you weren't having it. You hugged your teddy tight with both arms across your chest and wanted to walk on your own,"

"And I wasn't talking, right? You told me that before?"

"No: you really didn't speak at all for the first few months. The doctor said it was because you were in a state of shock. He told us to be patient. We knew you'd speak when you were ready," Molly said.

"There was no rush at all, Clare dear," Jim added. "We had all the time in the world for you. We talked to you, and sometimes you gave a little nod or a shake of the head when we spoke to you, so we knew you understood us. Once in a while, when you were playing with your teddy or when we were pushing you on the swing outside, you'd even smile. It was such a thrill when you said your first words."

Clare got up to refill her glass. She snapped on the light above the stove, but kept the rest of the apartment dark; she wasn't ready to see the job she'd done on her belly. Clare sat back down on the couch.

"What ... what was the first thing I said? Do you remember?"

Clare heard Molly and Jim chuckling with relief. They knew the worst of this crisis was over.

"We certainly do remember!" Jim loved telling this part of the story. "You said 'Molly mine.' Molly started to cry, like she's doing again right now sitting next to me, and I said, 'Yes, Molly is yours, and so is Jim.' I mean, you know, I didn't want to be left out of the moment."

Clare chuckled.

"And it stuck. I was Molly, and Jim was Jim; you were always an observant child, and I guess that's what you'd heard us calling each other. We felt it best to let you call us by our first names," Molly said.

"You had such a sweet way of speaking, like a little ... I don't know ... sing-song to it. By the time you started grade one, you were

CHAPTER EIGHT

talking just like the other kids. We trusted you'd catch up to yourself when you were ready. And you did. You always had your own way of doing things," Jim said.

"I've seen the new shrink a couple of times," Clare said.

"How was it?" Molly asked.

"She's kind of annoying, but not as bad as I thought. I may have been a bit on the rude side," Clare said. "I don't see how she's going to help me any, but I guess I have to keep going to get the judge off of my back."

"Just give it your best try. That's all you can do," Jim said.

Clare snorted. She was back.

"Clare?" Molly asked carefully.

"Yes, Molly?"

"Umm … Have you found yourself pinching anything of late?" Molly said gingerly.

Clare had no fight left in her.

"Just this sweet little figurine in the shrink's waiting room. I guess I was nervous and needed something to calm me down."

"I think you should consider giving it back. Apologize, maybe?" Molly said.

Clare could hear Jim sighing in the background.

"Leave it alone, Molly, she's been through enough tonight," Jim added.

"Well, I'd better go," Clare said. "I've got an early class tomorrow."

"Alright, dear," Jim said.

"Thanks … for everything," Clare managed, as tears filled her eyes once again.

"Good night. We love you," Molly said. "Dear? Just consider that this doctor may be able to help you. Not just with the stealing, but with the important stuff underneath."

After Clare hung up the phone, she drank the rest of her wine, laid down on the couch, and let her eyes close. She'd clean up her mess tomorrow.

50

NINE

*A*very arrived twenty minutes before her appointment with Dr. Mahler, which gave her plenty of time to unwind and just think. How many times had she sat in this very waiting room over the years? Avery knew the rhythm of psychotherapy from both sides of the couch. During the hardest times, the weekly psychotherapy sessions were a focal point for the patient, even a lifeline, for getting through the week. She felt that way right now. As the client progressed and brought her hard-earned self-understanding into her life and relationships, the sessions became gradually less essential and, at some point, unnecessary or even inconvenient. Avery remembered how that felt, too. Usually both client and therapist perceived when they are nearing the end of a course of psychotherapy, and then there was only the difficult business of saying good-bye.

Avery had had several courses of psychotherapy with Dr. Mahler in her lifetime, and several times they had said good-bye. The first round unfolded when she had just moved to San Diego to go to college following her brother's suicide and the unraveling of her family. Dr. Mahler still had dark brown hair with only a hint of grey when she first met him. Five years later, she returned to him as a graduate student in clinical psychology. The academic material had reopened old wounds, and she came to doubt she had the makings of a psychologist. Dr. Mahler's hair was greyer by then, but the same kind eyes sparkled behind the spectacles he had started to

CHAPTER NINE

wear. In tears, she'd confessed her fear that she would fail miserably in trying to help her future clients. *My dear Avery, tragedy and loss are the makings of the very best psychologists, as long as they know their own scars.* Dr. Mahler's words had stayed with her since then and gave her the encouragement she needed.

The third course of psychotherapy was in her mid-thirties, when she had a miscarriage in the fifth month of pregnancy. At least then she had hope of trying again. Yes, indeed, she was on to round number four of psychotherapy. As always, she felt a mixture of anxiety and gratitude when Dr. Mahler's door opened exactly on the hour.

Avery spoke for twenty minutes about her second session with Clare, and Dr. Mahler listened thoughtfully as always. He did flinch slightly at the mention of Avery's binoculars and his eyes opened wider when Avery spoke of the art advice she'd offered to her client. When Avery stopped talking, Dr. Mahler paused for a moment and looked into her eyes before he spoke.

"I like what you did, Avery. You made a mistake, you admitted it, and then you turned it into an honest opportunity to connect with that fiery, sand-kicking young client of yours. Perhaps some of your finest work yet. Now we'll not waste our precious time together talking about those supposedly-for-bird-watching binoculars of yours, but if you still don't feel safe around them, you can always bring me the key for the binocular cabinet to keep for a while."

Avery's face blossomed into a teenager's crimson blush. Dr. Mahler leaned back in his chair and exploded into deep belly laughter. The image of Avery peeping through her binoculars, and Dr. Mahler as her key holder, ignited a giggle in Avery, too. Dr. Mahler took his handkerchief out of his pocket and mopped his face.

"Ok, that was the comic relief we both needed. But let's press on. What was your thinking when you offered her the suggestion about where to go with her painting? It's unorthodox to solve a problem for a client, especially an artistic block like that, but I don't mind breaking the rules myself once in a while if it helps the client."

"I, I ... just saw this sequence of paintings in my mind. I had an overwhelming sense that I understood the darkness of her painting and how stuck she felt in it. She has nightmares about it, and I think she needed some help. Of course, she'd never admit that. I don't know, Dr. Mahler, I felt her unconscious was sending me a message and it reverberated in mine, and then these new images just arose in my mind's eye. Come to think of it, it was a way for us to communicate and get under the radar of her defenses."

Dr. Mahler looked at Avery intently.

"Yes, the crossfire of her defenses, defiance, pushing on your vulnerabilities—like this provocative mention of you running out of eggs. The fact that she didn't immediately dismiss your ideas makes me think you connected with her and made her feel cared for when she least expected it. You know, I think Clare will be a very important client for you, and you'll be important for her. Just keep those boundaries crisp and clean."

"Thanks, Dr. Mahler. Speaking of my unusual visions ... umm ... the strangest thing happened at my ballet class after our session last Tuesday."

The light appeared to shift into more subdued tones in the office just then, and she felt grateful for her long history with Dr. Mahler. She couldn't imagine telling this story to a new therapist. The thought of him retiring and becoming unavailable to her felt unbearable.

Dr. Mahler leaned forward, looking very serious now.

Avery told him every detail she could remember: the sculpture of Persephone, and the bird on her hand suddenly coming alive, Madame Paloma's encouragement, the studio key, the whole crazy story. Even Dr. Mahler, who'd heard just about everything, looked a little alarmed.

"Tell me again, Avery, how you felt when you saw the live raven looking at you from Persephone's arm?"

CHAPTER NINE

"I was frozen with fear. He looked mean, like he would hurt me."

"But then he didn't hurt you, Avery. Tell me how you felt when his wings brushed over you?"

"I felt really surprised; awestruck you could say. And then, I felt really calm and cared for, almost like I'd been caressed by something powerful that was trying to speak to me in some way. And, come to think of it, once the vision had come over me, everything went back to normal. It didn't take over my perceptions and spiral into some kind of a psychotic breakdown. It just left me filled with this incredible feeling."

"So this time, it was *foe* that turned out to be *friend*, like a trustworthy being who helped you along your way. Not the other way around, like in your dream about Clare. Does it feel difficult to know what or whom to trust? Even your own perceptions? Is that a part of what you are going through as your life is changing?"

"Well, I trust you even more. I trust Madame Paloma, for some reason. I don't trust Roland anymore." Avery's voice broke and tears began to roll down her face. "It's really not good when you can't trust your husband of thirteen years."

"Avery, I'm sad that you can't trust Roland now. But, please, let me ask you something else. Do you trust yourself? Can you count on yourself?"

Avery considered his question.

"Well, if you'd asked me that last week, I wouldn't be so sure. Everything was upside down. But now I guess I do trust myself. I trust that I'll figure things out." Avery wiped her face with the back of her sleeve.

"Do you think the raven has anything to do with your feeling that you can trust yourself?"

"Yes, I think the raven was some kind of a sign, maybe from my unconscious. The perception I had was like a part of myself that spoke to me, but was projected onto this statue. A symbolic statue of Persephone and raven, but nevertheless a statue, right?"

Dr. Mahler lifted his index finger and, without saying a word, rose from his armchair and walked to his overstuffed bookshelf. He pulled a magnifying glass out of his pocket and stepped on to his library stool. Squinting, he examined a series of grey-spined books with black lettering. Finally, he pulled a volume from the shelf, releasing a cascade of dust that danced in the afternoon sunlight. Dr. Mahler sat down and opened the well-worn book.

"The late Dr. Carl Jung, may he rest in peace, wrote this book, and I think his words will give us some food for thought. Let me see . . . the part I am thinking of for you, Avery." Dr. Mahler leafed through several pages marked with his penciled notes. "Yes, here it is. Listen to this, Avery. *The Raven is about rebirth, recovery, renewal, recycling, reflection, and healing. He signifies moving through transitions smoothly by casting light into darkness.* Let's think about this. At first, the raven looked a bit *creepy* to you, right?"

Avery smiled at Dr. Mahler's use of the word *creepy*, but he had more to say.

"This creepy, scary quality, it comes from a dark place in your unconscious that you don't yet know. It could even be a place that connects with darkness in someone's unconscious, someone you're close to. And that's very frightening—so frightening that you hid on the floor in a child's pose, my dear Avery."

Avery felt a chill down her spine.

"You're right, Dr. Mahler, it was probably my *shadow* that freaked me out."

"Yes, yes, my dear Avery! Exactly; it was your shadow that created this vision. Now, you might say to me, *Dr. Mahler, haven't I spent enough hours and big bucks in your office to bring all of that dark, shadowy stuff from my unconscious into the open?*"

Here we go again, thought Avery. Dr. Mahler was too excited to let his client participate in the discussion. Then again, in this state, Dr. Mahler tended to offer some of his most meaningful interpretations.

CHAPTER NINE

"I would say to you, *No, Avery, there's always more shadow that will arise during your life when it needs to.* So yes, the raven was scary, classical shadow material, actually, but then he surprised you and caressed you with his feathers. I think he's telling you that you are about to go through a huge transformation."

Dr. Mahler had risen to his feet to hold his book in one hand and point to it with the other, as if it held the answers to all questions.

"So you don't think I have schizophrenia?" Avery asked.

Dr. Mahler sat back down.

"Well, I have to tell you that with your beloved brother Sebastian's history, I've always looked out for you in this regard, and I've never seen any signs of that family risk showing up in you, thank goodness. I'd a glimmer of worry when you started to tell me about the raven's feathers moving with its breath, but the more you said the less worried I became. As you said, with schizophrenia, we'd expect an overall decline in your self-care and your perceptions. But what you described was a momentary fluidity in your perceptions, what non-Western cultures might call 'a vision.' So it's safe to say that I've crossed the question of *emergent schizophrenia* from my mental checklist. At least for now."

"Well, that's good to hear, Dr. Mahler. I didn't think so either. Schizophrenia took my brother. He couldn't fight it ... and everything else that was going on in our family."

"I know, Avery. I never met your Sebastian, but I feel for him that he suffered so terribly and that you lost him like that."

"It must be time for me to go, Dr. Mahler. I feel I've been here forever."

"Well, you're right. You've been here a long time. Let's wrap up. I'll not look at my watch right now, having just spoken about your late brother. It wouldn't seem right. Let's just trust that it's time to say good-bye for today."

"I'll see you next Tuesday, Dr. Mahler. And thank you." Avery stopped at the office door. "I think everything you said is true. I can feel it. But there's something else about ravens, too, you know. They *are* known to bring light, but they also steal things, like shiny ornaments; kind of like how Clare steals things."

Dr. Mahler suddenly brought his hand toward his head, but then stopped himself before touching his hair.

"To be continued, Avery, for sure."

TEN

Avery looked up at her reflection in the glass doors at the entrance of San Diego's International Airport and stopped dead in her tracks. *Is that how I really look?* She saw a slight middle-aged woman, chin pressed tightly to her chest, shoulders stuck in an exaggerated shrug, and hands buried in the sagging pockets of a belted sweater. Her brow, exposed by hair pulled back into a ponytail, was lined with serious wrinkles, and her mouth was set in a hard line that looked unfamiliar to her. Mercifully, the automatic doors parted and the image slid out of view. *Reality check?* No wonder she looked like a burned out, defeated version of her previous self. It had been more than a fortnight of forced politeness and anxious silences between her and Roland since that night when she had brought home the failed pregnancy tests.

Rolling her shoulders to ease her painfully tense muscles, Avery made her way to the arrivals lobby. She palpitated her neck as she scanned the board for Delta flight 746. This long-awaited Friday was just the relief she needed. Her old college roommate, Nazrin, was arriving from Vancouver to spend the weekend. The two women had stayed in touch, but they hadn't seen each other for almost six years.

Avery had met Nazrin twenty years earlier, a lifetime ago it seemed now, when they were both studying at San Diego State University. Nazrin was different from anyone Avery had ever known. Every day, the poised Nazrin, clad in fabrics modestly covering her head and body, sat at the front of their *Culture and Art History* class;

CHAPTER TEN

occasionally she raised her hand to ask a thoughtful question. When Avery returned to class after missing a whole week because of a bout of the flu, she needed to photocopy someone's notes. The studious stranger was her obvious choice. Avery bought Nazrin lunch in the cafeteria to thank her. They lingered until the janitor tapped her on the shoulder and pointed to the *We Are Closed* sign. By then, they were permanently knitted into each other's lives. They had instantly trusted one another. Avery poured out details of her life that had taken years of psychotherapy to collect and organize. And Nazrin, too, told her she had never met a friend with whom she felt comfortable enough to share the unedited version of her life. Until now, such disclosure was limited to tiny, chewable bits of conversation with her parents until the pained expressions on their faces told her they could go no further with this emotional topic. Nazrin and her parents were Bahá'í, a religious minority in their native country, who fled from Iran during the Islamic revolution, when the Ayatollah Khomeini government clawed back the rights of Iranian women and persecuted those practicing non-Islamic religions. Avery felt sick when Nazrin described herself huddled with her parents in a cellar that smelled like fear and urine to escape from the Revolutionary Guard. The guardsmen wore military caps and dark sunglasses, policed the streets, and raided homes. For several days, Nazrin's family stayed in the cellar with little in the way of food and water, smuggled in by sympathetic friends who risked their lives. Finally, one night they were able to make their journey out of Iran sitting on crates in the back of a delivery van. Nazrin's family ended up in a refugee camp in India, where gaunt children listlessly kicked around a half-inflated soccer ball. Nazrin told Avery about the moment when their airplane accelerated on its take off from New Delhi, and she saw her father sinking into his seat, eyes closed and tears running down his cheeks as his lips moved in prayer. Curious and eager not to miss anything, seven-year-old Nazrin pressed her face against the window when the plane touched down in Abu Dhabi to refuel. Avery loved the part of the story when Nazrin stuck out her tongue against the glass of the airplane window and saw one of the many men in white robes on the tarmac look up at her and stick out his tongue in return. Clearly, she'd always been a rebel. Finally, Nazrin told her, there was the climactic descent into the sea of lights that was Los Angeles.

At that very first cafeteria lunch, Nazrin told her that being an Iranian-American child in the 1980s was much better than what she'd escaped, but "it hadn't been all lights, sparkle, and freedom." Nazrin's parents prepared her as best they could to be peacefully assertive when faced with the expected taunts in the schoolyard, and reminded her that the Bahá'í people spread peace. But at age ten, when she walked to school proudly wearing her first rose-coloured Hijab, sent from Iran by her grandmother, three boys suddenly surrounded her. "Hey, towel-head! You should wrap that thing over your ugly brown face so we don't have to puke when we see you."

On that day, Nazrin raised her schoolbag, heavy with the many books of an intelligent and studious young girl, and swung it around her, knocking the boys in their heads. "You're stupid childish boys who will never grow a single pubic hair. You will stay chubby white dumplings just as you are now."

One of the boys looked down at his crotch before he ran away, yelling, "She's put a spell on us! Let's get out of here, guys!"

Nazrin, a strong girl who was far from the image of light and peace her parents encouraged, was never again bothered—at least, not by those boys.

Now, Nazrin's plane was scheduled to land in ten minutes. On the television monitor blaring nearby, the CNN anchor was discussing the travel ban and all the passengers being held up, or worse, being refused entry and being separated from their families. *Or withheld from their best friends?*

Yet surely, Nazrin would not have a problem. She was an American citizen employed as a journalist at the University of British Columbia's Global Reporting Centre in Vancouver. She met her

CHAPTER TEN

Indo-Canadian husband, Raj, around the same time that Avery and Roland began dating, and all four of them became good friends. Nazrin and Raj were both studying at San Diego State's School of Journalism and Media Studies. "I'm completely in love with this Raj," Nazrin told Avery when she came home one evening. She and Raj had just completed an assignment together on diplomacy between India and Iran after the Islamic revolution. "It turns out to be more than a diplomatic relationship between us," Nazrin said with a wink.

Nazrin and Raj married in a colourful ceremony reflecting both of their cultures, with Avery standing beside her best friend in a glorious, yellow Persian silk gown and a translucent hijab that floated around her face and body like a dream. When Avery looked over her shoulder at Roland sitting in the audience, he made a somewhat embarrassing swirling motion around his head with his arms to mimic Nazrin's hijab and then gave Avery a double-thumbs up. It was not the first or the last time that Avery felt irritated by Roland's borderline insensitivity to cultural subtleties, but she'd said nothing. She rationalized that he meant no harm and was ten times better than his exceptionally judgmental parents.

At the ceremony, Nazrin's father blessed his daughter and son-in-law with a Bahá'í teaching: *Dear all-merciful lord, thank you for your desire to behold the entire human race as one soul and one body. Nazrin and Raj stand before you today as two humans with beautifully different faiths to celebrate their unique love, their joined bodies and souls.* When Nazrin's parents kissed the bride and groom on their foreheads and sprinkled pink and yellow rose petals over them, Avery felt a surge of sadness that she didn't have parents like this. She later realized that Nazrin's mother, Diya, had a keen and generous heart that somehow awakened Avery's hunger for an emotionally available maternal figure – even before Avery fully understood it. Come to think of it, from the day of the wedding forward, Diya had made a point of including Avery at family events in Los Angeles, and referred to her as a *second daughter*.

Two years after this ceremony, Nazrin stood up for Avery when she took her vows with Roland. Hers was a classically white and crystal occasion, beautiful in its own right, but Avery missed the sparkling jewels and coloured fabrics of her friends' ceremony. She remembered standing behind Nazrin and Raj as they spoke their vows and seeing their interlaced arms and hands, wheat and brown, appearing from underneath layers of colourful, sheer fabrics.

Avery's mother wore a tailored charcoal suit, more fitting for a funeral than a daughter's wedding. After several glasses of champagne, she cried as she told Avery and Roland that she missed her son Sebastian more than ever and needed to leave early. Avery later thought that her mother always had a knack for missing opportunities; she had overlooked the chance to befriend Diya, who, of all the wedding guests, might've helped a woman terminally mired in grief to reconnect with the world of the living. On the other hand, Roland's and Avery's fathers had bonded with each other at the reception bar, where they remained throughout the celebratory speeches and glass-chimed kisses of bride and groom, until Roland's father had to escort his stumbling new friend to his hotel room before the wedding cake was cut. From then on, the two fathers remained in touch and spent an annual golf weekend together. Roland joined them one year and said the event involved far more drinking and bullshitting than golfing. *Funny that Roland, of all people, would've said that*, Avery thought. She smiled to herself at the memory of her husband sleeping off his so-called golf game on the overnight lounge chair of their deck just a few days ago.

Just as Avery was relaxing into these vivid memories of her friendship with Nazrin, the image of a cocoa-skinned baby interrupted her thoughts. *You can't ignore me any longer,* the chubby-cheeked little girl shown on a steady stream of Facebook photos seemed to be saying. She'd never met the daughter that Nazrin had given birth to

CHAPTER TEN

five years earlier, or the son who now must be three years old. The busy lives of two working and traveling journalist parents had taken over, and Nazrin and Raj had little time to see old friends. At least, that was the official story that Avery liked to tell herself. Besides that, there was the business of Avery's late miscarriage, which, no matter how guilty she felt about it, left her reluctant to visit any happy young family, even Nazz and Raj's.

Finally, Nazrin had broken the unspoken stalemate: Raj had some time off from his assignments and had offered to take care of the children so Nazz could fly to San Diego to see her best friend. For a moment, the airport bustle disappeared and Avery felt completely alone with herself. *Truth? Nazrin has this beautiful family with a loving husband who is completely enamoured with her and their children, and I am a middle-aged barren woman left behind in her wake.*

Avery shook her head and glanced up at the arrivals board to see that her friend's plane had finally landed. The ugly feelings dissolved as she felt her cheeks warming with anticipation. A silly-happy smile curled up the corners of her mouth. Minutes later, Nazrin poured into the arrivals lobby with a stream of passengers, wearing a chic pencil skirt cut just above the knees and a distinctively Persian, turquoise silk blouse. A hijab-like scarf was draped loosely around her gorgeous face and dark eyes. With that smile that always lit up her whole face, she strode assertively forward in tall brown boots and collided with her beloved friend as if by magnetic force.

"Avery!" Nazrin embraced her over the chained walkway that separated arriving passengers from the welcoming crowd. The two friends shimmied awkwardly towards the exit hall, where a full-body embrace was finally possible.

"Oh, Nazz, you look so gorgeous."

"I'm so glad to see you," Nazz said, returning the giddy laughter. "I'm also a nervous wreck. Even though I used my American passport, I'm so paranoid about crossing the border."

"I know! I hate that you have to feel this way. Every day, people are being held at the border and questioned for hours. It's ridiculous," Avery said. "Come on, let's take this bag of yours and get the hell out of here."

"Yes, let's, before they change their mind about this mouthy Iranian journalist lady."

Arm in arm, the two women took the airport doors to the parkade. By the time they merged onto the Pacific Highway toward La Jolla, they found themselves stuck in Friday afternoon traffic.

"I've been really worried about you this last while. Have you thought about what you're going to do?" Nazrin always cut right to the chase. If Avery were a more paranoid person, she would consider that Nazz and Dr. Mahler were working in cahoots. Or maybe she just needed as many people as possible to tell her the unadorned truth at this point in her life?

"Thought about it?! I'm obsessed with thinking about it, but I've absolutely no idea what to do, Nazz. I feel so stuck right now, like I've been cheated. I always imagined Roland and I would have a baby together, and we were so close to that happening just five years ago. If it's too late for me to conceive a healthy baby, I could definitely consider adopting. But Roland's nixed that option, too. 'Don't want someone else's child,'" Avery said, mimicking Roland with a sour expression on her face. "You know, I'm so upset with Roland that sometimes I can barely look at him. But am I ready to give up on thirteen years of marriage? And, as if that's not enough, I feel seriously middle-aged and unattractive all of a sudden. I just about fainted when I saw my reflection earlier today."

Someone honked behind them, and Avery stepped on the gas.

Nazrin put her hand on Avery's shoulder. "You're human, and you feel frazzled right now. But Avery, my dearest friend, my sister, you're the most beautiful and accomplished woman I know, with the compassion and patience of a saint! You of all people would ... I mean, you *will* be a great mother. I *hate* that you're in this terrible position. You and I, we'll figure it out, like we've always figured out everything."

Nazz fell silent for a moment, and out of her peripheral vision Avery could see her friend's face contorting into deep-thinking mode. "Roland's really pissing me off! If I weren't a faithful Bahá'í woman who doesn't believe in violence, I swear I'd slap that husband of yours. Actually, in this case, I might just slap him anyway and ask God for forgiveness after."

Roland should be scared, Avery thought to herself.

Avery took a deep breath as she visualized a displeased driver riding her bumper in the rear view mirror and, as soon as it was safely possible, she moved out of the fast lane. Something about Nazrin's anger made Avery feel breathless. Her own instinct was to swallow hard and push it all down.

Just then, a seagull with angry eyes flew directly toward the windshield. Avery swerved to avoid hitting the creature. The sharp *ha-ha-ha* call of the distressed gull flared up like a siren and then quickly disappeared into the distance. Her heart beat wildly. She saw it again: Persephone's stone raven in the ballet studio morphing into a live creature flying toward her. The flashback was so real that Avery cowered in the driver's seat, her hands bolted onto the steering wheel in an automatic defense. *What's going on? What's all this mean? I just need everything to stop!*

"Insane bird defeated by excellent shrink driver with keen reflexes," Nazrin said, laughing and shaking her head. Avery turned her head to look at her nonchalant friend. Didn't Nazrin see that this was a crazy, scary close call? Or was it? Avery suddenly doubted her perceptions.

"What's the matter, Avery? You look like you're going to be sick. Do you think we should pull over for a minute?"

Avery nodded and started to traverse lanes of traffic to pull over at a gas station that mercifully appeared at just the right moment.

Avery released her seatbelt, took off her sunglasses, and moved herself around to face Nazrin.

"*What is it,* Avery? It's me, talk to me!"

Avery sat motionless, eyes closed now.

"I've come all the way from Vancouver," Nazrin tried again.

Still absolutely nothing came out of Avery's mouth.

"Avery, what's wrong with you? You spend your whole day advocating for your clients, getting them to speak up to you and whoever else they should be telling how they really feel. But in your private life, you suffer from this … this paralytic passivity that's so frustrating to watch. Why are you accepting all of this? Why aren't you confronting Roland? Why aren't you asking him, *what the hell happened* four years ago when *we* were pregnant *together*? And then *we* miscarried, you should say to him. Ask him, make him answer you! *Demand* to know how you're supposed to feel when he says he never wanted a baby? You can't just roll over to the other side of the bed and cry and say absolutely nothing! You're crushing your spirit, Avery. And you're my best friend, and I can't allow that to happen! I'm begging you, speak up for yourself!"

Avery sat up, a sudden fire in her eyes. "Stop yelling at me. I'm freaking out here, and I'm scared, ok? Can you wrap your mind around that?" She surprised herself with the sharp words that unblocked her throat. "Didn't I tell you about my father screaming absolutely vile words to my mother, breaking things and slamming doors, and … Sebastian standing up for her and for me, and me wiping the blood from his face with a cold cloth. Didn't I confide all of that in you?"

"You did. And I remember every painful moment you shared with me," Nazrin reached for her best friend's hand. "But that part of your life is over, Avery. It's all ghosts in your head. Believe me, I know all about ghosts that spin fear; I have many of my own. But the reality is you chose a husband who is far from perfect, but he's not violent. And even if he were ever violent or you were faced with

CHAPTER TEN

a violent man, God forbid, you'd call 911, you'd fight for yourself, you'd press charges, *you'd make it stop*. It's safe to speak up now. In fact, what's *dangerous* is to keep swallowing your anger and allowing this fear that lives in your bones to stand in the way of saying and doing what you really want."

The two women embraced. Avery looked over Nazrin's shoulder to see *Cold Wine and Beer* illuminated on the window of the gas station convenience store. She started to laugh.

"I'm not just your most-loved sister, Nazz, I'm your only sister. The other ones must've all run away from home when you yelled at them like this. And do you know what? After this radical new form of shove-it-in-your-face psychotherapy you are practicing, *this* sister needs a drink. I'll be right back."

"You go right ahead. I'll drive," Nazrin said leaning her head out of the car window. Her mischievous smile told Avery they were back to normal. "I'm not trying to be a candy-assed psychotherapist, Ave. Just a brutally honest investigative reporter."

Avery returned a few minutes later with a grocery bag. She sat it down on the hood of the car while Nazrin watched from the driver's seat. She took out a jumbo-sized travel mug and held it up to show Nazrin. Then she took a bottle of the gas station's finest and only chilled white wine, unscrewed the top, and poured as much as she could fit into the mug. Still not stripped of all of her conscientiousness, Avery poured the rest of the wine into the grass, put the bottle in the recycling bin marked *glass*, and the neatly folded paper bag in the bin beside it for *clean paper*. Nazz rolled her eyes from where she was watching. Finally, Avery got into the passenger seat, and held up the oversized travel mug in her friend's direction.

"Cheers, Nazz! I'll put the GPS on for you," she said.

Avery took a large sip of cold wine. With her other hand, she automatically clutched the side of her seat; of the many things that Nazrin did well, driving was not among them.

When Avery and Nazrin finally pulled up the lane of the Frontieras' home, Roland stood at the top of driveway, waving with one hand and clutching an iced drink in the other.

"Well, if it isn't our favourite Iranian friend in the driver's seat," Roland said with a nervous smile, as Nazrin started to get out of the car. He downed the rest of his drink, and gave Nazrin a quick hug before taking her bag.

"And if it isn't my favourite Republican corporate financier! And you see, Roland, despite your friends' hard work to replace Obama with a dementing fascist dictator who overcontrols the borders, I still managed to climb back over the wall from the free land of Canada to see *y'all* without ever disturbing the beautiful new hijab that I bought especially for this occasion!"

Avery saw Roland glance at his empty glass before he responded.

"Oh, yes ... and so it begins. I missed your sharp tongue, Nazz. I suddenly feel much more awake." He dropped Nazrin's bag like a dead weight in the hall and gave her an exaggerated bear hug. Was this an attempt at disarmament? Avery smiled as the gas station wine percolated comfortably through her innards. She stepped around Nazrin's bag and followed Roland upstairs to the kitchen with her friend behind her. Tonight she wasn't going to be that person always picking up everyone else's baggage.

When Roland turned around he was wearing a conciliatory smile.

"So, ladies, I made three kinds of pizza, Caesar salad, and there are beers and pretty well any other cold drink you can think of in the fridge. I thought we'd eat out on the terrace. And since Nazz is already on a roll, how about we occupy the debate positions we took on our pizza nights many moons ago at San Diego State. Nazz can be the bleeding-heart-spend-all-the-money-on-everyone Democrat sitting on one side, and I will sit across from her as the someone-has-to-keep-the-economy-going Republican. And ... my Avery can sit at

CHAPTER TEN

the head of the table between us, because she likes to be in the middle and make everyone happy!" Roland put his arm around Avery and gave her a squeeze. She felt loved and appreciated, irritated, and, yes, *enraged*. Nazrin lifted her eyebrows and, for a split second, she made eye contact with Avery before her eyes locked onto Roland.

"Thank you, Roland, for having all this food ready for us. I'm actually starving. But come to think of it …" *Uh-oh, here it comes,* Avery thought, feeling both amused and nervous.

"*My* Avery is a strong Democrat who helps the vulnerable every day. So, she can take that seat at the head of the table. Avery, am I right? Would you like to be the strong Democrat representative for a change, rather than the peacemaker this evening?" Nazrin offered her a conspiratorial smile.

The image of the angry seagull passed through Avery's mind. This time she stared down the creature and did not swerve. *Get the hell out of my way,* an interesting new voice sounded in her head.

"Yes. That's a great idea, Nazz. I'm livid with our administration right now in more ways than I can count, so being the Democrat at the table is the perfect way for me to vent. Thanks, Rol, for setting it all up, so sweet of you. I just realized how ravenous I am as well," Avery said, putting her arm around Nazz.

"No fair: two Democrats against one Republican." Roland poured himself a Jameson on the rocks. He must've stopped at the specialty liquor store again, Avery thought. And what was the unstoppable Nazrin going to do next? Despite her earlier rendezvous with the gas station wine, Avery felt wide awake and alive to a palpable shift of energies in her home.

"Oh, Roland," Nazrin laughed, "Your problems are much bigger than that this evening. Remember, I live in *Canada* now, so I will be sitting across from you as a representative of our Prime Minister Justin Trudeau's Liberal government. Let's see, where shall we start? You screwing us over by reneging on NAFTA? The issue of respect for the contributions of immigrants?" She pointed to her hijab and then raised both of her arms up in exaggerated exasperation.

Roland looked hurt, but then he laughed and ushered the women to the terrace to serve them dinner and drinks. He'd always been a good sport. As the evening unfolded, Avery felt strong in her position, though she also felt herself softening to the qualities of Roland she loved the most; his playful rendition of the quintessential gentleman spoiling the ladies, the boyishly full-toothed smile that still lit up from behind his salt and pepper beard, and the conviction he showed in his well-formed arguments, which always sounded convincing and dependable, but never angry or threatening. This gentle appreciation of her husband felt like her hand was softly brushing over him, retracing the familiar places she'd discovered years ago, when she was falling in love. Avery hesitated in this moment, before the loving feelings ebbed away into waves of loss and a premonition of saying good-bye. For the first time, she considered that it would be hard on Roland if she left him.

"And what does our Democratic representative say about this point?" Nazz suddenly asked. Avery had completely lost the thread of the political discussion. The truth was that even back in the San Diego State days, she'd only short-lived interest in this type of political debate, especially compared to Nazz and Roland. Her mind always tended to drift past the intellectual verbosity of it all to places where human feelings, stories, and relationships moved her. A question occurred to her at this very moment. *Why had she never voiced her preference to do something else with their social time once in a while when they were all students at San Diego State, not even to her husband?*

"She can't comment until after dessert is served!" Avery improvised as she got up from her chair. Roland placed his hands on the table, ready to push himself up.

"It's ok, Rol. I've got this. You've done enough," Avery said, wondering if he could see the sadness in her eyes.

CHAPTER TEN

Predictably, after a few hours, the evening that had burst into a hot political debate, mostly between Roland and Nazrin, began to smoulder when the liquored-up Republican admitted defeat to the mercilessly sharp sobriety of the Liberal Canadian and the inspirational Democrat.

"You got me again, Nazz. Just like the old days," Roland said as he affectionately rubbed her shoulder. "The rest of the night is for the women's department only, because this crusty old Republican man is going to bed."

Avery and Nazrin moved across the terrace to where two lounge chairs looked out to the sparkling lights of San Diego.

"It's funny he should say women's department, isn't it? We claimed that term years ago when we decided what, and what not, to tell our husbands," Nazrin said, squeezing her best friend's hand.

"Did you ever tell Raj, Nazz?"

"No, I never did." Nazrin responded, her face shadowy and her head bending into the shape of shame. Nazrin was still holding her hand in the darkness, and this time Avery gave it a long squeeze. She'd held Nazrin's cold hand just like this more than fifteen years ago when they were waiting together in a procedure room at the San Diego Clinic for Women's Health. Nazrin had just met Raj when she discovered she was pregnant with the child of the only man she'd ever known intimately. Abortion was an unspeakable sin for a Baha'i woman—and a Hindu man for that matter—but the women's department of two had decided it would be a greater sin for a naïve young woman in the early days of her university education to continue a pregnancy with a manipulative young man who had pressured her into sex. Neither Nazz nor Avery had thought it would be possible for Raj to overlook this "mistake," or, at least, not hold a permanently altered perception of her. So there was no possible good to come of telling Raj, they had concluded, in the judgment-free zone of their friendship.

"And you, Avey, did you ever tell Roland?" Nazz asked into the darkness.

"No; I haven't even told Dr. Mahler," Avery said quietly. Nazrin was referring to the only university course that Avery had ever failed. Had it not been an elective, it might have cost her her academic career. Just after Avery met Roland, she'd been drawn into an affair with her charmingly erudite, much older English professor, who turned out to be married. Meeting Roland was the final straw of disenchantment with this paternal figure, who gradually exposed himself to be even more ill-tempered and harsh than her own father. He failed her on her final exam a week after she ended their affair. Avery could still hear his final words: *It will be fine, my dear, it's all part of your education.* She'd earned at least a B, and probably an A, but was too ashamed to appeal her grade. She told only Nazz about her mistake.

"Maybe it would help you if you told Dr. Mahler," Nazz said.

"No, I want him to keep liking me. Not that he'd judge me, but every client is allowed to edit out at least one story."

"Especially if it has been stamped *secret and shameful* by the women's department."

"Oh, Nazz ... our time has gone too fast," Avery said, as they sat over a last lunch before their drive to the airport.

"Yes, it has, Avery, but I've savoured every single minute. Plus, I can't remember the last time I slept through three nights in a row! Raj will not have been so lucky."

"Avery ... there's one more thing I really want to talk about while I can still look you straight into the eyes," Nazrin started. "It's about this bird flying over you in your ballet studio. I'm ...." Tears pooled in Nazrin's eyes, as she reached across the table for Avery's hand.

"I know," Avery responded. "I understand. You're scared that something is happening to me like it did to Sebastian. There was a

CHAPTER TEN

moment when Dr. Mahler and I had the very same thought ... but I ..."

Nazrin started to say something, but Avery wasn't finished yet. "I'm definitely a little stressed out ... well, a lot ... but I'm not crazy. I'm not schizophrenic, thank God. I don't know exactly where I'm going, but I know I'm headed somewhere important for me. The best I can understand it for the moment is that I had a vision from somewhere deep in my unconscious. I know it sounds weird, but it's like that raven spoke to me—not in words, of course, but a deeper, nonverbal message—and I feel like I need to listen, or at least, pay attention."

Nazrin relaxed into her chair, her intelligent brown eyes unwavering. Avery realized that both Dr. Mahler and her best friend were nervously watching her walk along the edges of reality. And yet, her own husband didn't have a clue about what was going on for her.

"Avery, I see it now. You're ok. You know, in my culture visions are pretty normal, almost like a dream that happens when you're awake. I just remembered something from my childhood that I haven't thought about in a long time. My grandparents had this tapestry hanging up in their living room with a huge bird in flight. It looked something like your raven, come to think of it, and the rug had all these ancient symbols around its edges.

"I was still very young, maybe six or seven, and I was fascinated with this bird. And a bit freaked out, too. My grandfather noticed me staring at it, and he told me that the wall hanging was about an ancient Persian fable. He told me it was the story of the Huma bird, and he said it was a very kind creature, and I needn't be scared of it ever again. I can't remember exactly what he said, but I read the fable when I was a bit older at school.

"So, Avery, the point is that the Huma bird is this fabulous, compassionate creature that's constantly in flight and represents the freed spirit. People rarely see it, but if you're lucky enough to catch a glimpse of it, or even its shadow, happiness will come to your life.

So maybe you're transforming, Avery, like your Dr. Mahler thought when he read to you about the raven. You have to free your spirit from its cage first, just like the Huma bird did. It's the breaking out and the not knowing what's next, that's the really scary part, and I see that this is happening for you right now, my dear friend. But if you had the good fortune of seeing the Huma bird, I would say it'll turn out well. You'll be happy again, my dear sister, if you allow it for yourself."

The two women were silent on the drive to the airport. When they embraced by the security gate, Avery felt Nazrin's heart pounding in her chest.

"I'll watch for you to come out on the other end of security," Avery said before Nazrin stepped into the line-up and quickly disappeared around the corner into the security zone. Avery hurried along the foyer to the exact vantage point from which she could catch one more glimpse of Nazrin. She waited. Finally, emerging from the long, twisted line-up before the security belt, Avery spotted the back of Nazrin's head again, enveloped in a soft orange and crimson hijab. Nazrin must've felt Avery's eyes on her, because in that instant, she turned her head to smile.

As if no one but Avery could see, Nazrin freed her left hand and arm from under her silk shawl to demonstrate the movements of a bird. She bent at the waist, her arm gliding toward the ground with the back of her hand and fingers cupped upward. After a moment of hover, she stood straight and raised her left arm as high as she could to show the bird soaring away. Prompted by the serious-looking officer at the front of the line, Nazrin turned away and leaned down to remove her shoes and put her personal items into a plastic bin. Avery waited until she glimpsed Nazrin's left hand wave one last time, her exotic dangle of bracelets sparkling on her wrist before she disappeared into the terminal.

PART II:
Fall

ELEVEN

Life is unbearably dull without Nazrin, Avery thought as she fidgeted on her chair in Dr. Mahler's waiting room. Today, the threadbare arm rests irritated her fingers. Many years of sunlight slanting from the window above the filing cabinet had drained the colour out of the 1970s landscape painting. There was never anything new or fresh in this room to catch the eye. She should just take the matter into her own hands and arrive early for her session with a bouquet of vibrant flowers and a colourful glass vase for the top of the filing cabinet. Then again, was her unusual grumpiness more a reflection of Nazz withdrawal? It wasn't just Avery who missed Nazrin. Roland did, too. He mentioned more than once that it was refreshing to hear Nazrin's sharp opinions around the table, that it reminded him of the irrepressible young people they'd been when they met. He was right about this. Nazrin had a way of revitalizing everything around her, including Avery's spirit.

The moment Dr. Mahler opened his office door, wearing his disarming smile, she regretted her critical thoughts about a room that was as unpretentious as its owner. Besides, he'd never allow her to decorate his office with a vase full of fresh flowers. And if she tried, she'd be subjected to a lengthy analysis of her family-of-origin dynamics that were now showing up in their therapist-client transference relationship and that, *ultimately,* were responsible for her wanting to bring him flowers in the first place. *Hardly worth the trouble*, she sighed. Instead she dutifully followed Dr. Mahler

CHAPTER ELEVEN

inside and sank into his well-used therapy couch with a renewed sense of appreciation.

"Tell me what's on your mind, Avery?"

Avery felt like standing up and stomping her feet, her irritation was so palpable. Instead, she spoke.

"I feel like I just haven't been able to settle myself down since Nazz left. I'm so irritable and annoyed, even picking little arguments with myself."

Dr. Mahler leaned forward and crossed his arms over his knees.

"It feels like so much happened in one short weekend. I guess I'm still trying to make sense of it."

"Yes, an eventful weekend with your dear friend Nazrin who, if I recall correctly, specializes in speaking her mind. Tell me what happened. Maybe we can sort it out together."

Avery nodded slowly, feeling as if a soft blanket of comfort had just descended upon her. *Now she was really ready to talk.* Recollections spilled out of Avery in unstoppable free fall. Dr. Mahler barely had a chance to nod while Avery raced around the bases, from being confronted by Nazz about her paralytic passivity to this week's instalment of flying creatures, this time aiming at her windshield. She finally felt herself slowing down when she admitted that this new lens through which she saw her husband that night with Nazz reminded her of why she once fell in love with him. And seeing Roland like this, she told Dr. Mahler, that old love just stopped her in her tracks. And even worse than that? She saw for the first time how he would struggle without her. I mean, *if I actually left him*, she heard herself saying for the first time out loud in the safety of this room. The echo of her words set off a dance of nerves that landed in the pit of her stomach.

"This rapid fire of images and emotions helps me to see your experience, my dear Avery. No wonder that you're left feeling unsettled."

"So what do you think about what Nazz said to me?" She could see that Dr. Mahler was hesitating about answering a direct request for his opinion. He looked down at his knees, as if they held answers, but then he started to nod, and Avery knew he was going to play slightly outside of the rules of psychotherapy.

"You know, Avery, I'm glad that you have this dear friend who cares for you enough to give you the honest feedback that most people would keep to themselves. I know that for a sensitive individual like you, her strong words and all that anger felt a little overwhelming, but perhaps we can also think about it like a form of emergency shock treatment to reignite your spirit."

"So you agree with her now?" Avery snapped. Her rational self knew he was right ... so why was she feeling this childish pout forming? The same irritation that she'd felt in the waiting room welled up inside of her again. A foreign impulse came over her; she wanted to get up and kick Dr. Mahler's trash can across the room.

"Avery, please tell me what's happening inside your head right now. Your face is contorted, and you look like you'd like to give me a good shake or something for saying what I just did."

"I feel so irritated, I don't even know what to do with myself. I know you're right, that Nazz was right, but it's still making me feel annoyed, *mad*. I feel like ... like Nazz kicked a hornets' nest, and now everything is swarming around me, buzzing in the most irritating way. And after all that, Nazz just gets up and leaves! I don't know where I'm going, but I can't go back to ... to how I was. That's what I mean about how everything feeling so unsettled, so ...."

"So what? Don't think, Avery, just say what occurs to you."

"So ... so *soul-crushingly boring* now."

"Ok, Avery, let's see where we might go with this. Please close your eyes. Take a deep breath and allow yourself to swim freely through your mind. Can you remember any other time in your life when you felt so soul-crushingly bored, irritated, unsettled, as you do right now? Move freely and without judgment or expectation, and tell me what you see ... "

CHAPTER ELEVEN

This isn't going to work today, Avery thought, but she felt so desperate that she surrendered. She closed her eyes, inhaled deeply. She then exhaled through her mouth and imagined her breath cascading from the top of her head, through her body, and into her toes. *Ok, soul-crushing boredom that makes you want to scream, and kick, and throw things.* And then the answer came to her.

"Avery, where are you now. What do you see?"

"I'm at the beginning of the summer after I finished grade nine. I haven't thought about this moment since ... I can't remember when ... I'm in my room in my family's home, sitting on my bed, and I'm looking at my suitcase. My stupid, packed-up beige suitcase with duct tape over the ripped part; my silly old suitcase that isn't going anywhere. I'm getting up now, and I kick the useless old bag so hard that I'm sure my big toe is broken, or badly bruised, anyway. It hurts so much, frustrates me so much, that I start to cry. I throw the glass of water on my bedside table across the room, and it shatters in the corner. I'm going to get into trouble on top of everything else ..." Avery saw her bedroom with the pink shag carpet and the poster of *Wham!*

"Where is it that you aren't going now, Avery, with that worn out old suitcase all packed up?"

"I'm not going to Dance Escapes! I hated my family at that moment. They ruined absolutely everything. Here I was supposed to go to summer camp with my friend Shelly, just once do something really fun away from all the craziness at home. I did everything that I was supposed to do. I saved money from babysitting to pay for half of what it cost. But now, it doesn't matter. I'm not going anywhere. Shelly cried on the phone when I told her. So here I am stuck in this boring, stupid bedroom by myself, with nothing to do. I'd already imagined myself dancing, and there was going to be a lake for swimming after the morning classes. And even a few boys were signed up for the camp, too. It was going to be so great. I packed my two-piece bathing suit, and two new leotards and dance tanks. But I'm stuck here in this shitty house, this boring place with my depressing family. They ground me down to nothing when I was so, so ... ready to fly, to be free, just for once, just for the summer," Avery said, covering her eyes with hands wet from tears.

"Avery, why aren't you going now—to the summer dance camp that sounds wonderful and you were so looking forward to?"

"Because Sebastian's been hospitalized. It's his second time. He stopped showering, his beard grew scruffy, and he stared out the window, talking to Jesus. So Mum called an ambulance. Sebby was pretty angry about that, so he's not talking to any of us right now, not even me."

"Avery, this is very serious that your brother is psychotic and has to be in the hospital. But why can't you go to your summer camp?"

"Because 'all bets are off,' as my father said; 'We don't need another one going squirrely on us at some summer dance camp.' My mother jumped right in, taking my father's side, of course, and she told me, 'You're needed at home now, to help out and to visit your brother every day so he can recover and come home.'" Avery felt her mouth twist in anger.

"And how are you feeling about this decision your parents made?"

"They are making me hate them ... and hate him. They're stealing my time to be a kid and be crazy and even make some mistakes, I mean just little ones, even. They're holding me captive in this deadly, boring, and depressing place."

"How very sad, Avery, and how desperately boring and lonely. And so your healthy, strong, beautiful, independence-seeking teenage spirit was put inside the cage of a bewildered family with a very ill son who took over any space they had for you."

"Yes, that's it. I can't go back to that time; I can only go forward. Even if I don't know exactly where I'm going." Avery felt a bit calmer now, but also very tired. Anywhere else, she would have felt embarrassed about how childish her words would have sounded, but here

83

CHAPTER ELEVEN

with Dr. Mahler, they both knew what regression to a childhood trauma looked like and how necessary it was for making progress.

"And as far as breaking spirits out of cages, my dear Avery, do you ... believe in second chances?"

There was no need here for fancy new vases or fresh-cut flowers when Dr. Mahler had the tried and true simple tools to look into her heart.

Avery was still thinking about her session with Dr. Mahler when she made her way back to her office. Balancing her wallet and deli sandwich in one hand, she unlocked the door to her waiting room, turned on the floor lamp with her foot, and sat down on one of the armchairs. She told herself she'd close her eyes, just for a few minutes.

When she woke up, her unfinished sandwich was still in its wrapper in her hand. *Why did everything look so different?* It was as if she were seeing this room for the first time. Her surroundings felt so surreal that she questioned whether she was still asleep and this was a dream. She checked the clock on the coffee table, which told her twenty minutes had passed. This antique clock had been her grandmother's on her father's side—a wise woman with a shockingly white chignon pinned on the top of her head, who had always understood Avery better than her own parents did. Avery closed her eyes for another moment to shake off the unreal feeling. The rhythmic sound of the clock ticking transported her to the feeling of complete safety she'd felt as a little girl when she fell asleep on her grandmother's couch.

Relaxed by these soothing sounds and images, Avery looked across the room to the cherry wood bookcase that housed her collection of figurines. Why did she have so many beautiful pieces in her waiting room of all places, while Dr. Mahler chose stark realism? Avery focused first on the dramatic flamenco dancer showing off a crimson fan held above her head, a figurilla Avery had seen displayed in the window of a tiny shop in Sevilla many years ago. *"Casi libre,* almost free," the old woman suddenly standing beside her had said, as she beckoned Avery to come in *simplemente para observar,* just to take a look. Placed beside the flamenco dancer was the elegant pewter replica of the Austrian Prince Eugene arrogantly perched on his rearing horse, purchased at the double-its-value tourist price in the gift store at Vienna's Belvedere Museum. Worth every Schilling!

Suddenly, she was on her feet. *What the ....? Where's my Italian David??* Within a millisecond, Avery's nose was almost touching the shelf. Infuriated, she located a tell-tale clearing in the shape of a circle in the thin layer of dust on her shelf. "Uh huh!" she muttered, as she touched the circle of dust with her index finger. The results of her investigation were obvious, and there was no doubt now that she was fully awake: *That miserable, defiant, snooping little thief snatched my beautiful white marble David right out from under my nose!* Avery swung her office door open, marched into the room, and fired her purse onto the couch as hard as she could. She made her way to the filing cabinet and pulled Clare's file, as if that would be of any help at all.

Avery began to calm down as she flipped through Clare's file. She'd known Clare was a thief when she accepted her as a client. Avery thought of Dr. Mahler's utilitarian waiting room. How unwise she'd been to put her precious things within reach of a young woman overflowing with anger and entitlement. Yes, it was like she'd left her unlocked Cadillac in the parking lot of the detention centre!

TWELVE

*A*very opened her balcony doors and stepped outside. The autumn sky had become overcast since noon. It definitely didn't look like beach weather for Clare today! *The binoculars stay locked up inside,* said a voice sounding like a much stricter version of Dr. Mahler. It was five minutes to four, and Avery searched for figures on the shoreline. Just dogs and garden-variety beachcombers. Perhaps Clare would be on time today, and the rhythm of their sessions would become more regular? Avery was about to go back inside when she picked up a musky whiff. She heard a dog barking in the distance, and wondered whether a skunk had made its way into the landscaped area around the lobby of her building. Avery followed the smell and peered over the railing of her second-floor balcony to see puffs of smoke floating above a mass of copper hair. This wasn't quite the Californian skunk Avery had expected. There was Clare, sitting cross-legged on the garden bench below, savouring a drag from a good-sized joint. Avery glimpsed an ear bud cord dangling beneath the mess of curls. Each time she took another puff, Clare leaned back her head and the tops of her sunglasses appeared. Clare must know her psychologist's office was somewhere above where she was sitting, and surely she *couldn't* have missed that there was a balcony.

Clare's head rolled back again and her grey-green eyes opened widely above her sunglasses. As she saw Avery leaning over the railing, Clare lifted her joint in her psychologist's direction and

CHAPTER TWELVE

mouthed, "Want some? Makes you less uptight." Then Clare moved to the sound of her music.

Avery stepped out of sight and inhaled five times, trying to get the best of the diluted fumes, before she closed her office doors. Hadn't she read a federal report documenting a rise in pot-smoking among middle-aged parents of teenagers (or young adults who still acted like teenagers)? Now she knew exactly why.

It was nine minutes past four p.m. when the scent of Clare wafted from Avery's waiting room to her office. Clare came in without being asked and arranged herself on the couch. She took off her sunglasses and offered Avery an uncharacteristic smile.

"So, I'm pretty chill for our session today, Doc," Clare offered.

"Yes, I can see that. Tell me, how you have been doing this past week?"

"Fine. Remind me again, *why* am I here?" Clare asked, slouching. *Only Clare and Angelina Jolie could look attractive with such bloodshot eyes*, Avery thought, as she prepared to get to work.

"Well, I remember you explaining to me that you were seeing me because you are a thief. So, Clare, speaking of this, I'm wondering if you have had any urges to steal since we started to meet four weeks ago?"

Clare sat quietly for a moment.

"Umm ... Not that I can recall. I haven't been in a lot of shops lately," Clare said, looking confused, even uncertain. "Now, wait a minute. Can you remind me of what happens if you find out I've stolen something?"

"Well, Clare, you are here to overcome your problem with stealing. I do have to provide an opinion to the judge after you complete your course of psychotherapy with me. I would have to be honest and fair in my report. So us talking about when and why you have urges to steal is an important part of that," Avery said evenly.

"And what happens if I fail psychotherapy and keep stealing and you write that in your report?"

"I'm not sure, Clare. Sometimes a judge will order community hours or a suspended sentence. I don't want to scare you, but it's serious, and it can affect things like your right to travel abroad. You might like to talk to your lawyer about this, too, and make sure you understand the legal part," Avery stated. "Now have you felt any such urges to take something, Clare?"

"Umm, well, like I said, I have been staying out of the shops. I mean, I don't really steal stuff from people, just from stores that have plenty more. It was just kind of a crazy, risk-taking thing I was doing to see if I could get away with it, but I'm over it now. What kind of community hours are you talking about?"

"There are many different kinds of community placements. It would be up to you and your probation officer to decide. It could be working at a soup kitchen or helping elderly individuals in their homes. But, of course, that's why you and I are working together, to prevent all of that and find out why you felt attracted to taking these risks."

An image of a disgruntled Clare, ladling pea soup to the unfortunate recipients passed through Avery's mind. *That might not work out so well*, she thought.

"You're kind of freaking me out right now. I mean, it's not like I said that I've stolen anything in the last while since the court thing," Clare said, sounding more defensive and less stoned with every word she spoke.

"Ok, so you say you haven't stolen anything since we started to work together …"

"We're not working together," Clare interrupted, mocking Avery's tone. "You like to think you're in charge and if you say I'm still stealing in your report, then I have to go and ladle out soup to some homeless person … when, when …"

"When what, Clare?"

89

CHAPTER TWELVE

"When I'm the victim! I'm the one who's been cheated and stolen from, but nobody seems to give a shit about that. So I take a little something here and there to make myself feel better, and you people make this big deal out of it!" Clare shouted.

"What's been stolen from you, Clare?"

"Um, let's just see ... my childhood, maybe? That's not a good thing to have go missing, now is it?" Clare rubbed her red eyes, making them worse.

"It is a terrible thing to have go missing, Clare. How did your childhood go missing?"

Suddenly Clare looked serious.

"My mother got breast cancer and died on me when I was four. My grandmother took care of me for a little bit, but then she couldn't anymore. She was frail and sad, and then she got sick or something." Clare stared into her hands.

"I'm so sorry, Clare, that your mother got so sick and died. She must have been a young woman still. What happened after your grandmother couldn't take care of you anymore?" Avery saw that Clare was digging into the palm of her left hand with the nails of her other hand.

"We ... we tried to find my father. But, you see, it turns out he's an asshole. And he wasn't interested in raising me, so I went up for adoption. I tried to find him again when I turned twenty one, but he just told the adoption agency that he was ok 'to give up his parental rights and declined to have contact with me,' something like that, the official letter said."

"I can't even imagine how hard that must've been for you, Clare. You lose your mother and your grandmother, and both times you try to reach out to your father, he isn't there for you." Avery noticed that Clare had drawn blood from her palm.

Clare sat with her head bowed, hair toppling to her lap. A tiny pool of blood formed on her palm, which she touched with her index finger. She sat that way for several minutes before she tilted her face upwards. "I'm not going to cry for you. I'm not going to cry for anyone. As you can see, I'm picking away and making a mess of my hands. You're making me tired today, doctor, and I was having such a good time before I got here."

Clare pulled several Kleenex tissues from the box on the table and pressed them into her palm. She brought her legs up onto the couch and lay down on her side, her right hand was covering her face.

Clare looked much younger than her age, a sad child who'd given up. As Clare's breathing became more even, her right hand slipped off of her face and fell loosely off the couch. A mix of dark emotions and pot had put this young woman to sleep. Avery felt an instinct to cover Clare with the throw blanket at the end of the couch, but she knew it was best to refrain from doing so. What kind of a father would abandon a little girl after her mother died?

At ten minutes to three, Clare was still sleeping.

"Clare … Clare, it's time to wake up," Avery said softly from her armchair.

"What happened?" Clare jolted awake, sat up, looked at the drying wound on her left hand and then made eye contact with Avery.

"You told me about what happened with your parents and your grandmother, and then you fell asleep, Clare. It's ok. This happens sometimes."

"Oh yeah, I remember that now. We could keep talking now, Doc, if you want?" Clare appeared confused.

Avery knew exactly what she needed to do to move Clare's therapy forward, but for a moment she struggled. The pull to let her stay and talk was strong, but she couldn't give in to it.

"I'm sorry, Clare, but our time is over for today. I'm hoping that if you're able to come right at four o'clock next Wednesday, we can pick up our talk then and use all of our time together. I'd also like to talk to you about the picking of your hands, or anywhere else on your body where you might hurt yourself. Some people do this to

CHAPTER TWELVE

relieve internal stress, but we might find another way that doesn't leave you with injuries."

"I guess time's up. My bad," Clare said. Without another word, she rose, opened the office door, and, to Avery's surprise, closed it gently behind her.

THIRTEEN

In the right light, at the right time, everything is extraordinary. Since her teens Clare had made a habit of memorizing her favourite quotations, and tonight these words of the nonconformist photographer Aaron Rose streamed through her mind. She lay on her bed, bathed in the extraordinary light of this night. Filtered through the slats of her Venetian blinds, the harvest moon cast playful lines of light on the naked body of her lover. There he slept beside her on a jumble of white bed sheets; she'd have to throw the entire smelly mess into the washing machine first thing in the morning. *Well, this dance is definitely over,* Clare thought, suppressing a chuckle. The young man's long, dark hair was no longer twisted into the sexy braid he wore sitting at the bar. When she'd caught her first glimpse of him from the back, his white shirt revealing hints of a chiselled body, she was pretty sure he'd be doing it for her by the end of the night. He now glistened with sweat and snored contentedly. Small pits of drool were accumulating in the corners of his mouth. *They go from sexy to disgusting so damned quickly.*

Clare felt restless now that the sex was over and extracted her hand from his. She slipped out of bed and wrapped herself in the white silk robe she'd abandoned on the floor earlier that evening. Standing in the breeze of her balcony doors, Clare soundlessly rolled up the Venetian blinds. The moonlight poured into her studio apartment, colouring it the shade of honey. Clare turned toward the bed to ensure that the flood of light hadn't woken up her spent man.

CHAPTER THIRTEEN

Suddenly, he turned over, and a wave of trepidation came over her. But then he was still asleep, and Clare sighed in relief. Turned on his side, he was also no longer snoring so obnoxiously. He looked more and more aversive to her, so much so that she had to look away. Clare savoured the moon as a private moment, and she didn't want to deal with asking him to leave if he woke up. *You are a cold bitch.* But in truth, she just didn't care.

Clare padded barefoot across the room, opened the drawer of her desk, and retrieved a faded, black and white photograph. She held it close to her face, hoping to find even the tiniest detail she might have missed the other times she'd done this very same thing. There she was again: the beautiful, smiling woman caught somewhere, sometime, holding a chubby-armed little girl high over her head. It was the only photo she had of herself with her mother. Clare wondered, as she had many times before, who'd taken this picture. Could it have been her father, that complete asshole of a man who she had tried so hard to find but who wanted nothing to do with her? Clare released the bitter taste in her mouth and smiled again as she thought about how she and her mother looked so wrapped up with each other in the photo; they probably wouldn't have noticed the person behind the camera anyway. Clare tried to hang on to the moment, but as always, this feeling of complete love faded to despondency. She'd been the apple of her mother's eye? Why was it so impossible to hold on to love? Maybe tonight would make a difference, because she had a plan.

Clare held the corner of the photograph between her pursed lips, and leaned down to pick up a canvas stored under her desk. She brought it across the room to her easel, and swivelled the easel so that it faced the moonlight. Clare felt for a pushpin in her easel drawer, discovering it with a prick to her finger. She affixed the photograph to the canvas frame so she could look at the painting and the photo at the same time. She had the perfect solution to the unfinished painting. Clare moved her painting stool to the side of the easel so as not to block the moonlight and sat down. Illuminated in the moonlight, the painting appeared to be in motion, clouds floating over basil green hills and mint sea foam spraying up from the ocean. The finely articulated sea spray looked like it was catching in the clouds.

It was that faintest whisper of a conversation with heaven, she thought to herself. She knew all about the sparkling promise of a child's search for answers from above, relentless attempts that had inevitably ended in disappointing monologues with God. Clare had given up on religion long ago, but from time to time, a fleeting image of sitting safely tucked in between her mother and grandmother in church made her question her faith all over again. A few strategically placed flickers of gold leaf glittered like water in the moonlight. She felt her edges melting as a smile blossomed on her face. It looked just like she had hoped. *I think Momma would like it.* The painting finally looked like that ephemeral place, the place that she couldn't actually remember or locate in her waking life, but that floated past her at night in wispy dream fragments for as long as she could remember.

When she was twelve, Clare had heard about lucid dreaming and how to get good at it. Her plan was to soldier fully alert through her dreams, good and bad, so she could see and remember everything. She learned about foods that would help this brilliant way of dreaming, like dark cherries and full-fat yoghurt, and incantations to be spoken at bedtime, apparently necessary to build the confidence she needed to stay lucid to her dreamscapes. Clare began setting her alarm to wake her exactly four hours after she went to bed, when she'd turn on the lights to write feverishly in her dream journal and then lie back down to induce a second round of dreams. At this point in Clare's admittedly extremist pursuit of dreams, Molly and Jim became worried. They sat her down one evening after dinner and asked her if she might like to see a counsellor about her dreams and about how, *ever so understandably, our sweet darling girl* still missed her *real mother.*

CHAPTER THIRTEEN

Clare was offended by this suggestion and her parents backed off. It struck her now how good they'd been to her. She'd a habit of resenting them, simply because they were a reminder of her real parents, one of whom had died on her and the other who had no interest in being in her life. She felt a wave of gratitude for Molly and Jim wash over her; she'd have to learn how to love them as they deserved to be.

Clare remembered how, one night, after her alarm went off at one in the morning, Jim came to her bedside with a thick sketchpad and a fresh set of drawing pencils. *Maybe it would be easier to draw what you have seen?* he suggested in his strong Scottish accent, and then padded quickly back out of the bedroom before she had time to open her mouth. That night, at fifteen, Clare decided to become an artist. The dream sketches flowed effortlessly from her mind's eye, unhindered by words, grammar, spelling, and exacting thoughts.

Enough of all this thinking! The harvest moonlight would not last much longer, and it was time to unleash her uncensored self. Clare closed her eyes for a few seconds and took a deep breath before she began to paint. Checking the black and white photo, she painted a side view of her mother, lying relaxed on her back on the ocean's shore, holding her little girl high, careful to capture the exact expressions on their faces, matching dimples and all. In a trance now, she filled in her mother's rose-coloured blouse that smelled like lilacs in the springtime, the loose white shorts that doubled as a bathing suit for quick splashes in a freezing cold ocean, and the pink-and-yellow dotted sundress allowing the free movement of young Clare's chubby arms and legs.

Clare painted traces of a blanket on which her mother lay; it was the well-used, soft grey comforter that had been taken from their cottage for this day at the beach. *It's no matter, we'll shake out the sand when we get home and it will smell much better for it, just like our day at the beach.* Had her mother really said something so fantastically carefree? In her mind, her mother's voice sounded like a happy song, different than the manner of speaking Clare was used to.

Clare worked frantically to keep up with the powerful images gliding through her mind. There it was now: A simple basket perched beside mother and child that would've been filled with lemonade in a recycled glass milk bottle; egg sandwiches cut into triangles; and her teddy bear, whose name was . . . Yes! It was Finley. She felt tears fill her eyes at this discovery of a name to call her teddy bear.

The canvas that had taken months to prepare and a lifetime of dreams to envision was finished. The moonlight had stood by her, Clare thought gratefully. She felt tears streaming down her cheeks, tears that she'd held in since that day of black and grey, holding her grandmother's hand at her mother's funeral. Clare folded herself down onto the old rug. *Good night, Momma.*

A few hours later, Clare woke to sunlight and the young man leaning over her, his long dark hair gathered into a messy man bun.

"I love your painting, but are you ok, beautiful?"

It took Clare a moment to gather her senses. She again felt hopeless. Last night was over. For a split second, she pictured herself cuddled into Piérre's arms and telling him about how much she missed her mother still, even eighteen years later, but instead she exploded.

"Get the hell out! Can't you see I want to be alone?"

This was not the first young man who would gather his things and get the hell out, looking like a dog who'd been kicked hard enough that he wouldn't be back.

Clare spent the better part of Sunday in bed nursing her emotional hangover. She let herself doze off and hoped for more dreams, but nothing came. Then again, it was no wonder that her rich repository of dreams and creativity was exhausted for now. She decided that her newly finished painting would be called *Love Lost*. Panic pulsed

CHAPTER THIRTEEN

through her body. Clare reassured herself that naming the painting didn't mean she would have to move it into her public portfolio.

In the late afternoon, Clare finally got out of bed, made herself a cup of coffee, and meandered out on to her balcony. She moved her lounge chair to face the finished painting. *Ok, so now what?* She could keep looking at the painting all by herself and lick her wounds. Clare certainly would not take it to any of her art professors for discussion, because they were too stupid to understand its importance; any of their ideas for developing the painting further were completely unwelcome.

Suddenly, an image of Dr. Frontiera's sympathetic face washed over Clare. Although her instinct was to dismiss this thought of her annoying doctor, another part of Clare rose up to play the devil's advocate. *She does seem to know something about art. She's paid a lot of money, too much if you ask me, to just sit there and be non-judgmental. You're kind of stuck about what to do next now that this painting that took you years to come up with is finished.* It will be like a test, Clare negotiated with herself. If Frontiera couldn't handle her painting or couldn't tell Clare something she didn't already know, then her psychologist was just another impostor. She went inside to slide her dried painting into an oversized portfolio bag. Then she turned her attention to the messy pile of linen on her bed, delighted at the prospect of removing every trace of the young man's smell from her apartment.

FOURTEEN

It was ten to four as Avery read her progress notes for Clare. She suddenly realized that she was clutching the ballet studio key that Madame Paloma had entrusted to her, a key that Avery wore like a precious pendant on a thin gold chain around her neck. She loosened her grip to see that the key was now imprinted on her sweaty palm. *The unconscious speaks*, she smiled to herself. Tonight would be the perfect evening to unwind with a solitary barre workout. The thought of having the ballet studio to herself felt strangely exciting, a little like the anticipation of a secret rendezvous.

Avery heard muffled sounds coming from her waiting room, and then a loud voice that distinguished itself over the soundproofing. "Oh, shit, that hurt! What a complete pain in my ass!" she heard. Clare had arrived.

Avery checked her watch. Three fifty-eight. This was the second time in the past ten minutes that she'd smiled. *We are not yet past all the drama, but at least she is bursting noisily through the doors on time. This is progress.*

When Avery opened the door to her waiting room, only Clare's head and shoulders were visible behind a large black portfolio bag placed upright on the rug and leaning against her knees. The bag looked like a large shield, but today the warrior's eyes said something different. Avery detected vulnerability in Clare's furrowed brow.

"Hello, Clare; please come in."

CHAPTER FOURTEEN

"The portfolio was a big pain … to bring all the way here. I can't tell you how many times I almost tripped over it."

Clare stood up, gripped the handle of the bag decisively, and flexed her bicep to transport it into the therapy room. Rather than sitting down in her usual place on the couch, Clare stood and surveyed the room. Her eyes stopped at Avery's desk situated near the veranda door. Avery's desk chair was pushed in neatly under the desk. Clare used her free arm to pull out the chair from behind the desk.

"This'll have to do, I guess," Clare said, as she lifted the portfolio bag onto the seat of the chair and leaned it against its tall back.

Without a word, Clare undid the wraparound zipper. Avery suppressed a gasp as a painting with many layers of colour and emotion was unveiled. Clare backed up to sit on the arm of the couch, still facing her painting, but now from a comfortable distance. She didn't turn to Avery before she spoke.

"I just finished this painting, and I didn't have anyone else but you to show it to," Clare began. *Good to know*, Avery thought, *in case I might think I was specially chosen.* The whisper of a therapeutic bond was finally in the room. Avery took a seat in the armchair next to the couch so that she and Clare were sitting side-by-side, facing the painting on its makeshift easel.

"Please, tell me about your painting, Clare," Avery said. Clare glanced at her, inhaled deeply, and released a long sigh.

"This is my mother, my real mother, and me at the beach, when I was little—somewhere, I don't know where," Clare started. Her voice sounded far away, as if she been drawn into another sphere.

Avery waited for Clare to continue. Clare, too, sat quietly before she spoke again. "Ok, I've decided that I am going to tell you about it."

Avery braced herself. Her heart ached for Clare's battle to maintain control over the raw emotions spilling out from her painting and into the room. "I'm glad. Please do tell me."

Over the next half hour, never once stopping to turn toward Avery, Clare did just that. Clare didn't provide a coherent account, nor did Avery expect one. Instead, Clare painted a collage of memories and impressions: the swoosh of light-pink paint layered smoothly over white to do justice to her mother's crisp summer blouse in the sunshine; her lighter toddler skin on chubby limbs in contrast to the hint of tan on her mother's leaner but still soft-skinned limbs; the tiny yellow dots on her sundress, to which she had added a hint of gold leaf, just here and there, to show the reflection of sunlight; and her mother's dark brown sandals, abandoned beside the comforter on which she was lying.

Clare's usual blanket of sarcasm and defiance had lifted as she pointed out the elements of her painting, reflecting years of dreams and yearning, as well as the techniques she used on lightly brushed corners or the textured contours of driftwood nearby. Avery listened carefully to whatever fragments Clare offered about her early life, her childhood of lucid dreamscapes, the final transfer of the black and white image onto the painting during the harvest moon night, and the frenzy to paint the details that suddenly spread over the canvas to fill gaps in her memory.

Clare got up only once to touch her mother's dimples and then her own on the painting, offering proof to Avery of their physical likeness. Not that any proof was needed; they were, without a doubt, mother and child. Finally, Clare moved around to sit on the couch, crossed her arms over her chest, and looked up at Avery.

"So, that's it. I'm not sure it was worth bringing in."

"Clare, it was very much worth it to me. I'm a little in awe of the beauty of your painting, but more than that, I can't imagine a better way of learning about you and your mother through your own eyes. Thank you for sharing all of this with me."

Avery saw Clare's face soften, but then her brow furrowed again. "So, what do you see in the painting, being a shrink or a psychologist or whatever you want to call yourself?"

CHAPTER FOURTEEN

"I call myself a psychologist. Hmm ... I see that you and your mother loved each other very much, and I think that you were once in beautiful and carefree places together. And I feel very, very sorry that you lost your mother at such a young age."

Still turned toward her painting, Avery saw Clare lift her sleeve to roughly wipe her eyes. "Well, I know all that already, that's why it's called *Love Lost*, but ... but thanks ..." Clare said, fighting for composure. "That's one of the regrets that I said I might tell you about one day. I mean, that she died so young, and I regret, I hate, that it's so hard to remember her."

"Yes, that *is* truly a terrible loss."

There were only five minutes left in their session. As Clare sat quietly, her eyes averted now, Avery studied the painting to find a path to help Clare out of immobilizing loss. She needed to offer a nurturing thought that Clare could take home with her today.

"You know, Clare, I wonder if you have any memories at all about what your mother called you. Did she have a special nickname for you, the way that mothers sometimes do?"

Clare started to shake her head with a sarcastic expression, as if to rid herself of a question not even worth considering. But suddenly, she sat frozen with her eyes wide open, as if she were seeing something for the first time.

"Clare? Are you remembering something?"

Clare nodded with an excitement that washed away the defiant lines usually on her face.

"I remember something new—or at least, something I forgot I knew! My mother called me 'my windmaker'! I think she called me this because I would run away from her really fast, like if we were playing at the beach or something. I still remember that happy movement in my legs. She'd just run after me, laughing and laughing. When she caught up with me, she'd put her arms around me from behind, pick me up, and kiss my cheeks. And that's when she'd say to me something along the lines of, 'I have to run very, very fast behind you, because you are being carried by the wind.'

"I loved the idea of being carried by the wind, even then. But it got even better, because my mother believed that it was *me, my spirit*, I think now, my fast-moving legs, that were making that wind happen in the first place. I don't know exactly how she said that to me, but I sure remember how it felt. And then it became a thing, every time I ran away from her down the beach or down this moss-covered trail to the cottage, our home I guess. She'd call after me, 'I've my little windmaker to catch,' yes, that part I remember completely, those were her words, *my little windmaker.*" Clare's cheeks were flushed with the story as if she had just run through the wind.

As her face started to fall into sadness, a psychic stumble from the highest high back to the reality of being alone with her spirited mother long gone, Clare suddenly checked her iPhone. "I better start packing up so I can get out of here on time." Clare stood and moved across the room.

When the portfolio zipper stuck for a moment, her anger returned. "The other regret I have is that my real father is a complete asshole. But that's a story for another day."

Just as Avery was about to say good-bye to her client, Clare turned around. "The part I'm going to tell you about my father is the story of a *shit storm*, not the story of a *windmaker*," Clare said with a grin.

Avery smiled back. *She can smile ... and she looks like she's safe to go home now.* "I'll be ready to listen to all that you want to tell me. Thank you for sharing your painting with me today. See you next week, Clare!"

Clare hurried out of the office and through the waiting room, her portfolio bag banging against her legs and the furniture several more times. Avery felt air tunnelling through the therapy room and out the open balcony doors. Clare's mother had known her windmaker very well, but now she was more like a gale-force whirlwind of a young woman.

FIFTEEN

You need your ballet more than ever now. Madame Paloma's words echoed in the still ballet studio. Avery was reassured by the familiarity of her bare feet on the cool wooden floor. In the fading afternoon light that spilled through the tall windows, Avery could make out the shapes of autumn leaves cascading to the ground. Her hands grazed her ballet tights as she assembled herself at the ballet barre. She faced away from the Persephone statue and instead looked out through the full-length windows into the gardens and forest behind. Avery's body felt heavy and tired, yet still dutiful to her instruction. Her thighs bent into their first perfect diamond shape to begin her series of *demi-pliés*. Avery's right hand seemed to be waking up to Madame Paloma's recent correction, and now it graced the barre *light as a feather*. Each *plié* felt as if the rhythmic movement was squeezing just a little more tension out of her body. *This is so what I need.*

By the time her series of *demi-pliés* was done, Avery felt energy returning to the movements of her body. The apples of her cheeks were lifting with a familiar smile of pride. *Alors maintenant on va brosser les pieds,* Avery heard Madame Paloma's voice. With her right foot alive through the arch but solidly grounded into the wooden floor, Avery relished the first brush of her left foot forward over the smooth ground until her toes formed a point and traced an exact half-circle on the ground.

CHAPTER FIFTEEN

Et encore mes petits etudiants, les rondes des jambes; this time she recognized the inflection of her childhood ballet teacher, Monsieur Gregoir. Avery thought about how her ballet lessons ended abruptly after Sebastian fell ill for the first time. "All of the family's energies need to be focused on him, there isn't time for the luxury of ballet," her mother had told her with tears in her eyes.

Who was she or Monsieur Gregoir to argue with that? He called home and did his best on her behalf. The night after the decision was made, she went into an angry frenzy of *rondes-des-jambes* on the shag carpet of her bedroom that left her with blisters on the soles of her feet and a pit of resentment in her stomach.

Let it all go: you are home now. I think I do believe in second chances. Tonight, the smooth floor seemed to offer healing to old wounds. Avery did an extra set of ten before she pivoted and repeated the exercise on the other side.

Avery checked her posture first in the mirror just behind the ballet barre on which her hand still rested, and then in the mirror on the other side of the studio. Across the room, the last of the day's sunlight reflected in a parade of sparkles on the mirrors, giving the impression of Avery's silhouette in the foreground. She felt proud of the dancer's figure that she projected, the studio key on her necklace sparkling like a gem. How different her reflection appeared to her today, grounded in her lifelong love of ballet, than it did a few weeks ago when she collided with her harried self at the airport. Despite the roadblocks of her childhood, Avery still felt and moved like a ballerina. *I'm so at home here.*

Warmed up, Avery decided that it was time to move into the deeper bends of the *grands-pliés* series. She remembered how Monsieur Gregoir told his students to imagine they were standing between two panes of glass, straight as soldiers; with each perfectly formed *plié*, their bodies would move up and down but never touch the glass. Avery closed her eyes to bring this visual to mind and to imagine the artistic beauty of fading sunlight on sheets of glass with a perfectly poised dancer standing between them.

When she opened her eyes again, she looked across the room to her reflection with the hope of confirming the desired straight alignment of her first *grand-plié*. But this is not what she saw. In what felt like an electric shock pulsing through her body, Avery saw not her own reflection, but that of a smaller, golden-coloured figure. Then this mesmerizingly golden figure, a little girl, turned her face slightly, tilted her chin upward, and looked at Avery imploringly. Still halfway down the bend of her *plié* with her right arm extending toward this golden child, Avery panicked, closed her eyes, and buckled forward. The sound of shattering glass exploded in the space around her before she folded onto the floor.

It took all of Avery's courage to open her eyes and look across the room. There, among sparkling chards of glass, she made out the figure of the little girl, crumpled now as if her skin were covered by tiny, creased bits of gold leaf. She was sprawled out on the wooden floor across the room, just like Avery. Surprisingly, Avery was overcome by a sense of calm and an urge to make connection with this collapsed child. Her right arm reached up for the ballet barre and her fingers circled around it. She pulled herself up and walked across the room, unafraid of the shimmering field of shattered glass. Avery moved toward the little girl, who was facing away from her. The small, crumpled body moved evenly with her breath. Avery bent over to reach toward the forehead of the child with the gentle back of her hand. With the sun almost set, it was becoming harder and harder to discern the outlines of the child in the reflection of the mirror in front of her. Before her hand could touch the little girl's forehead, the child's figure disappeared into what looked like a cloud of fairy dust, as did the chards of glass on the ground.

Avery crouched down to touch the wooden floor where the child had lay, or where she thought she had been lying. The floor still felt warm as she pressed her palm upon it. Baffled, Avery sat down and

CHAPTER FIFTEEN

checked the soles of her feet, still heated from their brushes with the wooden floor. They were smooth, velvety even, without any signs of cuts or embedded chards. Night was beginning to pool in through the windows and threatened to surround her. Avery rose quickly to turn on the studio lights. Everything looked absolutely normal. Even the Persephone statue with the raven still sitting on her extended hand was innocently set in stone.

Why am I not freaking out? Avery thought to herself, as she stood in the middle of the room that now looked unremarkable, just like Madame Paloma's dance studio always did. Was she in some elaborate dream? Having some Persian transformation vision? Was this finally the psychotic break that she had dreaded since Sebastian became ill, knowing always that she, too, might carry the fearsome genes? Maybe she and Dr. Mahler were wrong to rule this out? Avery shrugged her shoulders, not feeling a connection with any of these interpretations. *I wonder what Clare is really trying to tell me?* This thought passed through her mind so clearly that Avery could swear it had been spoken out loud. Yes, this was exactly the question she should be asking herself.

SIXTEEN

*I*t was nearly dark when Avery turned up the cobblestone lane. She was relieved that Roland's jeep was not in the driveway; she wouldn't have to muster the energy for a superficial conversation before drawing the hot bath she craved. Even better than this option would be coming home to a husband who took one look at you and asked, *what happened to you today? You look like you just saw a ghost.* She had already calculated how long it would be until she saw Dr. Mahler again: he was on holiday next week, and it would be thirteen days before she could tell the story of the golden child who had appeared in the ballet studio this evening. Avery had thought about phoning Nazz about what had happened, but the story just seemed a little too worrisome, especially after she had just reassured her friend of her sanity. Besides that, the demeanour of the little girl in her "vision" was decidedly fragile, and Avery felt an odd sense of protectiveness about exposing her. She felt disconcerted as she locked the front door behind her.

The hall light was always left on this time of year, when sundown came earlier and earlier, but what surprised Avery was the beam of light appearing from under the door of Roland's office at the far end of the foyer. She walked gingerly toward the closed door. *Could he be home? Where was his Jeep?* She gently knocked and waited before she crossed the threshold to Roland's private space. She hadn't been in this room for a very long time—*five years, actually*, her inner voice suddenly reminded her. She felt like a stranger in her husband's

CHAPTER SIXTEEN

world as she scanned the polished mahogany desk with papers neatly stacked on the leather blotter and the tall bookshelves filled with encyclopaedic volumes and a gentleman's memorabilia. Avery sat down on the leather desk chair, which was turned away from the desk as if he'd hurried out of the room. She could still smell a trace of Roland's cologne. Avery swivelled around in the chair, aware that if she were to hear the front door opening, she'd feel caught like an intruder.

Avery looked down at the elegantly detailed desk drawer with its ornate handle and remembered the exact moment she'd last been in this room: the night she was discharged from the hospital after her miscarriage. Roland had helped her to bed, but when she awoke grief-stricken a few hours later, he was not beside her in bed. She'd padded down the stairs and through the foyer, where light showed behind the door slightly ajar. Without saying a word, Avery had walked into his room, sat down on his lap, and nuzzled her face into his neck. She remembered his reassuring smell, and, at that moment five years ago, she was sure that this man was her rock, with whom she would soon have a child. *Avey, I didn't hear you coming. You surprised me. What are you doing up?* He had embraced her with one arm and used the other hand to close the desk drawer to make more room for her on his lap.

Avery now felt an uncomfortable sensation in her stomach as she stared at the drawer. She checked over her shoulder before she moved her hand toward it. She tried to pull the drawer open, but it was locked. She snatched back her hand quickly, as if she'd burned it on the stove. *What are you doing? Are you trying to make things even worse?* Her hand shaking, she reached for the pull-chain on the desk lamp. In a split-second decision, Avery decided to leave the chair facing away from the desk, just as she'd found it. She closed the door as quietly as she could, even though she was certain that there was no one at home but herself to judge her actions.

SEVENTEEN

On a handful of fall days, Santa Ana winds cascade from the mountains to warm the California coastline and make for perfect golfing weather. With his hands burrowed deep in his pockets, Roland leaned back against the trunk of a sycamore tree and allowed the pleasant breeze to waft over him. From his lookout on the hill, comfortably hidden by the mature branches of the tree, he could look through his binoculars down into San Diego's Holy Cross Catholic Cemetery, where a small gathering of people encircled a deep hole in the ground. Six pallbearers were lowering a simple pine coffin suspended by ropes to the rhythm of the minister's barely audible words, his right arm conducting dramatically above his head and his other holding the bible.

Over breakfast, Avery had told him about a funeral service she had to attend in the afternoon at Holy Cross, but then she said nothing more about it. The service had to be about one of her people, he figured, the ones she helped in her office but can't say much about. Avery called it her "office," but it looked more like a European sitting room. Although he once felt proud of his wife helping her clients, what transpired there was a complete mystery and didn't particularly interest him anymore. Roland knew that Avery was telling him the truth—honest to the bone, that one was—and he wasn't entirely sure why he'd even stopped here on the way to the golf course. He just didn't know what was going on with her, didn't understand her. Following the brief weekend of lightness when that ball of fire

CHAPTER SEVENTEEN

Nazz had visited from Vancouver and kicked up the debates of their youth, Avery said less and less to him, her expression so serious, sad, and withdrawn.

Shielding his eyes from the sun with his right hand as he ventured out from his hiding place, he could see her familiar, slight person even without his binoculars, clad in black skirt and generous sweater. He stepped back into the puddle of shade cast by the tree and lifted the binoculars: there she was, holding a long-stemmed, white rose in her right hand, ready to cast it on to the descending coffin like the rest of the entourage in the circle. She was by far the most elegant person there. A memory of his parents commenting favourably on Avery's class and poise the first time he invited her for a family dinner suddenly flashed through Roland's head. Standing beside his dignified wife, he made out an elderly man in an oversized charcoal suit, bent over with grief. Avery extended her left hand to graze his shoulder in support. There she was, sprinkling her compassion around her. *The old guy must be her client*, Roland thought, *and he probably just lost his wife or something.* The idea of losing one's wife caught him off guard, and there was a part of him that wanted to run down the hill and be with her. But he couldn't do that. He would just watch a few minutes longer.

As Avery lowered her left hand, he caught the glint of her wedding band in the afternoon sunlight. At least she's still wearing his ring. He felt relieved, yet also uncomfortable, spying on his solidly honest wife as if she had some big secret to hide. He would take her somewhere fabulous, even if just for a weekend; he would make her laugh the way he used to when they first met. Impressed by this sure-fire solution to saving his failing marriage, Roland's mood brightened. By the time he reached his Jeep, where his golf bag hulked in the back seat, his longing for his wife had left him again.

Later that night, Roland blew up the cobblestone lane with the razor sharp wind whistling through his uncovered Jeep. Not undeservedly, he thought, he was getting his face slapped with an ice-cold hand. He caught broad brushes of purple and yellow in his headlights, an impressionist painting of the lavender and sage he and Avery had planted together along the laneway when they were still happy with each other. He clenched his mouth, raised his chin to face the wind, and pushed the pedal to the floor.

Roland saw himself as a boy, chin held high, running the bases with his legs flying behind him, all while watching the baseball arching toward the fence at the back of his school. The intense freedom of this moment was breathtaking. His dad was going to be so proud! He looked up into the blue sky, still tracing the path of the baseball, when suddenly, he felt his body hit something hard. Darkness obscured the vivid feelings of his victory run. On the edges of this liquid blackness were faint sparks of light like distant electrical storms. Roland squinted in the glare of a flashlight. *Shit!* This is going to be a DUI for sure, he thought, as an image of his father shaking his head in disgust passed through his mind.

Wait a minute? What was all of this stuff around him? His left arm was covered with pieces of clay pots, and there was a plastic bucket and a gardening glove strewn over his passenger seat. He touched his painful forehead with his right hand, setting off another cascade of debris. There was a dark figure behind the flashlight, and Roland automatically searched for his wallet. As he began to come to his senses, he felt a grin of utter relief on his lips. The slight figure holding the flashlight was his gentle Avery in her dressing gown. He'd crashed through the doors of their garden shed. When she moved closer, Roland saw a different person than the Avery he expected, who looked much scarier than the SDPD.

"What the hell do you think you are doing? You come crashing through our garden house in the middle of the night smelling like a distillery. When are you going to grow up? When are you going

CHAPTER SEVENTEEN

to start thinking about how you affect other people? Like me, for instance?" She flicked on the light switch in the garden house, which miraculously still worked. The extent of the damage seemed to infuriate her more.

"Avey, calm down, I'm gonna fix everything. Why are you so mad? It's just a garden shed; no one got hurt. And I'm ok, thank God!"

"Well, I'm not ok. I haven't been ok in a while, in case you hadn't noticed." She threw a garden shovel across the shed.

Roland had never seen her like this. He didn't even dare take off his seatbelt and try to get out of the car. Instead, he sat immobilized in the driver's seat, while Avery exploded into a stream of his wrongdoings: The promise of the baby when they were getting married, and then the cold nonchalance of his mention that he never wanted a baby in the first place when she came home distraught with the failed pregnancy tests a few weeks ago. And then there was the absolutely mind-blowing insensitivity about her miscarriage and, worst of all, his goddamned arrogant presumption that she was just going to be ok and everything would go on as normal, as if nothing happened here, as if he just got to make all the decisions.

Even worse than the nauseating hangover-meets-concussion headache that threatened to split his brain into pieces, Avery's angry and unsympathetic words were circling dangerously close to a normally fortified place within Roland that was inclined to agree with all she said. *Extreme danger, lock down or run away,* the sirens in his head were sounding. Roland robotically nodded along to the rhythm of his wife's words, hearing none of them; instead, he lifted his consciousness to another place. While Avery was ranting around the garden shed, he was busy planning the rebuilding of a bigger and better garden house that would make her realize that his crash was really a blessing in disguise.

EIGHTEEN

*A*very woke to the sounds of hammers and saws. She remembered then that Roland had ordered lumber on the weekend and asked her what her dream garden shed would look like. He told her to think big. When she came home last night from her ballet class—just a regular class, with normal dance friends and no appearances by any other creatures or beings—Roland and Matt were sitting around the kitchen table, bent over the shed plans.

As she was getting into her car later that morning, Roland had rushed over to tell her that he and Matt were taking the rest of the week off from work just for her, to finish rebuilding the garden house. For a moment, his boyish grin and enthusiasm, complete with overalls and a new carpenter's pencil lodged behind his ear, disarmed her and made her smile. This was all the encouragement he needed to lean in and kiss her cheek. Avery hovered in that moment, smiling at her winsome husband. She clung to the feeling of comfort and stayed there for as a long as she could. But her good feelings disappeared in the clouds of anger, betrayal and sadness that rose up from within her and refused to be silenced.

Lacking her usual Tuesday session with Dr. Mahler, Avery had phoned Nazrin instead. She told her what had happened after Roland ploughed through the garden shed in the middle of the night and what a relief it was to finally stand up for herself and say all of what needed saying to him. Nazrin was her usual supportive and

CHAPTER EIGHTEEN

opinionated self, but her voice became softer when she asked Avery whether, in the days following his crash, Roland had tried to talk to her for real about what she had said to him.

"No. I thought maybe, just maybe, Nazz, he would take my hands into his like he used to, look me in the eyes, and even just ask me how I was feeling, say he was sorry, or even just acknowledge what had happened between us; any of that would have helped. It's like for him, it never even happened."

"I don't know that he even really heard you, Avery, that your words even reached him. It's so strange; I do think he cares for you still, but he just isn't capable of facing these deeper issues. It's like he's in an emotional lockdown. I'm sorry he isn't there for you, I'm sorry about the whole thing."

There was a deeper message in Nazrin's words, a profound sadness embedded in her tone; she'd lost hope for her best friend's marriage to a man who was also one of her oldest friends.

By the time Avery arrived at her office, the morning fog had lifted to reveal a brilliant autumn day. Wrapped in her cardigan, she took her coffee out to the balcony and surveyed the shoreline. Clare's amazing painting of herself as a little girl and her mother together on a beach somewhere came back to mind. Wherever this scene had played out in real life, it seemed different and far away. *It must be so strange, so unnerving, not to know where one's early years were spent,* Avery thought, knowing how important it was for her to pinpoint her childhood with Sebastian at the family beach house on Northern California's coast.

Avery knew it would be naïve to expect smooth sailing in Clare's psychotherapy, but she hoped some of the roughest storms were behind them. Yet, when she opened her office door she found a disgruntled looking Clare sitting in the waiting room. Eyes averted and brow furrowed into a scowl, she was slouched on her armchair with her legs and various bags sprawled out in front of her. Before Avery could utter her usual welcome, Clare rose to her feet to grab her belongings, stomped wordlessly past Avery, and planted herself on the couch.

"Well, Dr. Frontiera. Guess what? It's time for another show and tell." Clare reached deep into her pocket, burrowed around and finally pulled her hand back out of her pocket in a loose fist. In one smooth motion, Clare unfolded her fist and slapped her hand down flat on the table, like a seasoned poker player with a winning hand. When Clare lifted her hand, the first thing that Avery saw were the pink lines of a pregnancy test that now lay exposed on her coffee table. Still looking down at the familiar white plastic tab, Avery inhaled sharply. She felt Clare's eyes drilling into her.

"Yeah, I know, it's kind of ironic. I end up with what you're looking for and you get that downer result that I had my fingers crossed for this morning. Too bad we can't just magically switch."

Avery's heart pounded. Clare was absolutely right. *My entire being wishes that this were my pregnancy test.* "I'm glad you brought in your pregnancy test today so we can talk about it. You were saying that you took the test just this morning?"

"Yup. My period is a week late now, so I thought I better check." Clare looked searchingly into Avery's eyes. "But listen, you look pretty torn up. How are *you* feeling about all this?"

"I honestly do appreciate the concern you're showing for me right now, Clare; thank you for this. But we just need to stay focused on you, your pregnancy test, your thoughts and feelings."

"I get it," Clare said abruptly, with a dismissive gesture of her hand. "You know, I actually don't need to talk about my pregnancy with you, come to think of it. I'm just gonna kill it, like my mother should have done twenty-three years ago."

Avery winced.

"If you've changed your mind about talking about your pregnancy, that's your decision, of course, but I'd really like to understand

CHAPTER EIGHTEEN

why you think your mother should've ended her pregnancy with you. What makes you feel that way, Clare?"

Avery saw Clare shifting uncomfortably on the couch, as if she were having an argument with herself about having blurted out this thought.

"It's just that getting rid of me at the get-go would have spared a lot of heartache ... all around."

"All around?"

"Yeah—for my mother, for starters. Can you imagine how, on top of knowing she was dying, she had me to worry about? And no father to speak of ..." Clare's expression shifted from sadness to anger.

Rage can be the comfortable blanket that protects, even suffocates, the devastating loss that rests beneath it, Dr. Mahler had said when, years ago, he gave her advice about a terrifyingly angry client. *Don't let the fish get away, Avery.*

"Yes, it must have been an unimaginable worry, and so sad for your mother to know that she wouldn't be there to raise you and protect you."

Clare nodded slightly. She sat, eyes downcast, silent for several minutes.

"Clare, where are you right now in your thoughts?"

"I don't know where I am ... but I see these pictures, memories I guess, coming back to me from when I was a little girl, stuff I haven't really thought about for a long time ... I was like ... maybe four ... just after my mother died, I think ..."

Clare's brow furrowed; her eyes shut tightly and she stopped speaking.

"Can you tell me what you see in these pictures right now?" Avery asked gently.

"Ummm ... I'm with Granny—real Granny, not Molly's mum ... there's rows of old wood benches ... It smells ... musty and damp ... white candles everywhere ... flickering ... making spooky shadows ... crosses with Jesus on like ... cold stone walls ... It's a church I was in? ... Yeah, I'm pretty sure it's church ... There's this very serious man at the front ... Black clothing covers most of him ... He makes me feel like ... everyone's in trouble ... maybe that I've done something wrong ... He goes on and on ... words I mostly can't understand ... I hear him say my mother's name ... *Chloé* pops up from this blurry darkness of his voice ..."

Clare's eyes were still squeezed shut, but now a smile broke out over her face. "I love my mother's name ... Yes, I loved it even then ... Hearing the scary man in black say her name makes me feel a tiny bit better ... Chloé is like the name of a wildflower in a sunny meadow."

"What a beautiful way of thinking about your mother's name, Clare. What else do you see, do you feel, sitting there as a little girl with your granny in church, and the stern man in black speaking about your mother?"

"Now I feel like he's saying mean things about my momma ... His face looks so stretched out and angry ... He's so big and serious ... I feel like he's yelling ... I'm scared and bored, too ... I look down at my feet dangling from the bench ... got my shiny black Sunday shoes on ... my granny's grey wool stockings sag ... all wrinkly around her knobby ankles ... I see her scuffed up old shoes ... I'm squeezing Granny's hand to make sure she is still ... still with me and won't let go ... I'm still so scared ... Oh no, so scared that ..." Clare buried her face in her hands.

"So scared in that church ... that what, Clare?"

"I peed myself and now look at me, I'm just stuck sitting in a warm puddle. Gross." Clare said with embarrassment washing over her face. "What a strange thing to be remembering, but I can still kind of feel it now."

Clare opened her eyes and looked at Avery.

"You were only four years old and you must have been terribly frightened, Clare. It's a normal reaction for the body to just let go

CHAPTER EIGHTEEN

like that when you're terrified, even for an adult, but *especially* for a young child who has just lost her mother. I'm just so glad that you had your grandmother to hold on to at that moment."

Tears rolled down Clare's cheeks.

"My granny wrapped her cardigan all around me and we had to leave quickly after that—you know, with the pee and everything ..."

"Yes, of course, that sounds like exactly the right thing to do for a little girl in a truly difficult situation like that. I'm glad your granny wrapped you up and got you out of the church."

"The sweater felt good on me, and I thought it looked like a long dress, right down to my shoes when I was walking. But there was something else I was supposed to do ..."

"What was that, Clare?"

"My momma ... my mother was in the front of the church in this big wooden box, a casket I guess, and I think I was supposed to go up there with my granny to ... to say good-bye, I guess to pay my respects to her, I'm thinking now. But I'm kind of piecing together that this was the part that was just too scary for me and why I peed myself," Clare whispered.

"That would've been terribly scary for a four year old girl, Clare. I'm guessing it may have been a very traditional church, possibly Catholic, where even young children pay respects to the deceased person in her open coffin. But ... come to think of it, do you know what?"

"What?" Clare asked, appearing somewhere between bewildered and hopeful.

"It was a good thing, an adaptive thing, that you peed and had to leave before visiting the casket. Your understandable feeling of terror, and your losing control of your bladder because of it; they ended up getting you out the door before it was time to go to the front of the church. And as I hear your story, I have to tell you, I'm so glad that you got out when you did."

"Even though it may come from a well-intentioned religious tradition, asking a young child to face a parent who has died would have been even more traumatizing, could make such a huge loss feel even worse. No four-year-old girl is ready to handle something like that. An adult might be able to handle it, and at least they could make a decision about whether it's a good thing or not for them to pay their respects in this way." Avery hoped she sounded as convincing as she felt.

"I … I hadn't thought about it that way. You're saying that seeing my mother in her open casket would've done more harm than good for me. I feel kind of relieved about that."

"Yes. It was hard enough for you as it was! Devastating actually. So, yes, I think it's much better to remember your mother's smiling, loving and very much alive face, like on your painting, and the way that her name made you think about wildflowers."

Avery waited as Clare leaned back into the couch, took a deep breath, and closed her eyes. She looked peaceful as the breeze drifted in through the open balcony doors. Suddenly, Clare sat up and reached for the pregnancy test still on the coffee table. "And what about this, then?"

"I don't know, Clare. I just hope that you'll make a decision that is truly good for you. I know you were angry with me before when I wouldn't talk to you about my personal feelings about your pregnancy, which I can understand."

Clare nodded but didn't appear ready to explode.

"I just would hate for you to make a decision out of anger at me—or your dad—and, worse still, because you were so angry you wished yourself away. Having talked about all of this today, Clare, I can really see now what you meant about undoing yourself, about wishing you'd never been born, that this would have spared a lot of heartache; all the pain your mum felt leaving you behind and all the pain, the sadness, and the fear you felt about her not being there anymore."

CHAPTER EIGHTEEN

Clare pulled the sleeve of her sweater across her face. Avery searched through Clare's words and images to find something, anything, meaningful that might help her to start pulling herself from the pool of loss always threatening to drown her.

"But you know what, Clare?"

"What?"

"Your mother wanted you. There was so much pain for you after she died, and I can still see that pain in you now. But that isn't the whole story. I know this because I got to see your painting. I saw it with my own eyes and heard about it in your own words just a week ago, so I'm pretty certain of what I'm about to say to you.

"You were so loved by your mother, and you were the apple of her eye. And in spite of her dying so unexpectedly young, and all the hardship that came after, that love also still lives inside you, it's in your heart, just sometimes it's hard to find with all the sadness in there. That love shows up in your dreams and now it's in your painting."

Clare looked like a painting herself at this moment, framed in her red curls, with her grey-green eyes wide open now and standing out like Swarovski crystals. *If your mother could only see you now.*

Clare started to smile, ever so slightly, her eyes averted and her cheeks the pink of wild roses. For a moment, she looked to Avery like a shy child who had been given a compliment.

"So, are you also kind of saying that I should keep my baby?"

"Only you can decide if this is the right time, the right way for you to have a baby. I'm here to listen to all of your thoughts and feelings about this, if and when you want to share them. But it's your mother who got to make that decision about you. And she did choose. She chose to have you and love you, even if your father bailed or whatever happened there. But she didn't know then ... and didn't get to choose when she would die. She must have imagined a long and wonderful life with you, Clare, her little windmaker."

Eyes still averted, Clare rose from the couch. She picked up the pregnancy test and stuck it in her pocket with a long sigh.

"I need to just go now. I know we have more time, but I'm really ... full, and I just need to walk and think. I can't talk anymore today."

"I understand, Clare. You look very tired."

Clare nodded and walked toward the office door. Her hand on the doorknob, she turned around again as if some inner voice was insisting that she face Avery. Avery could see Clare's throat moving as she swallowed hard.

"I suck at saying 'thank you' ... and I'm even worse at 'sorry.'"

"Well, you're in luck, Clare, because one of the things I'm kind of good at is hearing even the quietest things, even the softest whisper of a thank you or sorry."

As Avery wrote her notes in Clare's file, she noticed how slowly her hand was moving over the page. This short sprint of a session had worn out both client and therapist. Avery looked up from the page to notice that the office door had been left open, and she got up to close it for privacy before her last client of the day arrived. As Avery was about to close the door, something white in the waiting room caught the corner of her eye. Perched on the armchair was Avery's David figurine. She walked across the room to retrieve him when she saw the corner of a small white card protruding from under that statue's base. Avery picked up the figurine in one hand and the card in the other. There were no words, only a black-inked raven in flight with tears coming out of its eye. Avery carefully placed her David back on his place on the shelf and walked back into her office, mesmerized by the image on the card that Clare had left for her.

NINETEEN

*D*r. Mahler had barely moved in thirty minutes as Avery released all that had happened to her over the past two weeks. Sunburn marked the bridge of his nose. *If there is a punishment for therapists who took holidays away from their clients, this must be it,* Avery thought. Today, Dr. Mahler appeared to her more like a derby rider perched on a horse that was moving a little too fast for his liking. While his many years of experience allowed him to stay in the saddle and hang onto the reins, the fast-paced action of the session registered on his face. His eyes opened widely, his eyebrows lifted up high over his spectacles, and he pressed his lips together every time he encountered the next dramatic hurdle in Avery's story. When Avery described her fury about finding drunken Roland in the debris of the garden shed, Dr. Mahler squeezed his lips into a tight, straight line that said, *And then what did you do? Should I be scared?* Avery's account of the hand drawn card beneath the figurine released his lips into his signature warm smile. *Nice work, you are really starting to crack that tough shell of your client,* she imagined him saying—that is, if she had paused even a millisecond before moving on to the next topic. Yet, when Avery finally described the gilded child who had gazed imploringly at her in the ballet studio, Dr. Mahler's eyes stayed stuck wide-open as he sucked in his lips several times.

"Oh, my dear Avery, so much has happened to you over the past two weeks."

CHAPTER NINETEEN

Yes, all of this happened to me while you were suntanning on your sailboat, Avery thought. This knee-jerk jealousy for her psychologist's time caught her off guard, and she suddenly felt her cheeks warming.

"But let's cut to the chase," Dr. Mahler continued.

Here we go, he's back in control, Avery thought, realizing at this moment that she too had been clutching her knees so hard they were starting to hurt and her fingers were becoming numb.

"Tell me, Avery, in all that you have told me today, what feels most important for us to talk about?" Dr. Mahler asked.

Everything stopped inside Avery, and she felt her mouth opening.

"I need to talk about *her*."

Avery tilted her face toward Dr. Mahler, using the same imploring gesture of the golden child she had just described.

"And why is it, Avery, that when you remember her gentle beckoning, your eyes fill with tears?"

"I'm afraid I won't be able to find her again and, if I do, that I'll lose her." Avery had no idea why she was saying this or where it was coming from.

"And you've been missing her for a very long time?"

Avery nodded as she looked at Dr. Mahler. Could he imagine her too, the collapsed body of the girl on the floor of the ballet studio?

"I know this sounds really crazy," Avery whispered.

"Is she real, this little girl?"

Avery saw the tiny face again, covered in crumpled pieces of gold leaf.

"She feels so real to me, but I know she's not actually there."

Dr. Mahler exhaled, and the anxiety in his shoulders appeared to melt into the rolled up sleeves of his white shirt.

"Ok, so she feels very real from your perspective, like a very strong feeling that reflects in your vision of this little girl. What does she mean to you? Who is she to you?"

Avery felt paralyzed in her ability to see deeper into her memory of the girl in the ballet studio. Her inner voice discouraged her from doing so. *You are playing a dangerous game; look what happened to your brother.* Still looking into Dr. Mahler's eyes, she winced when her teeth hit her thumbnail a little too hard.

"Please don't worry about your brother for a moment and what all this means. You're not doing this alone, and I'll be watching out for you. This is an important moment to just say whatever occurs to you, Avery, whatever you see in your mind's eye and whatever presents itself."

Avery nodded, closed her eyes, and leaned back into the couch. Broken images of the little girl filtered through her mind like pieces of ripped photographs. There was the little girl's chin slightly raised, golden and gleaming in the evening light, and then this image drifted away again into a distant darkness. Moving closer now on her inner screen was the girl's delicate porcelain shoulder showing just a hint of the soft pink fabric of her ballet dress. Avery squeezed her eyes tightly shut, and then her words began to flow.

"She's so fleeting. I'm trying so hard to hold on to her, and she's giving me glimpses …"

"Tell me what she's showing you, Avery," Dr. Mahler's calm voice sounded from the distance.

"She … is so delicate and fragile, yet extraordinary and amazingly strong for such a little girl … I can see her unspoiled, porcelain skin on her shoulder … I see how she holds her chin so that the light reflects on it … I feel like I know her, like I really want to know her …" Avery said as she felt a surge of love come over her.

"She sounds remarkable, Avery, someone you could not help but love." Dr. Mahler spoke as if he could see inside her.

Avery felt a faint smile brushing lightly over her face and then fading away as she peered deeper inside of herself.

"You're very brave, Avery. Let us continue to walk through this together," she heard Dr. Mahler saying.

The thought that she was not so different from Clare suddenly arose. Had Clare not made a childhood career of lucid dreaming to

CHAPTER NINETEEN

configure whatever she could of her mother, and her mother's love for her, into a painting?

"Ballet saved me!"

Her own voice surprised her, and she almost opened her eyes.

"It's ok, Avery, you are moving in and out of your inner realm, sometimes thinking out loud. You are fluid right now, like a person much younger than yourself," Dr. Mahler reassured her. "So tell me, how did ballet save you?"

"It's ... it's how I speak what I can't say in words. I think it's how I learned to express myself in the first place."

Suddenly a new flurry of images was making noise in her head. More pieces of *her*? There were the girl's lips, lifted into an angelic smile. Then her small hands zoomed into focus; little hands held softly in the shape of a ballerina's heart, but mottled with that odd, flaked gold, like the sunspots of an old woman. Avery swallowed hard as an image of the girl's legs moved into soft focus. In her mind's eye, she traced the *plié* diamond of her thighs and calves, then the wide, rose-gold ribbons wrapped softly around her ankles, and finally she could see the upper edges of her ballet slippers. Avery gasped as she visualized glass chards protruding through the slippers. She could see all of her now, standing still in a pool of blood as long as she could bear it, her golden brow furrowed in concentration before she collapsed onto the floor.

Avery screamed and opened her eyes to a concerned looking Dr. Mahler.

"Her feet are hurt! They're bleeding, and now she won't be able to dance ... and all she has is her ballet. I should have stood up straighter, straight as a soldier between the two sheets of glass like Monsieur Gregoir taught me, and not broken through the glass." Avery's heart was pounding. "And ... and she shouldn't have been dancing on his grave!"

"No, no, no, my dear Avery, it's not your fault. You didn't hurt her. And you didn't hurt Sebastian. That vision was your childhood shattering around you and you losing everything that was important to *you*. But you have found *her* again now. She made herself known in a way I have never witnessed before. It's quite miraculous, really."

"It's all true, what you're saying. I see it." Avery felt a surge of pride.

"And maybe she can lose some of the crumpled gold leaf now, don't you think?" asked Dr. Mahler. "She's carried the burden of being the perfect golden daughter long enough. She must be tired by now, wanting to lead her own life."

"Exhausted, actually," Avery said. "And I do want my life back, even if I don't yet know exactly what that means."

Dr. Mahler's face spoke to her: *I think we have done our job for today.*

"But there's something more."

"I feared there might be," Dr. Mahler responded.

"She also has a connection to Clare that I don't yet understand. And the question of why she appeared before me now, at this point in my life and at this point in my therapy with Clare, just seems really important, too."

"Have you considered transferring Clare to another psychologist while you are figuring all of this out?" Dr. Mahler asked.

"No, Dr. Mahler, I don't think that would be the right thing to do. Clare and I are breaking through, and I'm not going to be that next person to disappoint her."

"It's just a thought, Avery. You and I both know that when we are this involved and feel that essential to a client, we might just be going overboard. We have to consider countertransference," Dr. Mahler said.

"Well, I'll think about it, Dr. Mahler," Avery said. "I think we're over time. I'll see you next week."

Avery gathered up her belongings and scurried to the door, feeling a little like an admonished schoolgirl. At the last moment before opening the door, she collected.

CHAPTER NINETEEN

"Thank you so much, Dr. Mahler, for everything. I'm so sorry for shocking you with all of this news. Once again, you've given me a lot to think about. I don't know what I'd do without you."

Dr. Mahler smiled, dramatically placed two fingers on his wrist for a moment, and then looked up at her from his armchair.

"Well, you don't have to worry about me yet. Even after today's action-packed session, it turns out, I still have a pulse. I'll see you next week. And in case you're wondering, I don't think it's a good idea for me to take another holiday week in the next little while, do you?"

Avery lingered at the door, unwilling to let go of the moment, appreciating Dr. Mahler.

"You're smiling, Avery. This is wonderful to see," Dr. Mahler managed to say before he surrendered to waves of laughter.

"Just one more thing, Dr. Mahler," Avery started and he turned from his filing cabinet to look at her. It was nine minutes to the hour, and the sanctity of the ten minutes between patients was already broken.

"Clare's pregnant," Avery blurted out.

Dr. Mahler raised his eyebrows and put his hands on his hips.

"You're just going to have to hang on to that news until next time!"

Avery scurried out the door. *He's right, he's right, he's always right.*

TWENTY

When Avery opened her office door to find Clare reading a magazine in the waiting room, she realized this was the fourth Wednesday in a row that her young client had arrived on time. Progress. Yet, surely they hadn't yet come to the end of Clare's theatrics. Clare heaved a deep sigh as she rose from her armchair, stretched ostentatiously, and gathered up her possessions with an air of hardship. Avery caught herself glancing at the cherry wood bookshelf housing her figurines. She had her own trust issues with Clare now, Avery thought, but today her David was exactly where he should be and appeared quite content to have been resettled among his figurine friends.

Without so much as a hello, Clare marched past and plunked herself down on the couch. While Avery settled into her armchair, Clare was busy unearthing something from her backpack. *More show and tell? What did her predictably unpredictable young client bring in today? Couldn't we just have a normal psychotherapy session for a change?* Avery longed for the normality of clients who are content to tell you how their week went and what's on their minds.

Finally, the rummaging stopped, and Clare pulled a thin file folder from her bag and flipped it onto the coffee table like a bad hand of cards.

"It's hard to believe, I know, Dr. Frontiera, but this is all that I have of him." Her forlorn expression cancelled Avery's irritation. On

CHAPTER TWENTY

the file folder, she read the words scribbled across the label: *Biological Father (AKA Asshole).*

"It looks like you want to talk about your father today, Clare."

"Yes, obviously," Clare moved over on the couch and patted the seat where she wanted her psychologist to sit.

Avery rose from her armchair, picked up her reading glasses, and crossed the room to sit down beside Clare.

"So, this is what we'll do," Clare started to say in a commanding tone, as she opened the file folder on the coffee table in front of them. The slight tremor of her hand hovering over the opened file folder did not escape Avery's notice. *The body gives you away every time.*

"I'll show you what I have in here and tell you about it as we go through it. And then you'll understand why I am such a completely pissed-off person."

And a sad and disappointed person, too, Avery thought, as she nodded her head toward the file folder. Clare pointed to a document, then slid the paper across the coffee table. Her hair brushed past Avery's face as she did so, sending a hint of summer lilacs. *State of California, Certification of Vital Record, County of Los Angeles Department of Public Health*, Avery read. *Name of Child: Clare Meghan Thomas. Date of Birth: December 14, 1996. Place of Birth: Miller Children's and Women's Hospital, Long Beach. Name of Mother: Chloé Eileen Thomas. Name of Father: Not Identified.*

The birth certificate confirmed what the Judge had said in his statement about Clare. Clare *was* born in the U.S. —not that far from San Diego, in fact. Yet, somehow Clare's earliest memories of being with her mother and grandmother sounded like they happened elsewhere. Avery struggled to put her finger on why the place of Clare's earliest memories felt so far away. There was something about the colours, the nuances of light, and the landscape of Clare's painting, even the language she used to describe the memories captured by her artist's eye, that reflected the blissful tranquility of a rural coastal community somewhere else—perhaps on the East Coast? Maybe after Clare was born just outside of Los Angeles, especially with her father not in the picture, Chloé had moved across the country to be close to her own mother and get help with her new baby? And then Clare didn't return to California until after her mother died, and she was adopted by Molly and Jim?

"So as you can see, Bio-Dad didn't even have the balls to name himself on my birth certificate." Clare used her index finger to rub the space on the form where her father's name was missing.

Clare's strong words jolted Avery back into reality. She realized only then how far away she had drifted in her thoughts, and this shocked her. What was she doing? These geographic musings were so far removed from the facts on hand, and how did they even matter in her role as Clare's psychologist? Why was she so interested, so driven even, to unravel the geography? Suddenly Dr. Mahler's comment about over-involvement with her client came to mind and heated her cheeks. *Stop playing detective*, she told herself.

Refocused, Avery sensed the bristle of Clare's anger beside her.

"So you're saying that, as best you can tell, your biological father chose not to be part of the picture right from your birth, Clare, and understandably this stirs up a lot of hard feelings for you. I can only imagine how unfair and disappointing it feels every time you look at that space on your birth certificate. No wonder this enrages you!"

Clare nodded and released herself from the stranglehold of her crossed arms. Avery felt Clare tensing up again as she reached forward to take another piece of paper out of the file folder. It looked as if it had been crumpled and then smoothed out, maybe more than once. One large corner had been ripped off and taped back on.

"It gets even worse, Dr. Frontiera. This is the clincher, this is where anonymous Bio-Dad earned himself his full name, Deadbeat Loser All-Around-Asshole!"

Clare stood up and brandished the paper, then slapped it down on the coffee table in front of Avery. "Read it." She paced around the room while Avery scrambled to read the official-looking document.

133

CHAPTER TWENTY

Written on a *California Department of Public Health's Birth Index* form, the letter was marked *Personal and Confidential* and addressed to Clare. It started off by *confirming that at the age of majority* she had the legal right to make a request of information regarding her *biological parents*, in her case, her *biological father*. Avery knew about this branch of the government that had fought for the power of unsealing adoption records and conveying the hopes of adopted children to their otherwise untraceable biological parents. Clare was not the first of her clients who had used this service to locate parents, but more often than not, these long-lost parents wanted to be found.

Avery cringed when she read that Clare had sent her request on December 14, 2017, the exact date of her twenty-first birthday. Clare must have been thinking about taking this brave action for a long time, had researched and gathered up all those official and painfully cold documents, and then sent in her formal request on the very first day that she was legally entitled to do so. That's how much she wanted this. Despite knowing the outcome of Clare's request, Avery found herself feeling more and more anxious as she read on in the letter. *My anxiety*, she thought, *must be a miniscule fraction of what Clare experienced when she found this letter in her mailbox.*

The final sentence must have been heart-stoppingly devastating. *While we were successful in locating your biological father, we regret to inform you that he has elected not to reciprocate your contact request and, therefore, we are also not in a position to reveal his identity to you.* In an automatic action, Avery put the letter face down on the coffee table. Clare bent over the coffee table, lips in a tight line as she methodically put the papers back into their file folder. Then she sat down on Avery's armchair, still holding the file on her lap, as if it were the most natural thing she could do.

"So, Dr. Frontiera, tell me how you felt reading that letter?"

Just roll with the punches, Avery thought. *It doesn't matter where we sit. It doesn't matter where Clare spent those first few years of your life. Honesty is the best policy. Just speak from the heart.*

"I feel absolutely devastated, Clare," Avery began. "You put so much effort and hope and courage into finding your father on the very first day that you were able to do so. I'm truly amazed by your resourcefulness at such a young age."

Clare watched her intently.

"Now I ask myself, how could any human being turn you down like that? That part enrages me. I don't know him, but it makes me want to hate him."

Clare seemed soothed by what Avery said, including this casting of judgment over her father, typically outside the domain of the all-accepting, empathetic psychologist.

"Thank you," she said, nodding her head. "But ... but, where do I go from here, Dr. Frontiera? I feel so stuck in all this anger."

"That's a really good question, and a hard one to answer," Avery responded. She didn't normally answer direct questions like this, but somehow Clare always pulled her in new directions she never thought she'd take. "What happened to you with your father will take a very long time to heal. All that understandable anger—and even deeper lies that hurt, doesn't it? In listening to you and in reading the papers you shared, I am struck by something that I think is very important and might help you."

Clare was leaning forward in Avery's armchair now, enough so that the file folder cascaded down onto the carpet.

"You did everything right: you left no stone unturned, you put yourself way out on a limb. When you're rejected like that, it's in the human condition, especially for a child, even an adult child such as yourself, to assume that it must be your fault somehow. That you're not enough for him or that you should have tried harder—kind of crazy thoughts that are very real but not actually true. Because, Clare, you are enough, just by being his child, and with all that you are now, you are more than enough. You are plenty. I'm sure your mother, your grandmother, Molly, Jim, all the people in your life

CHAPTER TWENTY

who love you and stood by you, would all agree on that point. What happened here is about him. It is *he* who isn't enough, and not you."

Slowly, the smile of being seen came over Clare's face, like that first ray of sunshine after a long winter's night. "Some people would say I'm more than plenty. They might even say that I'm a handful!" Clare said, starting to laugh.

Her eyes moved across the room to the clock, strategically placed for Avery to keep track of the time. "I see we actually have almost twenty minutes left together today, Dr. Frontiera," Clare said. "You know ... I just realized something ... there's some pretty badass pressure coming from sitting here on what is obviously your favourite chair. I don't know where we should go from here in what we were talking about, but I'm guessing that, as per usual you've got some ideas." Clare started to rise from the armchair.

How kind of you to let me sit on my own chair, Avery thought. She was drawn to the comfort of her own chair, the familiar sense of her position in the room, but she also knew what would be best for Clare and for the tenuous relationship still building.

"I'd like to stay where I am for today, Clare."

Avery waited for Clare to pick up the papers and settle back down on the couch beside her. Clare returned the folder to her backpack.

"Clare, we've spent a lot of time, much needed time, to talk about your experiences of losing your mother at such a young age and being abandoned by your father. I'm sure we will come back to talking about these losses again," Avery began.

Clare's eyebrows lifted with interest.

"It's completely understandable that such huge losses overshadow everything else. But sometimes, when you are able to look beyond these losses, you can find parts of yourself that help to make better sense of who you are and to come to feel more whole as a person. So I'm wondering, Clare, what else you remember about that time in your life after your mother died ... and before you were adopted by Molly and Jim? Do you have any memories at all about what happened in between?"

Clare took a deep breath and twisted her hair into a tight ponytail at the nape of her neck. She let go and disappeared once again behind the free fall of curls. "I wish I knew more. It's all so crazy foggy in my memory, and I keep trying to zoom in on the details of what I do remember, but then the images just disappear."

"Clare, it must be so frustrating when you want to know what happened early in your life. You're not alone in that. It's really difficult for people to remember what happened when they were young children, especially when there were traumatic experiences. I've learned that as much as one would like to, you just can't force memory. But I do have an idea. Please, let's try something a little different. I invite you to soften up on yourself, Clare, even close your eyes if you feel like it. Ok … so you do remember being in the church holding your grandmother's hand after your mother died. You were actually able to tell me quite a lot about that moment, right?"

"Yeah, I guess I was … I do remember telling you about that, and I thought about it several more times after that appointment," Clare answered. She let out a long sigh before she continued. "I … I can see it again, right now, my legs swinging from the bench where I was sitting in the church, holding Granny's hand …"

"Allow your legs to keep swinging … so it's just you and Granny now, holding hands and sitting on the church bench. Take your time, Clare. Stay in that moment and just let yourself remember the feeling of her hand in yours, your togetherness at that moment after you lost your mom and your grandmother lost her daughter. Stay with the sensation of holding hands and allow your mind to drift. Don't force it to zoom in, just allow yourself to keep holding your granny's hand and let your mind drift through that time in your life … No pressure, no expectation about having to remember details, having to remember anything at all … and just see if anything comes up."

CHAPTER TWENTY

After a few seconds, Clare offered a faint nod.

Avery suddenly felt awkward sitting beside her silent client, and wished again that she could move back to her usual armchair to see the emotions passing over Clare's face. Then Avery softened into the seat beside Clare and reminded herself of how daunting it could be to look into the uncertainty of vague childhood memories. For a split second, she saw herself again as a little girl, running on the beach toward Sebastian. She tried to hold on to this moment, but as always it melted away into nothingness. Finally, Clare spoke.

"Ok, I'm remembering something now. It's like a picture I've seen before, but I haven't talked about it or even thought about it, at least not in a long time. Does that make sense?"

"It makes perfect sense, Clare, that's exactly what a childhood memories feel like. Just try to speak freely about what you're seeing in whatever way comes into your mind."

"Ok … I'm sitting up on my knees now … My chin touches the wood … The wood feels cold, smooth … There are white, pretty doily things on the table … I'm face to face with chocolate cake … I can smell it now … White sprinkles are squished into the brown chocolate icing … My mouth is watering … I can't quite reach them, but I see candles coming up from the top of the cake …" Clare said. Her chin was jutting upward and both of her arms were raised to show how the cake and candles felt up high above her.

"Granny is standing behind me … I can feel her hands reaching under my arms, so now I can stand up and be safe … on the chair … Her hands smell like soap … One, two, three, four, five candles … for our wee windmaker to blow out … Granny's saying … I guess she and my mom both called me that…" Clare said, her voice quickening with excitement of this discovery. "Maybe Granny calling me that after my mother died to … to kind of keep her voice alive …"

Clare's voice trailed off. The room fell quiet for what seemed like a long time.

"I can see that keeping your mother's voice alive would be very important, and it does seem like it's still kind of alive in your head."

Clare nodded, her eyes still closed.

"Your fifth birthday, Clare. I'm hearing just how caring and careful your granny was with you when you were a little girl. Is there anything else that you remember?"

Clare swept back her hair and turned toward Avery, grinning now.

"My granny said, 'Make a wish, my little one!'" Clare said energetically. But no sooner had she said this that the grin slid off of her face. *Maybe that's the story of her life*, Avery thought; *as soon as there is something good to smile about it disappears into another loss.* Clare was gone again now behind her hair, and Avery could see that she was holding her head up with her hand, elbow digging deep into the fabric of her jeans with the weight of it.

"Please go on, Clare, if you can," Avery said.

Clare sighed.

"You see ... Granny is helping me now to blow out the candles ... She's laughing ... I'm giggling ... It's ... it's happy ... But then it wasn't laughing anymore, but different ... Everything changed from fun to serious and scary ... My stomach's sick ... Granny's coughing and coughing, and trying to get air ... I don't know what to do ... Then, there she is on the floor collapsed ... Pointing her bony old finger ... at the door ... like the door to the outside ... I have to help her ... I'm reaching up as high as I can on the door ... I can feel cold metal on my fingertips, the door handle I guess ... I jump up and just pulled down with all my might ... The door is open now and I'm screaming as loud as I can ..."

The blood-curdling scream startled Avery. Clare's eyes opened wide, and she turned to Avery in disbelief. Avery instinctively touched Clare's shoulder.

"It's ok, Clare. It's ok to scream. It just came back to you how scared you were at that moment on your fifth birthday, your granny coughing and gasping for air like that."

CHAPTER TWENTY

Avery sat quietly, her hands on her lap, looking at the wary young woman beside her. They sat like that until Clare breathed more evenly. Using the sleeve pulled over her fisted hand, Clare wiped her cheek.

"So you screamed in horror just now, probably much like you did on that day. Scared yourself all over again, and me a bit, too."

"True."

"You know, Clare, it's amazing that even at five years old, you had your wits about you like that to get the front door open. Your scream just now, it was about your horror, but it's also what we're programmed to do when we need help. Your granny really needed help, and getting that door open and screaming was the best thing you could do. Do you remember if someone came to help, or what happened next?"

"Yes! Someone came ... She was wearing a burly brown sweater coat thing ... It smelled like the barn animals ..."

After sitting there like that with her brow creased in concentration, the index finger of Clare's right hand shot up close to Avery's face and shocked her all over again.

"It was Auntie Aggie! From next door, the one who let me touch the sheep babies in the barn ... She tried to help Granny ... There ... there was blood in Granny's spit ... "

"Anyone would have felt terrified, but especially a little girl who only just lost her mum. Tell me what happened next, whatever you remember of it?" Avery asked.

Clare nodded slowly and tilted her face toward Avery. Maybe it was actually better sitting side by side on the couch, Avery thought, with her client deciding if and when she wanted to face her.

"There are parts missing ... I know Auntie Aggie helped Granny to get into her bed ... I think it was the same day of the coughing, but maybe not, I'm not sure of the days ... It was the day it snowed ... There is pretty snow falling outside Granny's bedroom window ... I climb into her bed, quiet as a mouse," Clare continued, sounding much younger and more vulnerable than her usual self. "I try to stop shivering under the covers ... The cool pillow on my face smells like the sunshine outside where we hang up the wash ... She's sleeping and ... I'm getting bored, I guess, so I start tracing her face with my fingers ... I remember that part really clearly ... Funny-shaped brown spots on her cheeks like ... splotches of milk chocolate ... I kind of play in the snow of her downy white eyebrows ... My fingers slide down her nose like on a slippery hill or a mountain side ... It's kind of like the ski jumpers on the TV ... My fingers jump off the end of her nose high into the air ... touch down on her lips ... I do a little finger tickle on her lips ... I'm lonely for her now ... and then I see her lips waking up into a smile."

"Your granny woke up and was smiling at you. Do you remember how that felt, Clare?" Avery asked.

"It felt like a big relief," Clare said wistfully.

"Did she say anything, Clare, when she woke up smiling at you?" Clare slumped forward, gone again into her past.

"Granny said, 'Don't worry ... *it's time*' ... I don't know what that means ... She asks me if I know that my mother's in heaven ... funny, I still don't know what that really means, either ... Granny is saying she's a little bit sick and isn't much fun to be with ... It turns out she was more than a little bit sick ..." Clare continued, these last words sticking in her throat.

"Granny said it's the right time ... We need to look up your father ... I don't think I got it, what that even meant ... what's a father? ... Granny is really patient when she tries to explain it to me ... She said that father's a nice person to take care of you, like your Momma did ... Granny is saying she'll write my father a letter ... and I say I can help by drawing a picture for father, whoever he is ... I really just want to stay with Granny ... that's all I remember about that part, and about my Granny, actually ... I don't think I lived there much longer ...

CHAPTER TWENTY

"You know, one thing I do remember is six candles on my cake with Molly and Jim ... I'm realizing now, just hearing myself talking about it and remembering stuff, that I must have been five when I was adopted. Yes, and that's what Molly says, too, and she told me that they were so lucky to get me and have me over the spring and summer before grade one. So that kind of fits together better, doesn't it?"

"Yes, it does. Somehow it's better, isn't it, when it fits together into a picture that at least makes some sense," Avery said. "So from what else you have told me over our time together, I am guessing that despite her best intentions, your grandmother didn't find your father?"

"I don't really know. Maybe he didn't want to be found. He sure didn't when I tried to find him on my twenty-first birthday. Or maybe Granny found him when I was five and he just didn't care about his little girl." Clare winced at her own bitter words. "The memories are so foggy. And then there's, like, this fast forward to living at Jim and Molly's. It's unsettling, like parts of me are missing in action."

"That sounds really important to me, parts of you missing in action. Maybe we can find even just a few of those missing pieces. You are doing really well, I think, with just letting your mind drift. Let's keep going with that for just a little longer.

"Tell me about a few of those blurry images that you can remember from living at your mom and granny's cottage, and maybe about how you found your way to Molly and Jim. Would that be alright with you?"

Clare looked into Avery's eyes and nodded.

We're on the same side, Avery thought, *and I think Clare is starting to see this.*

"Ok: so you described your grandmother's bed and how snow was falling outside her window. You've told me a bit about the barn, Aunt Aggie, the farm animals. What else can you see? Do you remember leaving there? Tell me anything that comes to mind. Colours, sensations, feelings, smells, anything at all that filters through your mind ..."

"When you say it that way, it makes sense. It ... it gives me hope."

Clare put her face in both hands with her elbows on her knees. She breathed evenly, content to silently walk through her mental space, as was Avery to just wait.

"It's snowing again ... The sheep have snowflakes melting on their fleece ... Now the snow is gone and I am stomping in the mud outside the barn, with my yellow boots making mud splats with my feet ... Auntie Aggie is holding my hand ... We're laughing ... I don't see the mud anymore now, but when I look down, I see my bare feet in tall, cool green grass ... they are touching my ankles, the pretty green blades ... It's like a meadow with tiny, white flowers ... I hear sheep somewhere and I feel sunshine on my face ... My curls are moving with the breeze, they tickle me and I'm giggling ... I am looking up from my feet and I see Auntie Aggie standing by the knobby wooden post of the clothesline ... There's this huge basket beside her on the grass with heaps of white in it ... And there she is, it's Granny ... She's sitting on some kind of a garden chair ... There's a soft, white blanket wrapped all around her ... I'm glad because she looks cozy ... In the sun, I can see little hairs of the blanket and the wisps of her soft, white hair like peach fuzz in the sun ... I'm running over to see Granny and Aunt Aggie ... but ... but I can't get there fast enough, the harder I run, the further away they are getting ... they are disappearing from me now ..."

Again an image of herself as a little girl running toward Sebastian on the beach flashed through Avery's head, and it, too, disappeared. *It's taken me this long, a lifetime really,* Avery thought, *to get this far with my own losses.* And still the fleeting images hold so much emotion, so much movement, so much power.

"You know, most of that felt really nice, like kind of peaceful and happy and ... alive. But that last bit ... it hurt, it sent all this stress

CHAPTER TWENTY

and sadness through my stomach when I was running across the meadow and they were disappearing."

"Clare, it must have been so hard for you to say good-bye to the cottage that was the first home you remember, and to say good-bye to your granny, to Aunt Aggie, the sheep babies, all of it. I'm glad you carry the happiness of those days, the peacefulness, as you say, of this country life with you, too. Now, do you remember anything at all about saying good-bye or any pictures in your mind about getting to Molly and Jim's before your sixth birthday? Let's just go a little farther with this before we call it a day."

"Ok," Clare said with a yawn. She slouched back into the couch, her head resting on the back of it, took a deep breath, and closed her eyes.

"It's confusing, all mixed up pictures ... coming and going ... Auntie Aggie's face is up close ... She's crouching in front of me, buttoning up my coat ... I'm breathing in the smell of the sheep ... something about being a good girl ... then the sound of rain all around me, but I'm warm in my coat and woollen socks ... My face is cool against the glass ... Trees and meadows are rushing by me ... A pretty woman in a fancy dress is smiling at me ... A little cap with a golden bird on it ... I can smell her perfume ... pretty-coloured Lifesavers in a little roll ... my face is pressed against the window ... I hear more rain ... Now, white cotton clouds and blues ... Is this heaven, where Momma is?"

"There's lots of greens, too ... and then something else, I don't know what it is ..." Clare was drawing shapes with her index finger in the air, her face tense, eyes still pressed closed. It looked like Clare was drawing a quick string of hearts with her index finger, over and over again.

"I have no idea what that's about. I think I'm done!" Clare said, opening her eyes. "That's all I can do today. I think I figured out quite a bit, but now I need to just chill out."

"Yes, I couldn't agree with you more. We've covered so much today, Clare," Avery said. "No wonder you're tired. I can't be sure, of course, but it sounded like you were remembering your travels from your granny's cottage to Molly and Jim's. Quite different from how you might see it now as an adult, but very much like it would look through the fresh eyes of a child."

"Yes; maybe in a car or a plane, I'm thinking, or probably both? You know what I never realized until right now is that the pictures in my mind are blurry and mixed up, but they are ... you know ... kind."

"Kind?" Avery asked.

"Yes; like, it's strange, confusing, and moving fast, but people were nice to me. I was still being cared for."

"Oh, yes, I can see that now. Auntie Aggie buttoning you up, you hearing the rain but warm and protected from it, the pretty woman smiling at you. You had a big trip to make, but someone must have organized it well for you, and the adults who saw you on your way were looking out for you. I'm so glad, Clare, that you had this kindness on your side with all you were going through and that you can feel that kindness even now. It's still a part of you now.

"Now Clare, I just have one more question for you, something you might keep thinking about. With all that you've shared and pieced together about your life as a little girl at your granny's cottage, when your mother was still alive and after she died, what of *that life* do you think is still a part of who you are today?"

Clare inhaled sharply.

"Freedom. Dirt and grass under my feet. Flying through the meadows like the windmaker I supposedly was, probably still am," Clare said, starting to smile. "I still love animals, even farm animals that other people find stinky. That simple, straight-up life, no pretences; it kind of appeals to me, even though I don't often admit it. And, I guess ... the love that I did get, being cared for, being allowed to be a little girl who just wants to play.

CHAPTER TWENTY

"You're right, Dr. Frontiera; it's easy to lose track of all of that good stuff when I am raging about my father or overwhelmed with missing my mother. But I guess these are some of those pieces that were missing in action. It's a strange business you're in, Dr. Frontiera. Sometimes I don't even know what's going on or why I feel different after being here."

"I can see all of that, Clare. The parts of yourself you are finding, I can see those in you. I really appreciate you sharing all of that with me. And, yes, you are right: every day I still learn what strange and wonderful things can happen in this room, regardless of where you're sitting."

"I will see you next week at the same time," Clare said in a playfully mocking tone. "You can have first picks on the seating."

TWENTY-ONE

*P*sychotherapists begrudge writing reports about their clients for outsiders, and Avery was no different. It was anywhere from uncomfortable to infuriating, to have to reveal anything that occurred in the sacred space where all should be private. Avery realized long ago that no matter what consent forms clients signed at the outset, they really had no idea what they would end up discovering about themselves during the psychotherapeutic journey or how exposed, even betrayed, they might feel by a report written about them.

All along, Avery had expected that Clare's lawyer would send a polite reminder for a progress report to put before the judge, but when the thick paper envelope from the downtown San Diego law firm had arrived in the mail last week, it was still unsettling. Essentially, the lawyer hoped that Avery could present evidence that Clare was a motivated client who figured out the psychological reasons for why she was stealing, showed remorse, and was no longer at risk for committing such petty crimes. If only it were that simple.

Avery had placed the lawyer's letter in Clare's file so that she could think about it again when she was preparing for today's session. She thought about how much progress Clare had made over the past few months, much more than Avery had envisioned when they first met. Indeed, what had occurred during the past few months between Clare and Avery was anything but predictable. Even now, were they still not dancing around the expected boundaries of psychologist and

CHAPTER TWENTY-ONE

client? An image of her failed pregnancy tests exposed on bathroom countertop flashed through her mind, and then there was Clare's positive pregnancy results, slapped down hard on the coffee table. She'd certainly not be writing about this in her report.

Somehow, Clare had gotten under her skin, and Avery was still not entirely sure why. Clare's turbulent twists and turns of anger, disappointment and sadness, and, yes, particularly her strong sense of entitlement, also had something to do with how she'd gotten herself into trouble for stealing. But there was so much more to the story, and how much of that did she want to tell in a cold, clinical report that would become a part of the court record? Therapists always wanted to shield clients from unnecessary exposure of their vulnerabilities, but Avery felt a surprisingly strong, perhaps overblown, sense of protection towards Clare. Yet the report had to be written, and Avery needed to drive the agenda today.

"Clare, there's something I'd like us to talk about today. It has to do with a figurine in my waiting room," Avery said as soon as Clare settled into the therapy couch.

Clare's body reacted immediately. Blotches of blush sprung up on her cheeks, chest, and arms. Her eyes opened wide and registered panic. It didn't take long, however, before her armour of defiance enveloped her. Avery was not surprised that Clare reached for her shields again in the face of this embarrassing topic. Clare's brow furrowed, her eyes narrowed, and her mouth set.

"I'm not sure I'll be staying for that," Clare shot back.

"Clare, I found the figurine returned on the armchair after you left last week ... together with the beautiful card."

Clare looked confused. The hand that had already been tightly wrapped around the strap of her backpack in preparation for her flight out of the room unclenched and returned to her lap. Her eyes averted, a person much younger than Clare spoke.

"How did you even know it was me who left it there?" she asked, still sitting on the edge of confrontation.

"Well, for one thing, the card just felt like you, Clare."

Clare sat quietly for a moment, and then she looked up with something different in her eyes than the defiance.

"I have a tattoo just like the bird on the card. I drew it out from a dream when I was seventeen," Clare said solemnly.

"Do you remember the dream still, Clare?" Avery asked.

Clare nodded slowly and looked serious.

"Yes, it was a dream I had after …"

"After what, Clare?"

Clare took a deep breath and, with what appeared to be a feat of determination, she opened her eyes and looked directly at Avery.

"I was still living at home then, and it was the summer right after grade eleven. I was angry about my asshole father—angry about everything, really, even angrier than I am now, if you can imagine that. I decided I deserved something special, so I went to this little shop that's just filled with beautiful things, the kinds of things I love, one-of-a-kind clothing, jewellery, handmade papers … you know, the 'objects of beauty' that I've been known to steal. There was a young man working in the shop … on his own. He was really nice, telling me he was a student at the university and that the shop was his summer job. And so …. " An expression of disgust distorted her mouth.

"And so what, Clare?"

With her chin still tucked into her chest, Clare opened her eyes and looked up at Avery. Her hands were tightly intertwined in her lap. She looked like a little girl who'd been caught doing something wrong.

"And so I decided to use my special talent on him," Clare said, swallowing hard.

"What is your special talent, Clare?"

"I'm pretty, and I know how to make men want me. So this guy in the shop, I just charmed him and flirted with him. I knew he probably wasn't supposed to have so many expensive earrings out

CHAPTER TWENTY-ONE

of the glass case at the same time, but I manipulated him by telling him I wasn't sure and needed to see them lined up together. He even let me try them on, and I was pretty certain that normally people aren't supposed to try on pierced earrings. He was complimenting me, saying that all the earrings looked beautiful on me but that none of them could possibly match the amazing colour of my eyes…"

Clare fluttered her eyes to make her point, but then rolled them upward. Avery was uncertain at this moment whether Clare was rolling her eyes at the stupidity of men or at herself for her behaviour. Maybe a bit of both.

"And what happened then, Clare, after you'd used your special talent to bring this young man to find you so attractive and make exceptions for you?"

Clare tucked her chin back into her chest and looked up at Avery.

"I told him that I wanted to try the hat that was on the shelf behind him with the earrings. When he turned around I slipped the antique emerald earrings, the ones I had known all along that I wanted, into my pocket. When he handed me the hat, I made a big show of modeling it for him with the earrings. Ironically, he said that the dangly aquamarine earrings with the floppy white hat would make my boyfriend take me out on a special date. He was obviously fishing to find out whether I had a boyfriend. I didn't have a boyfriend, and this nice young guy didn't stand a chance with me, either. I took a photo of the aquamarine earrings and told him I was asking for them for my birthday. He wondered if I wanted to leave him my phone number, but I said no. And then I just left!"

"How'd you feel when you left the shop?" Avery asked.

"Well … at first, I felt high. I loved the sparkle of the emeralds in the sun. I felt powerful, victorious, and pretty smart, too. And I had my usual rush."

"What kind of a rush, Clare?"

"Well ... I guess I can tell you this, because we're both women and, you know, we've even seen each other's pregnancy tests and everything."

Will my wretched pregnancy tests never go away from this room?

"Ok, so please do tell me about the rush, Clare."

Clare raised her eyebrows slightly. "It's a sexual rush, like I've turned myself on; it's not quite an orgasm but something in that direction."

"So using your beauty and charm to control a man turns you on in a sexual sense. Ok, let's retrace our steps. You start off in a state of anger, stemming from your understandably strong feelings of having been abandoned by your biological father. You've been wronged and someone has to pay, perhaps. From that anger, and the painful feelings of abandonment, you feel you deserve something special, you're at least entitled to something you want ..."

She stopped her interpretation when she saw Clare raise her right arm.

"Yes, exactly, you're nailing this, Dr. Frontiera," Clare said with a spark of excitement. "I feel I like I'm entitled to something beautiful, and I use my looks and my charm to get what I want. I just take control and my body responds with this feeling of sexual pleasure. An orgasmic bonus!"

My interpretation just got seriously hijacked, Avery thought, as she watched Clare revelling in her powers and avoiding the shame that had been uncovered just a few minutes ago.

"You've discovered an important part of why you steal and what you get out of it, Clare. But I don't think the story you set out to tell me is finished. What happened after you stole the emerald earrings? You told me you had an important dream that you drew into the image of a raven with tears and that you now have in the form of a tattoo on your body."

Clare's face fell. Her moment of excited revelation was lost, so much so, that Avery felt a twinge of guilt for using her therapeutic

CHAPTER TWENTY-ONE

talent on Clare. But when she saw Clare take a deep breath and lean forward, she felt confident again.

"It's not a big place, where I grew up, and a few days later, Molly mentioned to me that her friend who owned a shop in town had to fire her summer student because he didn't follow security rules and it cost her a lot of money when someone stole a valuable pair of earrings. These were Molly's words, I remember them exactly: 'You know that shop you love downtown, sweetie? They may have an opening for a salesgirl this summer, if you're interested. In any case, your birthday is coming up; maybe you should pick something beautiful for us to get you. Something beautiful for our beautiful daughter.'"

Before Avery could respond, Clare continued speaking.

"When Molly told me all that, I felt like her kindness was innocently dancing around my mean heart. I imagined how duped the guy in the shop must have felt when the theft was found out. And how terrible he must have felt about being fired. And the worst part was that he was so nice, that he didn't seem to have tried to get me into trouble. I even asked Molly if they had figured out when the earrings got stolen. But she said no, the owner of the shop said that the guy she fired had no clue about how it could have happened. I mean, it's a small town, and I ... I wouldn't have been that hard to find. He could at least have yelled at me."

Avery could see that Clare was struggling to tell the truth without falling into that well of shame. The deeper the fall, the more it would just fuel her unworthiness and so the defensive entitlement that got her into trouble in the first place.

"I can really appreciate how terrible you must've felt. So you had this incredible high after you stole the earrings, but then the high disappeared when you heard that the young man lost his job over it. And all that trust and kindness around you, both from him and your adoptive mother, really brought out these bad feelings. So much so that they showed up in your dreams, too."

Clare nodded as she swiped at her tears with one arm and then the other. "Dr. Frontiera, do you think I'm just a terrible person, a heartless bitch?"

"I know you have a big heart, Clare; you just hide it sometimes. Your big heart carries a lot of love and sadness about your mother, and it was precisely because you do have a big heart that you felt so terrible about causing the young man in the shop to lose his job. And you also felt terrible that Molly was ready to give you whatever you wanted. But I do think that from what we figured out today, that your stealing might bring more harm to you than you are able to imagine when you are in the throes of getting what you want."

"You're actually right. I kind of saw that it wasn't really worth it, stealing like that when I was seventeen. That's why I ended up getting the raven with the tears tattooed on my inner thigh … to remind me of the young man in the shop every day. It worked for a while, but then, it kind of faded away. I started to make up excuses in my head. Like, how could he have been so stupid to lay out all the earrings and turn his back to me? I guess I just totally disparaged him, like it was his fault, not mine. I even convinced myself that he probably ended up finding a better job for the summer. But lately, the guilt and the shame have come back to me for some reason."

"Maybe we should go back to the dream you had, the one that inspired the tattoo. Can you tell me about the dream?" Avery asked.

"I'll never forget this dream. I must have been holding the emerald earrings in my hand when I fell asleep, just thinking about what had happened. In my dream, I start off flying, effortlessly, impossibly high in the sky, and I still feel the emeralds in my hands, but now there are many more of them. 'How did that happen?' I wonder, as I fly along. I look out at my outstretched arms and realize that my arms are really wings. I am a beautiful, white seagull with diamonds, aquamarines, and emeralds decorating my feathers, like, embedded in them. It feels strange, beautiful, and powerful at the same time. The skies are a brilliant turquoise and there are soft, white

CHAPTER TWENTY-ONE

lines of clouds scattered here and there. I'm flying and searching for something, I don't know what. Suddenly, it occurs to me that I have no idea where I'm supposed to land. I realize then that my arms, I mean my wings, have grown too heavy. Now I'm lost and tired and alone in the sky. The sky darkens and suddenly, it's pitch black. I hit something hard, like a wall or a cold hard pane of a window, I just can't see what it is …"

"And what happened then, Clare, in your dream? Please go on."

"I feel hollow bones in my neck and wings cracking. I'm crumbling and splintering and shattering. I'm scared that I'm dying, not just as a seagull, but as me, that I'm actually dying. I give into the storm around me; I swirl around, completely out of control, and it is as if I'm spat out of the top of a whirlwind, and I am in flight again …"

"So you've survived a horrible crash and you're flying again. What happens then in your dream, Clare?"

"It's as if I've flown through the night, and the sun is coming up on the horizon. I look back down over my wings. They're not the white wings of the seagull anymore, but the black, shiny wings of a raven. I've become a raven. I look for the jewels on my wings, but they've disappeared, it feels like. I look one more time, and I'm elated to see that there are still sparkling beads on my wings, like many tiny diamonds glistening in the morning light, and I think to myself that I haven't lost everything. But when I see my wings more closely, they aren't diamonds at all, but beads of tears. I am crying and the teardrops are catching in my black wings. It's both beautiful and terribly sad at the same time. Kind of like me, I guess."

"You are beautiful and sad at the same time," Avery reflected.

"Yeah, it turns out I'm not the powerful, white, bejewelled seagull. I was lost, I crashed, and I almost died from the weight of my wings. And now, I'm just a shitty raven who got caught stealing and is so sorry, so sad."

"It's a very powerful dream, Clare. I don't need to interpret it for you because you already understand it. I just wonder about the last part. You know, ravens are very intelligent, and it sounds like you survived a terrible storm and that you're realizing the sadness you are carrying on your wings. It feels important to learn this about yourself, don't you think?" Avery asked. She decided even before Clare responded that this is where they should end, with the dream, leaving the powerful emotions it expressed to just settle in the safety of the room. Or was that what Avery needed to have happen? Birds had become a sensitive topic for her.

"Thank you for sharing this dream with me. I imagine we'll come back to it again. So my last question is, why did you steal from me, a woman, and why did you bring my figurine back to me with the beautiful drawing of the crying raven?"

"Are you that shrink who wants me to unearth my deeply buried lesbianism?" Clare burst into laughter.

Avery smiled ever so slightly in return, but then her eyes beckoned Clare to continue past her joke.

"Well, you're right: I normally just steal from men. You know, because my anger stems from my rage at Bio-Dad. But you—having to come and see you enraged me, too, and … I guess it threatened me in a way I didn't understand until this very second. I felt like you were going to blow the whistle on my game. That you were going to take away my mojo. And I hadn't even met you yet, but eyeing your naked David, I just took control over the situation. But then …"

"But then what, Clare?"

"But then you turned out to be nicer than I thought. And I felt bad that you're having trouble getting pregnant—or, that's what I picked up, at least. And, you know, you're actually helping me. I'm guessing I'm pretty close to the top of your list of the most pain-in-the-ass patients, but … you never gave up on me or transferred me to someone else."

CHAPTER TWENTY-ONE

"It's very brave and honest for you to tell me all this. I'm so very glad to hear that you feel what we are doing together here is helping you now. I feel really good about that, Clare." Avery said.

Clare's tears had stopped, but they still glistened, it seemed, with the emotional charge of the session and Avery's words of praise.

"You know, there's one more thing you might like to consider," Avery started.

She was taking a risk by not ending the session on this conciliatory note, but at the same time, she wanted Clare to keep thinking about the other possible reasons for why she stole from her female psychologist.

"I think there is another angle to think about. Your very understandable rage about being abandoned by your father, even when you tried to bring him back into your life many years later, is connected to your desire to bring men to their knees, to show them who's really boss. You may also hold some anger toward your mother. Anger's not always logical, especially for a child. You may harbour angry feelings about your mother leaving you alone in the world, even if she couldn't help it, or perhaps you feel that she didn't have the clout to make your father stay with her and you while she was alive, and to make sure he stayed in your life after she died."

Judging from Clare's crossed arms and expression, Avery's long-winded interpretation had annoyed her.

"You have said some really smart things today, but now you're losing it," Clare said, shaking her head in disgust. "I'm not having some textbook mummy transference to you either. Try living in the real world."

Without another word, Clare marched out of the office and slammed the door. Maybe Avery was way off the mark this time? Or perhaps an important seed had been planted? It was hard to know.

Avery stepped outside to take a few minutes on her balcony. She saw a burst of copper before she made out that it was Clare striding away from her office building and onto the beach. Suddenly, she stopped and turned around, her hand on her brow to look up at Avery standing on her balcony, confident that she'd find her. Amidst a flood of feelings, Avery raised her right arm to wave unreservedly to her client, who was likely riddled with emotion too. Clare hesitated for a moment before her hand unfolded into a peace sign. Avery replied with a thumbs-up. *Maybe fewer words next time*, Avery thought, as she turned to go inside and write her progress notes.

PART III:
Winter

TWENTY-TWO

*D*ecember in San Diego was a quiet affair, when locals broke out oversized sweaters to cope with extreme temperatures in the low sixties and occasionally surrendered their flip-flops for fashionable boots. On this last afternoon of psychotherapy before the Christmas holidays, Avery stood on her balcony, breathing in the crisp winter air and hugging Clare's file to her chest for the final session of the day. After the end of the long tourist season, she always loved her bird's-eye view of San Diegans taking back their beach boardwalks, the movement of their darkening outlines cast against the backdrop of palms in the rusty remnants of sunset. The strings of tiny white Christmas lights entangling the majestic trunks of the palm trees were all that was needed to set a festive tone.

Lingering in her favourite place of contemplation, Avery was still reeling from the unexpected phone call late last night. The house phone ringing for the first time in months had startled her where she'd fallen asleep on the couch. Didn't everyone just keep their landlines for the odd call from elderly relatives with bad news?

"Avery? This is your father speaking," the surprisingly frail voice had sounded from somewhere in her distant past. It was rare enough that her father sent a birthday card with a cheque in it, but he never called her. It was just too awkward.

"Is Mum ok?" Avery heard herself whispering automatically as a cascade of catastrophic images filled her headspace.

CHAPTER TWENTY-TWO

She shivered in the cool December air, more from this memory than the temperature.

The last Avery had heard before her father called last night was that her parents had separated, again, after a brief reunion of living together at the family's beach home. There was nothing unique about this most recent separation; it had unfolded the way it always did. There they would sit silently for hours in front of the television, Dad with the Scotch decanter, fancy ice bucket, and Madmen glass on his side table and Mum with her oversized bottle of wine within her reach. *God forbid should they have to get up out of their matching La-Z-Boys to refill their drinks.* Only rarely would one of their hands migrate toward the other's, almost imperceptibly so. When Avery was still living at home, witnessing this hint of connection between her parents in the living room gave her a fleeting feeling of hope for what was left of her family. But it never lasted. It was as if, as soon as they touched, an electric shock sent their gaze toward the fireplace mantel, where Sebastian's graduation photo rested next to the urn. When this happened, her father's eyes quickly averted and returned to the television, but not her mother's eyes; they stayed locked on to the image of Sebastian. For Avery, this moment triggered an almost unbearable longing for her brother, not only because she missed him but also because he'd evened out the balance of power in their family. "We need at least two of us to deal with the two of them," Sebastian used to say with that conspiratorial glint in his eyes.

To this day, that palpable yearning for her brother was mixed with a child-like surge of anxiety that she would be caught for stealing his ashes and refilling the urn with bone-coloured sand. While she preferred not to be found out in her act of teenage rebellion while still living under her parents' roof, Avery had no remorse about that night, when she snuck out of the house to set free the lovely ashen softness left of him. She could still remember feeling him cupped in her hand under the stars before she finally flattened her palm and let the wind carry him off toward the surf. Who knew that all the hard-edged horror he had experienced in his short lifetime could be distilled into this quiet softness she felt in his ashes?

Avery both longed for and dreaded these moments when her parents fleetingly reconnected, looking at that photo of their firstborn. And then it would all unwind. It was the same pattern that had been knitted and unravelled a thousand times to its perpetual state of imperfection. Something—really, almost anything—would trigger her mother into a memory of Sebastian as a child, and her eyes would tear up as she spoke about him. In a reflexive response, her father's hand would tense around his Scotch glass and his mouth would tighten in self-defence as he stared straight ahead, intently watching the mundaneness of strangers' lives on the television screen and hoping that his wife's emoting would cease. Her mother's persistence to keep talking about Sebastian in her sadly slurred words would finally cause him to explode. Neither of them could handle their separate wells of emotions freed by what was called the "devil's nectar" for a reason. It was always the same ugly, downhill fight. About whose fault it was. Who was the better parent? Who lost his temper with an already disturbed child and damaged him more? Who indulged him until he could no longer cope with anything in life?

Without fail, her father would storm out of the house, sometimes for the night and sometimes for weeks. When she was still living at home, Avery braced herself for the slam of the door. And then she did what any good daughter would do and helped her mother to bed. During her college years, when she had moved out of the family home, the fallout from their fights took the form of phone calls to Avery in the middle of the night and desperate arrangements to get the police to look in on her mother.

But the biggest problem for Avery in all of this was that no matter how hard she tried, how many crises she averted, her mother remained unresponsive to her daughter's love. Dr. Mahler had eventually helped Avery to realize that through no fault of her own, her

CHAPTER TWENTY-TWO

mother was incapable of grabbing hold of the child who was still alive. He finally made her see that she had to take distance from her parents' fights and her mother's desperation, *before this kills you, too, my dear Avery*. Despite all of Dr. Mahler's efforts to soften the guilt of stepping away from that family sinkhole, the bitter bile of self-reproach had come back up into Avery's throat last night, when she heard her father's voice.

"Your mother is in an institution now, a nice private facility."

An institution? It couldn't possibly be worse than the prison of a parent whose child chose to take his own life.

"She just wasn't able to manage on her own anymore, I had to do something ... let's see ..." Avery had heard papers rustling in the background. Surely, he'd have some cold hard facts to rationalize what he'd done ..."Yes, here it is in the doctor's report, Avery, you'll understand this better than I."

I don't think I understand anything anymore, the voice inside her head screamed as she pressed her eyes shut and felt the heat running down her cheeks.

As always, her father was relentless in establishing his case. He was the finest advocate in Mendocino County, after all; she had once read this about her father in a newspaper story. "Ok, here's what's wrong with her ... she suffers from a dementia with a course of marked deterioration, likely Alzheimer's type ... chronic depression, and cirrhosis of the liver ... all of which will require residential care ... you see, I had no choice, Avery."

"Ok, dad, I've got the picture," Avery finally managed to say out loud. Protectiveness and sadness for her mother pooled in her gut and threatened to wash away the walls she'd fought so hard to build.

But he wasn't quite done yet. "The final straw was when the neighbours had to get her out of the house after she fell asleep in her chair and set the kitchen on fire a few weeks ago. I'm sorry, Avery, your mother was saved, but the house burned down." Her father's voice was becoming steadier, more confident, than the frail voice she heard when she picked up the phone.

"So what is it you want me to do, Dad?" she had asked him.

"Well, there's nothing left of the house, nothing that needs doing there, and I took care of the insurance matters." He hesitated and suddenly an unfamiliar softness came over his voice. "It's just that your mother asked for you, she wants to see you."

The power that this handful of words held over Avery was stunning, even to her. *What? Me? She wants to see me?* Avery saw herself then as a girl, running on the beach as fast as her little legs could carry her, flip-flops, bucket, and shovel in a trail behind her, running to the back porch where her mother was smiling with her hand cupped over her eyes. She actually knew how to smile all those years ago.

"Avery? Are you still there?"

"Yes' tell Momma I'll be there before Christmas." Had she just called her mother "Momma" again, after all these years?

"All right then. You're a good girl, Avery …" he started to say, gearing up for a quick exit.

She knew that if she didn't speak up now, he'd be gone again into the night. "I was just wondering," she had asked him, certain that he could hear her swallowing hard, "are you going to be there when I come?"

She heard him clearing his throat and knew the answer would be no. "You know I would if I could, but my health won't allow it. The doctor insists I take my usual R and R in the Caymans for the next couple of months, you know, after all I've been through with your mother and the fire."

When Avery set down the phone and looked up, she saw Roland standing there in his pyjamas. He walked over and patted her on the shoulder. "I could hear your father's voice on the phone. You are a good daughter," he told her. "I'll have the Christmas tree up just the way you like it when you get back from your mother's."

CHAPTER TWENTY-TWO

Dr. Avery Frontiera, specializing in men who walk away when you need them most. Still shaking her head, Avery turned around to step away from the sanctuary of her balcony and into whatever Clare had in store for her today.

The shock of seeing her already there in the therapy room was chased away almost immediately by a gripping wave of irritation that threatened to express itself on Avery's face. Clare had let herself in and was sitting on the couch. Her shoes discarded on the rug, she sat cross-legged in bare feet, with a voluminous sweater covering her almost to the knees. Avery glanced at her bathroom door; it was closed and she was certain she'd locked it. It was three fifty-eight; Avery checked on the digital clock on her desk. She rarely ran late but, even if she did, all of her other clients knew to wait in the waiting room which, after all, was called that for a reason. *This must be what it's like parenting a teenager,* Avery thought, grasping for an approach to take in this unexpected situation. *Pick your battles, don't sweat the small stuff, understand that during the teenage years—or regression to the teenage years during young adulthood—opposition and rebellion at every possible moment are annoying but normal.* Avery decided she would let Clare's behaviour go without comment, at least for now. But Avery's cursory glance at the clock had not escaped Clare, who was observing intently from her perch, right index finger thoughtfully touching her chin. Was that a smirk coming over her face? Could this get any more irritating?

"Please … please, sit down, Dr. Frontiera. Don't mind me. I saw you were having your little moment out on the balcony, so I thought I would let myself in early and get all set up.

"Anyway, getting to the point here, I'm finally ready to talk about my pregnancy. I have to admire you, you know; you're, like, the most super controlled person I've ever met … I mean, not even asking me once about the whole baby thing since I shut that topic down a couple of months ago. Especially with our history of sharing pregnancy tests."

Avery felt her mouth opening and closing. There was no point in even beginning to sift through the layers of insult, presumption, entitlement, and general *shit-disturbing* that were hurtling across the room. Avery swallowed hard before she was able to settle back into therapist mode. What was this huge wave of defensiveness and passive aggression coming over her client? Why was Clare protecting herself with such determination today, when in the last few sessions she'd showed so much softening, so much progress, and had even thrown her a peace sign?

"So, obviously, I'm not going to kill it now," Clare continued, her face registering the faintest wince at her own harsh words.

Clare's hand reached instinctively under her sweater and lifted it to locate the bump protruding over the top of her low-rise jeans. Avery felt her eyes following helplessly to the ivory softness of Clare's pregnant belly. She reined herself in and resumed the expected eye contact. Too late. Clare's eyes shot down to her belly and then peered at her psychologist from underneath her raised eyebrows. Avery's cheeks blazed. She wished now that she had poured herself some water, maybe even something stronger, before sitting down.

"And ... and how are you feeling, Clare?" Avery stumbled in an awkward attempt to gather herself.

"I'm ok now. I puked a few times, but nothing too major. I made three different appointments with the Women's Health Clinic for an abortion, but I ended up cancelling all of them."

"It sounds like it ended up being a hard decision, figuring out what was going to be the right thing for you."

With her eyes averted, Clare nodded. When she finally looked up at Avery, tears were pooling around her eyes.

"And ... and best for the baby, too." Suddenly, Clare seemed to be gripped by another train of thought and lifted her hand so that its palm faced Avery. "But before we get into all of that ... I just ... I

CHAPTER TWENTY-TWO

just want to say sorry for being such a bitch when I got here today. I know perfectly well that I'm supposed to wait in the waiting room—just like everyone else."

"Thank you for saying so, Clare. I do know that you're aware of how it's supposed to work here. But why do you think you were behaving that way earlier on, when you are feeling sorry about it now?"

"It's like something that takes me over. I turn into this pissy, completely unlikable teenager, just stomping around and bullying anyone in my way to see how far I can push things." Clare appeared disgusted with herself.

"And how far could you push things?"

"Pretty far. To the point of complete obnoxiousness, I would say, and meanness, too, with that comment about our pregnancy tests. But then …"

"But then what?"

"But then, you're still here. You don't just kick me out of therapy and tell me you are going to fail me on your report to the judge. You're still sitting there, listening patiently and, like, really talking to me. It's so reckless of me to do that here, and it just wastes time. Especially when I have some pretty important stuff to talk about today." Clare's hand migrated to the bump on her abdomen, this time over the top of her sweater.

"And we'll certainly talk about that important stuff in just a minute, but maybe acting like that, especially when there is something really important on your mind, could be a way of protecting yourself?"

"I think you're right. Come to think of it, I've been doing that … like, forever."

Avery knew how hard it was for Clare to apologize and to admit that Avery, or anyone but herself, might be right. She felt proud of the young woman sitting before her, but then she imagined Dr. Mahler mouthing the word countertransference. Was this feeling of pride yet another red flag for over-involvement with her young client? She'd have to think about this later.

"You know, what you're telling me makes perfect sense, Clare ... I wouldn't blame you one bit if you just wanted to protect yourself from more pain about losing your mother, your grandmother, and then your father. It would be hard to know whom you can trust, who will stay with you."

"I ... I guess it makes sense when you say it like that, Dr. Frontiera. I mean, all that stuff was a lot to deal with ..." Clare covered her face with her hands and let out a long sigh.

"A huge amount of stuff, Clare. For anyone, but especially for a little girl just starting out in the world," Avery encouraged.

"I didn't even realize that this is what I was doing. What I'm still doing, I guess ... it's so stupidly defensive of me. "

"It is defensive, Clare, but I can't agree that it's stupid. I'm guessing that, without even realizing it at the time, it was a very adaptive, a healthy thing to do as a child. It actually made perfect sense to keep people at a distance, test them out again and again, until you could even start to trust them."

"Yeah, true, like poor Jim and Molly. I put them through a lot of crazy shit."

"And, of course, we really have to respect that even though all of this is becoming clearer to you now, sitting here with me and really thinking about it quite hard as an adult, in childhood, these things just happen naturally, outside of awareness. You did exactly what you needed to do without yet being able to realize it," Avery offered.

"I guess that's true. But now that I know, I should probably change it. Stop being such a bitch, I mean. That's gonna be hard for me," Clare said, cracking a smile.

"It's hard to change something that's been a part of your pattern for a long time. It's ok to be cautious."

"Cautious?"

CHAPTER TWENTY-TWO

"Yes: being careful, gentle and taking your time is what I mean, Clare. After all, this way of protecting yourself came as a reaction to some very tender and understandable feelings about losing people and about not trusting people." Avery knew that her young client was hardest on herself.

"Yeah …" Clare said, twisting and untwisting a strand of her hair around her finger. "I don't want to go to the other extreme and trust everybody, is kind of what you're saying, too. There are some really untrustworthy people out there who would take full advantage of that!"

A wave of anger flared over Clare's face, then dissipated, rather than building upon itself the way it had in past sessions. This was new, too.

"But anyway, that's not the point right now," Clare continued. "I told you about how I was being a bitch today because I realized it was getting in the way of what I really wanted to talk to you about. About what's, like, really, really important to me, but hard to talk about."

Clare reached over to the coffee table to touch her iPhone. It was three thirty-two, they could both see when the screen lit up, and today it was Clare who wanted to take control of the precious time left in her session.

Clare sat silently. Was that fear in her eyes?

"There's still quite a lot of time, Clare. Please tell me what you wanted to talk to me about today."

"I want you to adopt my baby, Dr. Frontiera," Clare whispered.

Suddenly everything Avery knew with certainty became unsteady and surreal; she gripped the arms of her chair to keep from falling. There she sat, staring at Clare's lips, struggling to make sense of the jumble of sounds spinning around her. Clare's words travelled through space in slow motion and reassembled. Yes, she really said that. *Clare wants me to adopt her baby.* Avery's heart leapt and then crashed. Everything she wanted and couldn't have had been wrapped

170

into a single sentence. *Not like this, it can't be like this.* And now, how was she supposed to manage this tender request, right after she'd encouraged Clare to step out of her protective armour?

"I … I …" Avery heard herself stuttering, stumbling.

"Wait. Just give yourself some time to think about it. I know it's a bit of a surprise," Clare continued, without a doubt trying to hold her ground and stave off yet another disappointment, this time about to be delivered by her trusted psychologist. Her words were strong, practiced, like a persuasive essay she'd been drafting and redrafting for some time. She wasn't ready to just give up.

"I've been thinking this through very carefully, Dr. Frontiera. I think we would agree that I've made progress," Clare said, swallowing hard. She was willing to offer anything…admission of fault, fear of disappointment, the faintest hope of trust…to have her request taken seriously. Avery imagined she could hear pieces of herself falling and shattering on the floor.

"There's been no stealing, I swear on my baby's life, for at least two months. The one thing I did steal, I've returned, as you know," Clare's rapid fire continued. "I know myself better, and I'm becoming less of a bitch. But I'm still way too immature and way too selfish to be a mother; I know you'll agree with that. The baby isn't due until June twenty-first, which is, like, way after when we'll be done and you've had a chance to write your report. So you won't be my psychologist anymore. So no conflict of interest there, you see, I thought of that, too. You won't get into trouble, and I could sign something promising not to make a complaint against you ever, even if you piss me off.

"The only thing is I really want an open adoption, I think it's called, so that my little girl can know me a bit, too, and even hear about what happened to my mother when she's older. But you'd be the official, full-time mother. And if you wanna be real, just for a second, Dr. Frontiera, you and I both know you want a baby and I don't think you have a lot of other options."

CHAPTER TWENTY-TWO

A beautiful little girl with grey-green eyes and her mother's curly red hair? *You can't have this.* The voice inside Avery's head was harsh.

"Clare ..." was all Avery could manage before Clare interrupted her once again.

"Wait! Just wait," she said, on her feet now. "And then there's the most important part of all ... You'll be a really, really good mother. You're patient and smart and kind and you actually give a shit; you've a great job that pays a lot of money, and you'll be like totally committed ... You are ... just someone I ... um ... kind of trust, but who isn't in the rest of my life, like ... like Molly and Jim. I'm not even going to tell them ... It would be too much for them to bare ..."

Clare sat back down, evaluating the impact of her words on her psychologist's face. It was as if Clare could see into the mess inside Avery, the stirring and debating, yearning and dismissing. Could she smell the ambivalence that could possibly lead to victory? Or to complete professional suicide, depending on how one looked at it? Avery could see in Clare's eyes this faint possibility of a win.

"And I think we already figured out that you can handle obnoxious teenagers—or immature young adults, same difference—in case she's anything like me."

Avery hadn't been prepared for what was happening in this room, despite the stream of ethics courses and workshops that had helped build her professional self.

"Clare, I want to thank you for speaking to me about all of this, for thinking about me as a parent for your baby. I'm very touched. I hadn't expected this. So you're right, I just need time to think about what you've said. And, also, we have to finish for today."

The second the final sentence came out of her mouth, Avery knew she'd made a mistake. Clare stood, snapped up her shoes and purse, and fought the tears welling up in her eyes.

"You know, you're pretty fucked up, just like the rest of us, Dr. Frontiera. This is a lot simpler than you think. Not everything fits perfectly into textbooks and that fifty-minute hour of yours," Clare said with a dignity that brushed shame over Avery's cheeks.

"I'm sorry, Clare. I honestly don't know the right way to handle this, but I do know that I would never intend to hurt you. We'll talk more."

"Ok." Clare turned to walk out the door, her shoulders held high.

TWENTY-THREE

There was an unspoken honesty in Northern California's rugged coast and mountains. The serene groves of redwoods reached impossibly high to knit dark green tapestries and filter the sunlight into softness. The long drive from San Diego to Mendocino gave Avery plenty of time to retrace her steps to this place of her childhood. She could have chosen to fly into Sacramento and rent a car, as Roland had suggested, but she felt compelled to stay connected to the ground and feel the distance in real time. Lying awake last night at Cantua Creek's only B and B, situated near the historic border between Northern and Southern California, Avery had decided that she would bypass the cinders of the family beach house and go directly to her mother's new home. She wanted to remember the beach house as it was before the fire, to care for her own memories before she faced what was left of her mother's.

Her high school guidance counsellor, Miss Allison, her sun-kissed crow's feet deepened by kindness, had dared to suggest to her parents that Avery return to ballet after Sebastian died. A few years later, when Avery was in her last year of high school, it was also Miss Allison who immediately understood about the geographical tipping point necessary for selecting the location of her college. It had to be far enough away to get some real distance from the family memories of the beach house; she needed to escape the reaches of her mother's blank stare, Sebastian's shadows, and the suffocating smiles of sympathetic neighbours. But the chosen college also couldn't be so far

CHAPTER TWENTY-THREE

from familiarity that Avery wouldn't recognize herself; the place still had to feel like a beach somewhere in California, a beach on which she could imagine meandering up the coastline to where she had left him.

The shiny brochure for San Diego State had brimmed with appealing course descriptions and smiling college students, oblivious to what all of her hometown knew had happened to their family. This fresh place in Southern California whispered to her the possibility of a new grip on life, a way to carry on.

Mendocino Memory Care Community was located at the end of a long driveway that wound through a meadow. Avery pushed the intercom button and identified herself. The gate opened slowly, then closed again in her rear view mirror; this security measure both comforted and frightened her. Even in December, the grounds were beautifully kept. Gawky Jeffrey pines closest to the front doors were decorated with simple silver ball ornaments. As a child, she'd loved these imperfect pines with their messy branches and knotted trunks that looked like the faces of grumpy old men. *Why do all these trees have the same name, Sebby? Don't worry, it's just their last name, Avey. Why don't you give each of these guys their own special first name?* What would it be like, she wondered, to be driving up to this facility with Sebastian beside her—but, then again, would their mother even have ended up here, had he lived?

The pleasant young woman at the nursing station, designed to look more like the reception area of a posh country inn, told Avery that her mother chose to have her lunch on a tray in her room today. *Some things don't change; God forbid she make some new friends over lunch.* Avery and the young woman, whose nametag identified her as *Nurse Iris, Memory Care Team,* walked together through the dining room, where several residents were still eating or staring despondently into the distance. One elderly woman had fallen asleep in her wheelchair, a red knit shawl over her lap and her mouth gaping as an attendant wheeled her toward the exit.

Chatty Nurse Iris, unabashedly proud to show off the fine facilities available to "the lovely residents," made Avery smile despite the nerves gathering in her stomach. They passed through a hall decorated with seasonal reminders for all denominations of the memory impaired: pretty silver-and-blue dreidel string lights interspersed with tiny traditional Christmas wreaths and red Chinese muslin stockings. At the end of the hall, French doors required a numerical pin code for entry. Iris said this was the Reminiscence Wing, reserved especially for the more advanced cases, but then she blushed and corrected herself to say it was for those who benefitted from around-the-clock care.

Nurse Iris slowed down and fell silent a few doors deep into the wing. She touched Avery's shoulder and pointed her to the door of the next room. There was a brass handle but no lock on the shiny mahogany door and a discrete but permanent doorstop to keep it half open, a compromise between safety and privacy. *Mrs. Elizabeth Jean Howard*, the nameplate on the wall to the left of the doorframe read. The dignity of her mother's full name spelled out, together with her preferred title despite the many years of marital woes and separations, brought tears to Avery's eyes.

From the doorway, she saw her mother perched on a vanity bench, her body angled toward the large window overlooking the facility's abundant gardens. Her silver hair fell in waves over her frail back, and her delicate profile was illuminated like a full-body halo by the afternoon sun. Avery knocked cautiously on the door. Her mother continued to stare out of the window until she finally spoke.

"You may take the tray away now," she said crisply without turning her head.

"It's me, Momma. It's Avery. Can I come in? I heard you were asking for me."

Her mother hesitated and then slowly turned. She furrowed her brow until finally the smile of finding an answer to a difficult problem broke out over her face. Avery was mesmerized by the glow

CHAPTER TWENTY-THREE

of her still-beautiful mother's warm expression. Was this finally her moment?

"Mary! You've come all the way from Colorado to see me."

Mary was her mother's older sister who had died ten years ago. Avery's smile wavered, dissolved. Suddenly, she felt her fatigue from the hours of driving and sleeping on a too-thin mattress last night. *I can't stop trying now.* She needed an approach to save the moment, and moved across the room to sit down on the window seat and face her mother.

"Oh, Momma! You've always told me that I reminded you of your older sister, Aunt Mary. But in the end, you decided to call me, your own daughter, Avery—you know, to avoid confusion, you told me."

Her mother's expression was blank, but then her eyes opened wide and she brought both hands to her face in surprise.

"Oh my God, my little girl came home from college just to see me! Avery, darling, how are you doing at school?" Her mother reached for her daughter's hands.

Avery darling. These simple two words melted her. Was this what it felt like for an addict in the depths of withdrawal to stick the needle back into their arm? Her mother's hands felt so soft against her own.

"It's going really well, Momma. I'm actually pretty well finished with school now."

"And what did you study, my dear?" her mother asked with an expression of interest so heartfelt that it filled Avery with a second wave of this dangerous drug.

"I studied to become a psychologist, Momma. I do my best to help people with emotional problems." Avery paused; had she just touched a wound that would spoil everything?

Her mother turned away and stared into the gardens, when suddenly a carefree smile breezed over her face.

"Well, it's not always easy to be the only child in the family—it can be a lot of pressure—but you've done it swimmingly my dear.

And, I might add, you've made your father and I very proud!" her mother declared, as if she had just made an amazing new discovery.

Avery was stunned. The woman who thought of nothing but her son had forgotten him completely.

"I'm glad I make you and Dad proud; I try my best."

Suddenly, her mother slumped and all expression left her face as she closed her eyes.

"I need to rest now. You may come again on a different day," her mother said. She was wringing her hands now and shaking her head slightly. Suddenly, her mother stood up, still agile in her physical movements. She walked to her bed and lay down, facing away from Avery.

"Maybe I'll go now, Momma, and let you rest." Avery lifted the throw blanket from the foot of the bed and spread it gently over her mother's slight person. Her mother's eyes were closed when Avery leaned over to kiss her sun-mottled cheek.

Avery felt a contentment that she hadn't experienced for as long as she could remember, maybe ever. Her mother's dementia had made her burn down her home, but it also helped her to find this protected place and freedom from the torturous memories of her son. *And now I do know that my mother loves me, that she's proud of me*, Avery thought, feeling the joyful melody of this favourite new song circling around her heart.

"Good-bye, Momma. Sleep well."

"You can take the tray now, Miss. You know I can't tolerate clutter."

You better take this gift and run while the going is good, Avery chuckled to herself. Some things about her mother hadn't changed at all. Avery took the tray from the table.

"Yes M'am!" she said, smiling.

In the hall, Nurse Iris waited to escort her back to the lobby. Would the nurse's feedback find its way into her mother's medical

CHAPTER TWENTY-THREE

chart for the benefit of the other memory care team members? Her smile suggested that she'd favourably rated Avery's visit.

TWENTY-FOUR

Clare's iPhone never lied about the facts. *Wednesday, February 14, 2019, three fourty-eight p.m.* She couldn't argue about how much time had passed or that this was her last day here. Her thumb hit the home button and *Happy Valentine's Day Clare!* shot across the screen, setting off an explosion of stupidly happy crimson hearts. She snorted in disgust and tossed the phone back into her bag. Clare inhaled deeply, as she always did here, and looked around the room. Her irritation settled quickly, as if sponged away by the quiet beauty around her. She closed her eyes for a moment and tuned into the ticking of the antique clock beside her on the coffee table. Not in her wildest dreams had she thought it would end this way. The mental screenshots of her heel-dragging introduction to this waiting room still held every detail of those first impressions—not just the colours and the shapes, but that viscera of late summer heat she had felt in her body sitting in this very chair, and even the distinct bristle of her angry determination to disparage and resist everything.

Clare remembered all of this with razor sharp exactness, yet the feeling in the room was different now, softer. She felt connected with the little girl clutching the bouquet of wildflowers on Raeburn's painting, her big chocolate eyes so sad and wise despite the hint of smile on her lips. Clare had to admit that just sitting here gave her comfort. Almost a half-year had passed since she first stepped into this room, all vigilant, ready to criticize, and impossibly defensive.

CHAPTER TWENTY-FOUR

Just months later, here she sat on her personal favourite of the three armchairs, the fingers of one hand playfully tracing the familiar, carved details of the chair's arm and her other hand resting lightly on her pregnant belly. With only minutes to spare before the therapy room door opened, she felt compelled to look around just one more time, to absorb every detail. Suddenly, her eyes filled with tears, and she realized that what she was really doing was saying good-bye to all of this.

For a few weeks now, Dr. Frontiera had been talking to her about their soon-to-be ending therapy relationship and how it was important to talk about all the feelings that came up. "Ending?" Clare had repeated softly when Dr. Frontiera first said this. The heaviness of this word stuck in the back of her throat like toffee that had been chewed in too much of hurry before swallowing it down. Her strong reaction had surprised, even annoyed her. After all, it was no shocker that these sessions would come to an end in the four to six months of psychotherapy prescribed by the judge. And, in fact, it couldn't be forgotten that when she first started all of this therapy business, kicking and screaming, she just couldn't wait to be released from this pointless exercise. This nasty string of sarcastic self-reproach had rampaged automatically through her head for what seemed like a very long time as she stayed motionless on the therapy couch. And all the while, Dr. Frontiera had just sat there, patiently waiting for Clare to continue speaking, her face full of all that kindness and unending understanding.

It was when she looked back up from the harsh tirade in her head and found Dr. Frontiera's warm eyes waiting for her return, that Clare heard *it* distinctly for the first time. At this moment it was not Dr. Frontiera's words of encouragement that she heard, but a new voice, an altogether different tone chiming up from within *herself*, a softer and gentler version of her that had been building up before it could express itself. This voice was mellow; it told her to *be chill* and patient, to realize that she'd been through a lot and it was ok—really, it was expected—that she be nervous about leaving her safety net and going it on your own. "It's just that ... endings are hard for me," she had said out loud, the sound of exposing her inner voice surprising her.

She felt her lips curling up ever so slightly. The hint of proud smile also surfaced on Dr. Frontiera's face and told her that she saw it too, the victory of that moment. It wasn't that she'd never be harsh with herself again, or flare out at some man who touched a nerve, but now Clare could see her hurt more clearly, she kind of recognized the shape of it, and she had a choice about how she would speak to herself. All that slogging through the harsh reality of her childhood, all that pain she hated to admit but had exposed to this patient and kind woman sitting with her, it had taken seed in her somehow. And *that* was the reason for all of this. *Turns out it wasn't a pointless exercise at all.*

Clare pulled her iPhone from her bag. *Three fifty-five p.m.* In exactly five minutes, Dr. Frontiera would open her door one last time. Clare shifted in her armchair and felt the flutter of her baby. She closed her eyes, overwhelmed by the road still ahead of her, with the scary-sounding birth and the open adoption. That was something she'd talk to Dr. Frontiera about today. She remembered now that moment in their first session after the Christmas break, when Dr. Frontiera had given Clare the final thumbs down about adopting her baby. That was after Clare had worked so hard, even researched all the strangulating rules that psychologists had to live by, to make her strongest argument. Using her most mature voice, she'd asked Dr. Frontiera to consider that the adoption would occur long after their therapy relationship had ended. Feeling more heated by the fear of Dr. Frontiera saying no, then she had told the super responsible doctor to get her head around the fact that Clare was perfectly willing to go to another psychologist if she needed more help in the future, you know, to avoid that supposed "conflict of interest." *There's no conflict here, we both want the same thing,* she wanted to

CHAPTER TWENTY-FOUR

yell out, but didn't. Of course, she doubted anyway that she would ever need another psychologist. Nor would she ever find a psychologist like Dr. Frontiera; that part of her thinking she swallowed on impact and didn't speak out loud. Clare had even promised to never complain to any authorities about Dr. Frontiera adopting her baby. There had to be some kind of a form like a pre-nup—shrinks had consent forms and release forms for everything—and she would sign it, no problem. No one would even have to know.

In the end, Dr. Frontiera's reasons for saying *no-can-do* weren't surprising, nor was the kindness and respect that she showed when she told Clare. Clare had wanted so badly to just hate on Dr. Frontiera at that moment, to be a completely miserable bitch to her for the rest of their time together. But she didn't do that. She didn't, not just because she'd found this new hold on herself, but because she saw the pain in Dr. Frontiera's eyes. She could see that Dr. Frontiera's decision hurt her as much, if not more, than it did Clare. *Mental screenshot.* There sat Dr. Frontiera, wrapped up in reams of red tape, her wrists painfully writhing in the shackles of professional psychology. *How sad*, Clare still thought now, as she sat in this room waiting for the last time—not just that this caring woman wouldn't be her little girl's mother, but that she'd cut herself off from this golden opportunity, from what Clare was pretty sure she wanted more than anything.

Clare hated all these theories and rules; she vowed that this essential rebel was a part of her she'd never change. She just wished she could liberate Dr. Frontiera, too, even if only by a fraction, just enough of a movement to crack the body cast her psychologist had created for herself.

Dr. Frontiera's door opened and startled Clare out of her thoughts.

"Please, Clare, come on in!" What child wouldn't want that warm welcome when they got home from school?

As Clare stood up, she felt tears roll down her cheeks. Damn, she'd thought she had this under control.

"It's ok, Clare, let's sort this out together."

"It's really just the hormones," Clare muttered.

Clare turned her face to wipe the tears from her eyes with the sleeve of her shirt. When she blinked her eyes open, she found herself face to face with white marble David, still sitting on the bookshelf where he'd been placed after she returned him, months ago. A smile came over Clare's lips. *Maybe things will turn out ok in the end, she thought.* Even David looked like he was starting to trust the situation, that he knew he wouldn't be kidnapped again by the kleptomaniac young woman who got off on feeling him in her skirt pocket. Who was that girl even?

This moment of eye contact with David hadn't escaped Dr. Frontiera, who was still standing in the doorway and started to chuckle.

"I only just put your report in the mail, Clare."

"Don't worry, Dr. Frontiera, I'm not in that biz anymore!"

As she walked toward the therapy couch, Clare felt it again, that new voice inside of her. *It's ok: endings are hard for you, girlfriend, but you're crushing it right now.*

PART IV:
Spring

TWENTY-FIVE

*D*r. Mahler sat silent for twenty minutes straight through Avery's play-by-play rendition of her last session with Clare. Finally, Avery sank back into the therapy couch.

"So it's over now," Dr. Mahler said. His eyebrows lifted slightly, as if he couldn't decide whether this should be a statement or a question.

"Yes, I guess it is. I think I did a good job with Clare in the end and that … you know, that I made the right decision. I'm just still working it all through in my mind."

"Alright, my Avery, let's talk about this. It's been quite the roller coaster for you over the past six months, so I can appreciate that it helps for us to go over the most important parts together, to help consolidate them in your mind. From what you've told me, this young woman was the most challenging client you've ever had in your practice and yet you persisted—both of you did, in your own ways—and in the end, she got better. Not just in that she gained insight into why she was stealing, so she can stop this defensive expression of her conflicts and not ruin her life, but in so many other ways that we know to be important. Many other young women wouldn't realize they are not yet ready to be a mother. And that's a good thing, right? To not rush into motherhood and to consider all of one's options. No one would argue with that, I think?"

"Yes, you're right, Dr. Mahler, I'm with you so far," Avery said, soaking in every bit of the good medicine. "Please … go on …"

CHAPTER TWENTY-FIVE

"All right," Dr. Mahler continued. "Over the past few weeks, you offered her a kind and thoughtful psychotherapy ending."

The surge of pride Avery felt at his words of praise and acknowledgement was almost embarrassing. She remembered then how confident she felt writing her final report to the judge. It was as if Dr. Mahler's words were cementing into place the pieces of her work with Clare that were dependable, that fell within the normal boundaries of psychotherapy. This was just the anchor she needed for all those other unexpected pieces for which there was no proper place in her report or even in her mind, the until-now uncharted territories.

"On the last day, she thanked me for everything despite her disappointment that I wouldn't adopt her baby. She made me a card. This time, it was a vibrant bird all in blues and greens. It was in flight, carrying an olive branch in its beak."

Dr. Mahler was smiling. They didn't need to discuss the card. Surely, by this point in his career, he'd received a whole trunkful of cards of his own from his grateful clients, including the one from Avery after her first round of therapy, a beautiful depiction of a ballerina curtsying her thank you.

"And in refusing to adopt Clare's baby and not even considering giving in to my own needs and desires and problems of the moment, we know I did the right thing?"

Dr. Mahler normally wouldn't answer a question like this and, in fairness, neither would she, if she were sitting in the therapist's chair.

"You know, Avery, I've been thinking quite a lot about what's happened here, Clare wanting you to adopt her baby. Normally, I don't offer an opinion, and I still won't, but maybe it will be helpful for you to hear another psychologist's line of thinking."

Not just another psychologist, but my guru, Avery thought automatically, as she felt her entire body edging toward every word he might offer. Dr. Mahler noticed her movement, and he smiled kindly.

"You're looking very enthusiastic on the edge of your seat, my dear Avery. What I'm going to say, it's not anything you don't already know, but maybe it helps you to hear where I've landed in my own thinking.

"Professionally speaking, you and I both live in ... let's just call it the land of clinical psychology. For better or for worse—mostly for better, I feel, from my experience of many years—we practice our psychotherapy in this place. And in this place, there is no possible road that leads to adopting your client's or your former client's baby. It is an ethical impossibility. Neither of us had to even open our ethics handbooks, as Clare's request is so far outside the realm. There is nothing even close to this that has come up in my entire career. What Clare asked is a completely impossible outcome."

Completely impossible outcome. There you go, it's wrong and you can't have it, final verdict, Avery thought. The flashback was instant, taking her breath away with its pain and beauty. Avery was seeing *her* again, her golden child, collapsing and crumpling into the field of glass chards, beloved soft rose ballet slippers shredded and stained with blood. Avery swallowed hard. She could swear she smelled the scent of the child's delicate porcelain skin at this moment. Avery took a deep breath and willed herself to sit up straight. She shook her head and looked at Dr. Mahler intently, searching for his solid ground.

Nothing was lost on him, and he nodded at her slowly until she returned to the safety of his support and understanding. She felt her breath becoming more even and her body relaxing, and so, too, Dr. Mahler's shoulders softened and his crow's feet crinkled to reveal a full-faced smile. Then his expression sobered as he engaged in an inner debate to decide if he should say anything more.

"I've tried very hard over the years to not lose sight of the bigger picture, the fact that looking through our glasses of psychotherapy, of clinical practice, it's not the only way of looking at things. You've painted a vivid picture for me of Clare, a free spirit who questions everything—who, in fact, lashes out against our many rules and boundaries. But I believe she also brings something else, some knowledge of you, your needs, and what you have to offer. So, I

CHAPTER TWENTY-FIVE

guess in fairness, I just want to say that I appreciate that from where she is sitting, in her world, the wish that you adopt her baby makes sense. In the end, just because we can see it, understand it from her side ..."

"It doesn't mean I can do this for her. Or for me," Avery said.

"Even if it hurts very much."

"I .... I miss her. I indulged myself in completely inappropriate fantasies of holding her baby, my newly adopted baby. I could see us; we would meet for coffee once in a while and talk about how the baby was doing. Yes, also completely inappropriate, I know ..."

"Avery," Dr. Mahler stopped her, "just tell me how you've been feeling without all that harsh judgment layered on top of it. We all have a right to fantasies and feelings. Our thoughts are just in our head and can't hurt a fly; this is the place to speak them out loud."

"Clare's plan just sounded so .... so nice, so idyllic, so hopeful ... and so non-rule-ish, so non-medical ..."

"Non-rule-ish? Non-medical? What do you mean?"

"It turns out that Clare was dead on. I can't adopt with Roland, so it would have to be alone. I'm pretty well too old and the agencies prefer couples, two parents. Even if my application is eventually accepted, I don't think I will ever make it through the waiting list and past other younger couples waiting to adopt. And I looked into IVF; it turns out Clare was right on that front, too. By my age, ninety per cent of the remaining eggs have chromosomal abnormalities. And then there's my history of the ..."

"The miscarriage, the terribly disappointing miscarriage. I remember that time in your life, Avery," Dr. Mahler said, handing her the Kleenex box. "It's like you have looked in every possible direction, being open to all the possibilities, and you've nevertheless come up empty-handed. And then Clare offers you this baby growing inside her young woman's body. No wonder that you harbour these fantasies, that even though you have concluded it isn't possible, it's so very hard to let go of this idea."

" I think I just have to be patient with myself. You're right, it's not like I've done anything wrong or made a poor decision; it's just that I have to get used to the fact that I can't reach out for the one chance I have left for having a baby."

Now it was the sadness and loss of giving up on having a baby that she had to deal with. At least what she was facing was clear and separated from knowing she had done the right thing in caring for Clare as her psychologist for the past months and in saying no to Clare's request. Avery began to gather up her things. She knew it was time.

"I will be here to help you through this loss or whatever else arises. Thank you for trusting me with your feelings and desires. It's a privilege." Dr. Mahler's moist eyes meant a lot to her.

Avery had one more thing she wanted to tell Dr. Mahler.

"Oh, and Roland is taking me to Victoria for a get-away this weekend, for my Valentine's present. I'm not sure why I am even going, but I am."

"I'm guessing it has something to do with the fact that you are a caring and committed person and that you aren't completely ready to give up."

Yes, Avery thought, always best to leave no stone unturned.

TWENTY-SIX

*A*very couldn't remember the last time she and Roland walked like this together, holding hands. There was a savoury, old-English atmosphere in downtown Victoria, with its charming pubs popping up at every corner and colourful flower baskets hanging from traditional lampposts. She had to admit that Roland had done his homework. He'd promised Avery she'd love this absolute gem of a Canadian city when he surprised her with the airline tickets just a few weeks ago on Valentine's Day. They hadn't been anywhere together since their trip to Ireland last summer, but Avery was tied up at a conference for most of that time, so Roland said it didn't really count. Things had been cold and distant between them with the exception of that one weekend when Nazrin visited in the fall. So when he made her dinner on Valentine's Day and she discovered the travel agent's package tied up with a red ribbon beside her plate, Avery's eyes welled up with a faint sense of hope for her marriage that she didn't think still existed within her. "See?" he'd said, when he saw the tears in her eyes, "*that's* my girl. I just knew I needed to take you somewhere special, just the two of us."

The flight out of San Diego was an easy three hours, and Avery found herself dozing off after the first-class breakfast and a second glass of champagne that she drank purely for the purposes of calming her nerves. What would it be like to suddenly spend two whole days with her husband when, at home, they ran parallel lives and no longer knew each other?

CHAPTER TWENTY-SIX

Roland was right when he said the last bit of their journey was *just a puddle jump,* because twenty minutes after they took off from downtown Seattle, their seaplane was gliding into the shimmering inner harbour of Victoria. When they taxied into the seaport, their airplane felt more like a boat from which sights along the shoreline could be seen at eye level. Avery saw kayakers paddling in flocks, turquoise-domed roofs of the old parliament buildings, and a fish market that was attracting more seagulls than people.

When they climbed out of the seaplane, there was a short walk through the tiny seaport terminal. A quick meet-and-greet with a white-haired gentleman wearing a navy blue suit, *Canada Customs* proudly embroidered in gold on his lapel, was all that was required in the way of security before he pointed to the old Empress Hotel and nodded with approval, "It's the finest in the city!" Roland was still glowing with pride for his choice of accommodation when they were crossing the street in front of the hotel a few minutes later.

It was an early spring day, and with the flawless blue sky behind the Edwardian outlines of the hotel and gardens, Avery had the feeling of walking onto a movie set. It was barely lunchtime by then, so they left their bags with the elegant receptionist who encouraged them to take a walk down Government Street until their room was ready. Avery felt a sharp shot of anxiety at the thought of checking into a hotel room when she hadn't been intimate with Roland since the month before the failed pregnancy test. She was almost giddy with relief at the thought of spending a few hours meandering the streets of Victoria before checking in. *We just need some time to get to know each other again,* she caught herself thinking. At home, they were used to camping at the far reaches of their king-sized bed. Would they do the same thing here at the hotel? How had they gotten to this?

As they walked back out through the revolving glass doors of the hotel, Avery's momentary relief gave way to an unbearable flood of sadness. She stepped out of the doors in front of Roland and hesitated there, feeling all that sadness flowing through her and pooling down her sunken shoulders, arms, and finally into the smallest extension of her hand. Roland was stepping out of the next glass-encased segment of the revolving door when, without hesitation, he stepped forward and reached for her extended hand. At this moment, she was grateful that she'd retrieved her wedding band from the rubble of the garden shed after Roland had crashed through its doors; she had decided to give it one more chance to sparkle on her hand.

That afternoon, it occurred to Avery that, at least when traveling, she and Roland enjoyed many of the same things. They both felt drawn into one of Canada's oldest bookstores, Munro's Books, awed by its neoclassical architecture, coffered ceilings, and stained-glass skylights. They lost each other in the bookstore for over an hour until Roland emerged with a political biography to find Avery sitting on a chair in a quiet corner bent over D.M. Thomas's *The White Hotel*, a small pile of other selections stacked on the floor beside her.

Afterward, they stopped to enjoy the music of a solo cellist under the arches of Christ Church Cathedral's massive wooden doors, where the acoustics worked perfectly in the musician's favour. They discovered an Italian restaurant called Zambri's, which they chose partly because they both liked the way saying its name several times in a row tricked you into thinking you could speak Italian. Avery sat across the table from Roland and noticed how handsome he still was: as always, his hair and beard were perfectly groomed. When she commented that she'd never seen him with a bare face, he told her she wasn't missing anything and scowled in exaggerated disgust, his expression seeming strangely familiar to her.

They followed the same unspoken rules. Keep it light. Stay away from sensitive topics and arguments of the past. Notice the things you once found attractive and charming about each other, and embrace the many good things that you must have held in common

CHAPTER TWENTY-SIX

at some point. And, yes, consume some decent wine, but just a moderate amount, and definitely not the complete blowout of a drinking afternoon that might unleash a tirade of past grievances. And so far, the game plan was working.

As if he'd just invented a new behaviour, Roland seemed delighted to take Avery's hand again after they finally left the restaurant. On the home stretch to the hotel, Avery noticed an antique black sign with gold lettering suspended from an ornate wrought iron hanger: *Out of Ireland.* Under the big gold lettering, in slightly smaller letters, it read: *Irish Importers.*

"I can't believe we missed this one the first time we passed." She tugged at Roland's sleeve.

"Oh, well. I can't imagine what we would see in there that we didn't when we were in Ireland last summer." He started to step forward. "I'm really looking forward to seeing our room."

"Come on, let's just take a minute. Some of us were working when we were in Ireland and didn't get to do a whole lot of shopping, remember? Plus, you've loved all things Irish since your schooldays, right?" Avery said, smiling.

"Sure, let's do it. Why not?" Roland said, smiling in defeat from behind his beard. "If you see something you like, I'll buy it for you, Avery. You deserve it, always working so hard to help everybody else but yourself."

Avery saw Roland's brow furrowing, sending another flash of familiarity from a face she hadn't studied this closely in a long time. Something irritating stirred inside her, and she wondered whether his remark about her caring for others was a compliment or something else. She let it go. *Keep it light,* Avery reminded herself.

"Now you *do* need to worry," Avery said, touching his forehead with her free hand to erase the furrow. "I have expensive taste!"

Roland followed Avery through the tall glass doors. The store smelled of fresh linens, white soap, and wool. He moved to the side of the store where men's clothing was on display. Avery veered to the other side, where an emerald green sweater caught her eye. As she touched it lightly, she thought, *This would look beautiful on Clare!* Avery shook her head, as if to jiggle out thoughts about Clare—or any of her clients for that matter—when she saw Roland over her shoulder. He looked thoughtful, even a little sad, as he ran his fingers along the strap of a man's leather and linen satchel bag. There was no trace of the smile he'd put on for her when she convinced him to walk into the store. Avery went to where he stood, startling him and causing him to blush. She was surprised to see his face redden. What was wrong with him?

"You should get yourself something, too," she said.

"You know, I used to wear a satchel like this when I rode my bicycle to the university," he said, a smile returning to his face.

He picked up a grey herringbone cap and put it on his head.

"And a cap something like this. I dressed like a local." His exaggerated grin faded into a boyish smile new to Avery.

"You *do* look like a local Irish lad." Avery responded genuinely. "I always thought it was a real feather in that cap of yours, a young man from California who just took off to somewhere completely different. I sometimes wish I'd done something like that myself before … before I got old and complacent."

Roland was looking at her intently, his head nodding slowly to the beat of her words. *Is this what he looks like when he feels heard?* Avery suddenly felt uncertain and embarrassed.

"Anyway, I was just looking at a sweater, and I think I'm going to try it on."

"Ok; come find me and show me," Roland said, turning away to check out a rack of belts with Celtic buckles. She smelled a trace of the leather mixing with Roland's cologne as he moved.

Avery took the emerald green sweater, as well as a long silk scarf in a mix of greens and blues that had been hanging beside it, and started walking toward the back of the store. The attendant, a

CHAPTER TWENTY-SIX

smiling young woman with a glossy head of red hair, pointed to the changing room and nodded with encouragement.

Avery took off her jacket and blouse, because this was the type of soft and long sweater that you could wear with leggings and little else underneath. She hesitated for a moment as she looked at herself in the full-length mirror. There was the soft, lacy bra she'd laid out the night before. She indeed looked rather pretty in this faint shade of pink, and her hand came up to touch the silky fabric. The afternoon light that flowed into the store through the large windows and glass doors managed to topple brilliantly over the large gap between the high ceiling and the curtain rod of the changing room, flattering her skin and casting shimmer into her hair.

Suddenly, she felt a flash of heat, and her cheeks and chest blushed a darker shade of pink. Avery didn't know if it was the thought of whether Roland would see her like this tonight—and the strange mix of pleasure, embarrassment and fear that rushed over her—or whether the heat was a sign of the beginnings of menopause. *I'm not ready for any of this*, she thought. Avery allowed herself to lean back against the cool wall to relax. She didn't know how much time had passed when she found herself quickly standing upright to pull on the sweater, drape the silk scarf loosely around her, and open the curtain.

Roland was standing right in front of her. He looked her up and down, and she blushed again.

"You've been a while. I was just coming to check on you," he started to say. "You don't usually wear that colour."

"Emerald green? Couldn't be more Irish," Avery said. "Do you … like it?"

"I do like it. I'm just not used to that colour on you. It … it looks nice with your hair," Roland said softly. "Why don't you just get dressed and hand it to me, and I'll go and pay."

Avery nodded, stepped back, and closed the curtain. She was much too warm now, and it was a relief to pull off the sweater and send it out through the curtain.

When she stepped out of the change room, Roland was putting his credit card back in his wallet. His expression had changed back to his gregarious comfort zone, and there was no doubt in Avery's mind that he'd been flirting with the young saleswoman.

As she joined him at the counter, Avery's eye was drawn to a display of Celtic pendants akin to the pewter medallion her husband had worn around his neck for as long as she'd known him. When they started dating, he'd told her it was given to him by one of his best lads at university before he returned to San Diego to start his Master's degree. Much later, when they were planning their wedding, Avery had suggested he invite his good Irish friend, but Roland said he'd lost touch with him and couldn't even find him on Facebook.

"Roland, look at this pendant; it's just like yours."

He looked startled.

"I didn't see you there. Yes, those are very popular in Ireland; everybody has one. I say it's time to go check out that deluxe hotel." He extended his hand.

"They're very popular and deeply meaningful where I come from," said the young cashier. "Would you like to look at it? They all have a special kind of message attached to them."

Avery was curious, although she could feel Roland bristling beside her.

"Sure, I'll take a quick look at this one," Avery said, pointing to the look-alike of Roland's, "and I'd like to see the card that explains what it means."

Roland sighed impatiently.

"Avey, it's really warm in here. I'm going to wait outside," he said quietly, as he turned his face away from her.

"I'll just be a minute," Avery muttered, a strange feeling of dread rising in her gut.

CHAPTER TWENTY-SIX

The young woman placed a white box with gold writing on the counter for Avery.

"There we go, we're all organized now," she said with a lovely Irish lilt in her voice. She popped the case open.

Barely looking at the pendant resting on purple velvet in the lower half of the box, Avery's heart began to race as she read the inscription printed on purple card in the top half of the box. *Celtic Knotwork. The interlacing lines of this Celtic knot stand for no beginning and no ending: the continuity of everlasting love and binding together or intertwining of two souls or spirits.* Her hands trembled as she snapped the box shut. Some fine lad who gave Roland a pendant like that. The feeling of faint hope she'd experienced earlier in the day about their marriage tumbled into a sick feeling of despair. What else wasn't he telling her?

"Thank you," was all that Avery could manage as she turned and left the store.

When Avery stepped out onto the sidewalk, she saw Roland sitting on a bench, his head in his hands. He didn't even look up at her.

"Why did you have to go and do that?" he whispered. "We were having such a good day."

"You're right, Roland, we were having the best day we've had in a very long time," Avery said, tears welling up in her eyes. *So this is what the last breath of a marriage feels like.*

"It's really not a big deal, Avery. You over-analyze everything." The only other time she'd seen Roland cry was at the funeral of his beloved grandfather, the one person he could run to when his father was out of control.

"You're crying, Roland, for God's sake," Avery said, as she sat down beside him on the bench. "So it must be a big deal."

"I don't know what to do now." Roland looked so lost that she took his hand and held it in both of hers.

"You know, if you loved someone in Ireland, I could've been ok with that," Avery said, "but that you are lying about it and wearing her necklace still, that's a problem. It makes me feel like I don't even know you … "

"It was a mistake, just a mistake. Can't you just forgive me and go back to the way we were?"

"I'm not sure," Avery said. "It's not just this …"

Roland jumped to his feet as Avery sat, startled into silence.

"If you think we're going to be talking about the baby again, you've got another think coming. I just can't, ok?" And with that, he turned away from her and walked quickly down the street toward the movie-set hotel.

On any other day, Avery would have felt charmed by Victoria's quaint "International Airport" and the sympathetic staff who'd helped her to secure the next flight home to San Diego. She guessed her fragile presentation and mention of a family emergency elicited a scurry of concerned activity behind the Air Canada counter. Did she have a bag to check-in, *dear?*, the middle-aged woman with the kind eyes asked. No; she had to move quickly and leave her bag behind, Avery responded, which set into motion another wave of concern and fingers pointing to the lovely gift shop, where she might just find what she needed for her travels home. As she held up her Nexus card at the security doors, the officer was most apologetic that they didn't have a separate line for their trusted travelers, but escorted her to the front of the four-person line-up.

The moment she stepped out of the security area, Avery's eyes locked on to the sign for Spinnaker's Restaurant and Lounge. *It's just one step at a time tonight,* she told herself. Only after the bartender poured her a second glass of red wine did she look up to notice her surroundings. There were trees growing inside the terminal; tiny birds flew to and fro among them until they found an escape

CHAPTER TWENTY-SIX

through one of the many open windows at the top of the glass walls. Her iPhone buzzed several more times: more texts from Roland today than in the entire past year. The image of him turning and walking away from her, the exact motion she'd seen the night of the failed pregnancy test, repeated itself again and again, like a film clip on a loop.

When he'd walked away from the bench, she'd stood and hailed a cab without even thinking. "That's a delightful shop, isn't it?" the taxi driver had mentioned as she settled into the back of cab with the *Out of Ireland* bag.

"Yes: takes you right back to Ireland," she'd said, before asking to go to the airport—the real airport, not the seaport, please. Avery took another sip of her wine and, without reading what Roland had written, texted him back: *I'm ok. I just need to go home.* She put her phone on airplane mode and signalled the server to fill her glass.

"Are you sure … you've time for another, ma'am?" the young woman asked quietly. She must have spotted the tears even before Avery felt them.

"I guess I thought I had more time than I do. I'll just pay up, thanks!" Avery gave her cheeks a quick wipe with the sleeve of her new sweater.

TWENTY-SEVEN

*B*y the time the taxi turned up her lane, it was just past three a.m.

"Must be nice to be rich," the cab driver muttered, as he craned his head out the window to take a closer look at the tall front doors illuminated by soft spotlights. Normally Avery would overlook such hostility, but not tonight.

"It's not as nice as you think. You have no idea what goes on inside."

Avery was barely out of the car when the driver stepped on the gas and sped down the lane. She looked up at the house she and Roland had worked so hard to build. Its rooftops glowed in the moonlight, showing hints of the coppery-rose colour of the tiles. Avery yearned for all those endless possibilities she and Roland had shared while creating their dream home.

Avery searched her purse for her keys as she walked down the path to the new garden shed with its geranium-filled window boxes. He could be so nice, and that just made all of this so much harder. Avery let herself into the perfectly organized shed. There was no time left for crying; she was on a mission. She found exactly the tools she needed, then ran to the house, moving quickly to pump up her courage. Her hands trembled as she unlocked the front door. Avery stepped over the Saturday morning newspapers that had come through the mail slot.

CHAPTER TWENTY-SEVEN

Avery hesitated at Roland's office door: sacrosanct respect for the privacy of others just wasn't working for her anymore. She shook her head, closed her eyes, and took a deep breath. Images and snippets of conversations spun through her head. She saw the golden child standing in a field of glass, beckoning her. *I never wanted a baby.* His words enraged her. She kicked open the door to his office and turned on the light. Avery looked at the desk drawer. *Enough with all this gentleness.*

As if she were watching a movie, Avery saw her left hand position the chisel into the thin crack along the top of the drawer. With strength, precision, and a frightening lack of remorse for her delinquent behaviour, she used the hammer to hit the top of the chisel. One, two, three blows: the wood gave way and splintered. Within seconds, Avery was able to slide out what remained of the drawer and place it on top of the desk. Inside the drawer was a thick, Manila folder neatly tied with string, labelled *IRELAND*.

Her heart pounding, Avery took the file folder and sat down on Roland's leather loveseat in front of the fireplace. The string was tied in a simple bow she undid with one easy pull. What more might she discover about Roland's previous life in Ireland? The first time he'd made love to her, that Celtic knot thumped against his chest. *She* must have meant a great deal to him. Was she that beautiful? Did she have shiny red hair? Why hide *her* from Avery for all these years?

Avery opened the folder and found an old black and white photograph. As she stared at the photograph, the room receded. The young woman on the photo, her wavy hair flowing around her smiling face, was even more beautiful than Avery had imagined. That must be her. But that wasn't the worst of it. The photo must have been taken from an intimate angle by someone lying down beside *her*, close enough to touch her dimpled smile, to smell her hair, and to catch this moment of her arms holding up a chubby little girl in a sundress. The little girl's tiny fist was partly plunged into her mouth and the rest of her gummy mouth was gaping wide open in pure delight. *That's what I wanted.*, Avery gasped, hearing the faintest traces of a little girl's giggles like fairy dust around her. Then it was quiet; just barren nothingness again.

Roland was a meticulous man who organized and labelled his belongings. She watched herself turning the photo over in slow motion, but then the pain rushed through her. There, in his handwriting, was the answer: *My Girls, Kilkee Beach, 1996.* She turned the photo back over to take a closer look at *her husband's girls.* There was so much love in this photo, and there was no doubt in Avery's mind that this delighted little girl was the apple of her mother's eye.

The apple of her mother's eye? Suddenly Avery remembered Clare standing before her in the therapy office, showing her beautiful painting of a mother engaged with her child. And, yes, Avery had told Clare, to help her to heal, that there was no doubt in her mind that she was once the apple of her mother's eye. Avery pictured Clare's painting of her mother lying on the beach, holding up her little girl, a work of art that had taken her years to create from a black and white photograph. *It's the only photo I have of me and my mother.* There were probably a million photographs like this of loving mothers holding up their babies. *It's bad enough as it is*, Avery tried to calm herself. *You are so hurt right now that you are making up crazy connections in your mind.*

Her hand trembling, Avery placed the photo on the coffee table. She could barely breathe, felt that her heart couldn't take anymore. Should she call 911? Was she about to have a heart attack? Or a panic attack? Or just splinter into a million pieces? *You just have to see this through: finish the job.*

Avery inhaled deeply, then exhaled slowly through pursed lips, just as she taught her clients. Ok. Next in the logically organized *Ireland* file, there was a white cover page labelled *Vital Documents.* *Vital; what an interesting choice of words*, Avery thought, as her back broke out in sweat underneath her Irish sweater. She peeled back the cover page. The top line of an official document immediately

CHAPTER TWENTY-SEVEN

jumped out at her: *State of California, Certification of Vital Record, County of Los Angeles Department of Public Health.* The name of the child on the birth certificate was *Clare Meghan Thomas.*

TWENTY-EIGHT

Frozen on the couch with the weight of the papers still on her lap, Avery stared out the window, disconnected from any sense of time. Listlessly, she watched the inky blackness in the windowpanes disappearing into purples and blues until only soft brushes of orange and pink remained. When the first rays of sun hit her hard on the horizontal, Avery's eyelids fluttered. Her head rolled back onto the back of the couch. Her last sensation was the mixed scent of Jameson's, cologne, and leather as the papers slid off of her lap.

Avery was falling now ... through thick billows of paper white clouds and brilliant blue sky, her eyes squinting against the bright light. Braced for the landing, she pulled her knees tightly to her chest. She was moving faster and faster, like a human missile gathering speed. Her skin was fiery hot when she broke through the surface of the water. The brilliant splashes of water caught against the harsh sunlight mesmerized her, like tiny sparkling chards of glass with hints of colour exploding around her in slow motion. Avery heard gurgling sounds and then nothing as she was carried downward into the depths of these disturbing waters, the light up above becoming dimmer and dimmer in the distance. She was spinning, first slowly and then quickening as if being sucked downward into the swirling motion of a drain.

Avery felt herself hitting something hard, and her instinct was to close her eyes and tighten her grip around her knees. The blow to her head had slowed her movement through the water, and Avery opened her eyes

CHAPTER TWENTY-EIGHT

to check her surroundings. She saw a man's fist and arm near her face, the rest of his person occluded by darkness and swirling water. The fist was coming closer now, so close she could make out his wedding band of gold and tiny black diamonds. Roland, help me, she tried to scream, but her mouth filled with water. His fist opened and from it escaped the Irish knot pendant. It floated away in the waters like a silver fish, as he, too, disappeared. He's gone now. She couldn't breathe. Panic streamed through her body. She pressed her face into her knees as her body slipped into unconsciousness.

Still inside her dream ... Avery was jolted awake by another impact. This time, the blow with the foreign object released the tight hold she had on herself, her arms letting go of her knees and then all of her limbs unfolding. This is the end; I'm dying. She could see herself now from down below, looking up, the outlines of her person spread out above her in the water like a starfish, dark and shimmering against the faint light still cast from where she'd broken through into the water. The feeling of panic that had come from the realization that she was drowning suddenly eased and gave way to the faintest sensation of hope.

Something was moving through the water towards the outlines of her starfish-self floating above. It was the shape of a young man. With a soft, wide-armed movement, Avery could see him enveloping the sea star shape of herself so that the stretched out limbs became discernible again as her legs and arms, her face and hair. She was in herself again now, no longer able to see her form from down below. His arms circled her waist; she leaned her head back against his chest. It was when she felt completely safe that Avery knew it was Sebastian. They were traveling swiftly into the darkest reaches of the waters and, as she felt him propelling them, Avery was filled with a distinct feeling of love. That they were in long, dark corridors of water taking twists, turns, and switching directions did not bother her, because she knew he was taking her somewhere better.

She must've fallen asleep in his arms, because when she woke up, Avery saw turquoise water illuminated by sunlight. Sebastian let go of her waist and took her hand, pulling her around to face him in the *water. She saw his beloved face. Elated, she grabbed his other hand, too, and pulled him close. His hair, wavy like hers, was floating around his face, but then she could see he was shaking his head. Sebastian released one of Avery's hands and pointed upward to the surface of the water.*

Avery felt the hand she was still holding, giving it the same quick double squeeze they had used to communicate as children. Come with me, *she was saying, but he shook his head again and then shrugged his shoulders in that same movement of childhood that meant,* sorry Sis, no can do. *Avery realized she couldn't hold her breath any longer. Sebastian could see it, too, and with both hands, he reached for her waist one more time and gave her the push upward she needed to propel to the surface.*

TWENTY-NINE

*A*very sat up on the leather couch, gasping for air. The sensation of wetness on skin sent her hands to her cheeks, only to find them dry. It was dark outside now, and streams of rain pelted against the tall windowpanes. Disoriented, Avery reached for the only light source visible in the room, her iPhone. It was just after nine at night. She must've slept all day and then well into the evening hours. Avery reached beside her to switch on the lamp.

In the glow of the table lamp, nothing in the room appeared familiar. Roland's painting of Graeme McDowell winning the US Open Golf Championships still hung over the fireplace, but the golfer's face and the way he was pumping his fist no longer looked triumphant. Instead he seemed angry, even desperate. For all these years, this elegant gentleman's room had harboured Roland's secrets of his past life and the daughter he'd abandoned. Ugliness had seeped into the walls of the room and stolen the beauty of its design.

If this weekend had gone according to plan, she and Roland would have been arriving home together tonight. Where was Roland, anyway? She certainly didn't want him walking through the door to find her with his coveted Ireland file. The memory of the photo of *his girls* on the beach brought tears to her eyes. Avery reached for her iPhone to open Roland's texts, the last one written about an hour ago. *I'm still at the Victoria airport, but it looks like we're fogged in for the night. How are you, Ave?* She wouldn't have to face him just yet, but then the realization that he actually thought he could hold a

CHAPTER TWENTY-NINE

conversation with her inflamed her all over again. *HUGE storm here, I know about CLARE and YOUR GIRLS,* Avery typed back angrily. Capitalized texts made people feel they were being yelled at, but in this case, that was exactly the effect she was looking for. A few clouds of thinking dots bubbled up across the screen. Then the movement stopped: the screen was empty.

How sore and dry Avery's throat felt. The last thing she'd had to drink was her second glass of red wine last night. She stood up, paper beneath her feet. *Oh yeah, there is more file I haven't even seen yet.* She opened the bar fridge and gulped a bottle of cold water. Sebastian had looked at her so lovingly in the water as he pushed her upward. *You will survive this fall. You're not as alone as you think. You must live the life that you still have.* Avery grabbed Roland's leather satchel and stuffed everything into it. She took his car keys from the desk and ran out into the rain.

THIRTY

*W*hy were these horrible storms given such gentle, feminine names? The unrelenting rains of tropical storm Rosalyn, she heard on the car radio, were causing severe flooding; atmospheric rivers were spilling over the highways in the San Diego area. People should stay indoors and avoid all unnecessary travel. It seemed not to matter to her, the usually responsible Dr. Avery Frontiera, that she was driving through the night in these dangerous conditions, and that the trip she was undertaking was wrong in more ways than one.

The only reason she knew where he lived was by a fluke. Years ago, as a graduate student, Avery had left a term paper in his office. The paper was due the next day to one of her more demanding professors, the kind who took off points for each day of lateness. When she finally caught Dr. Mahler on the phone, he was on his way out of the office. *Yes, Avery, I do see the large envelope that you are describing, but unfortunately, I must leave right now.* When Avery told him politely that she would get the paper at their next session, she heard the hesitation in his voice. If she were not studying to become a psychologist, he never would have made the exception that he did.

The Jeep hit another pool of water that splashed over the windshield. Avery gripped the steering wheel and tried to remember what she was supposed to do if she hydroplaned. At least Roland's Jeep handled the road conditions much better than would her own car. Several vehicles were scattered on the side of the road and in the

CHAPTER THIRTY

ditch. Police officers with fluorescent vests and flashlights guided the traffic at the turnoff for La Playa. While it was a relief to get off the highway, the streetlights were out on the strip to Point Loma; Avery had to rely on her high beams to illuminate the necessary landmarks. She recalled her surprise at finding Dr. Mahler's home when she was a student. Amid the dramatic ocean-view homes she'd imagined for her guru psychologist, Dr. Mahler's modest rancher was tucked away behind abundant trees that obscured the beach. *He must value his privacy*, she'd thought.

A windblown branch swiped the side of the Jeep, startling Avery so that she almost missed the next landmark: Point Loma Nazarine University. Avery glanced at the clock on the dash; it was eleven seventeen p.m. The closer she got to her destination, the more her heart was pounding. Her nervousness at this moment was less about what was still left to uncover in the Ireland file and more to do with her imposition into Dr. Mahler's private life in the middle of the night. But she was in a state of emergency. Although she was not the first person to be deeply disappointed by the secret life of a spouse, who else had ever lived through the shock of discovering that her up-until-then childless husband was, in fact, the father of her young psychotherapy client? Dr. Mahler was the one and only person locked into this secret with her. She couldn't expose Clare to Roland, and she could also not play God and reveal Roland to Clare. Whatever good, whatever healing from her painful trust issues Clare had taken away from her psychotherapy, surely this fragile new growth would not survive the news that her psychologist's choice of husband was that father who had injured her and abandoned her more than once. Once she had the chance to explain all of this, Avery thought, Dr. Mahler would understand her dilemma and accept her extreme behaviour. Well, maybe he would.

The heavy rain and gusts of wind were relentless. Pools of water scattered with debris became visible in her high beams around the darkened outlines of the university. Yes, she remembered, it was a quick left, right after the small university and then a right on a street that started with an L. *Lomalinda*, there it was now. *Go right to the end; you can park at the gates and come up the chip trail, where you'll find your envelope in the mailbox on the porch,* he'd told her all those years ago. He was drawing the line at the mailbox; she understood that he didn't want a client, not even a psychologist in training, to knock on his door. She still remembered hugging her term paper and taking a few sheepish glances into the front windows before turning to walk away.

Avery parked at the gates. As soon as she turned off the engine, it was pitch black. Another wave of panic pulsed through her. *Will he fire me as a client? Call the police?* Avery grabbed the flashlight out of Roland's glove compartment and twisted it on. *I'm going in*, she thought, as she grabbed the satchel from the passenger seat.

THIRTY-ONE

*R*oland's damp leather satchel squeezed tightly to her hip, Avery followed the beam of her flashlight to navigate the debris and puddles forming on the chip trail. The path winding through the trees felt longer than she remembered it. Finally, Avery reached the clearing in front of Dr. Mahler's house. Why was she surprised that his house was completely dark? What did she expect when it must be close to midnight? *Just turn around and forget this embarrassing mistake*, she debated. Avery recalled a movie, *What About Bob,* about the story of a very needy client acted by Bill Murray who followed his psychotherapist on vacation and showed up out of the blue at his summer cabin. This was not a flattering comparison.

She stood, soaking wet and bathed in ambivalence. It was when the dream image of Sebastian passed back through her mind—he propelling her upward to the surface of the water when she was unable to hold her breath any longer—that Avery was able to take the last few steps to the front door and put these other distracting thoughts to the side. *You don't have to do this alone.*

Avery finger-combed her drenched hair and shuffled her shoes on the doormat to slough off the debris. She knocked softly on the door and waited. Nothing. She rang the bell, appalled at its sound and the disturbance she was creating. And then, with a surge of desperation that ripped through her body, that internal dam of polite reservation broke wide open. She felt disconnected from her usual self. Who was

CHAPTER THIRTY-ONE

this person now who was pounding on the door forcefully in short bursts, interspersed with jamming on the doorbell, and doing this again and again like an ill-behaved child who wouldn't take no for an answer?

Finally, the lights in the house came on. She heard footsteps and the front door cracked open. There he stood frozen in the doorway, looking at Avery, his plaid housecoat belted at the middle, faded blue pyjama pants and Birkenstock clogs visible below. Dr. Mahler's mouth opened and closed. She tried to decipher the emotions crossing his face. Concern? Irritation? Uncertainty? A white-haired woman peered over his shoulder.

"Don't let that poor girl stand out there in the rain, Sammy. She's going to catch her death. Come on in, dear!" Mrs. Mahler beckoned as she moved her stunned husband out of the way.

Avery couldn't remember the last time a stranger had referred to her as a girl, but she instantly felt cared for. By the time Avery stepped into the front hall to take off her shoes, Dr. Mahler had regained his composure.

"Liz, this is Dr. Avery Frontiera, a colleague, and I'll have to believe there is an unprecedented emergency bringing her to our home so late at night!" Dr. Mahler looked directly into Avery's eyes.

He was sticking as close to the truth as he could without blowing her cover and revealing her as one of his clients.

"Oh my!" Mrs. Mahler shook Avery's hand. "As if the weather tonight isn't enough of an emergency by itself. I don't know how you and Sammy do it. Do you live close by? The phones and internet must be down, too."

"Please, call me Avery. I'm so terribly sorry to disturb you like this, Mrs. Mahler. I won't take up too much of your husband's time, if he's even able to speak to me at this late hour."

Mrs. Mahler smiled and patted Avery on the shoulder. She looked like she knew exactly what her husband would do in a case like this.

"I will show you to the study, Avery," Dr. Mahler said, "and we'll let Mrs. Mahler go back to bed. Thank you for your understanding, as always, Liz."

Avery envied the respect between Dr. Mahler and his wife, their seamless cooperation in the face of an emergency. She followed Dr. Mahler down the hall. He opened the door to his study and switched on the light.

"Make yourself comfortable, Avery. I'll be there in a few minutes."

Avery sat down on the brown corduroy couch. A crocheted blanket made up of a mishmash of colourful squares had been thrown over its back. A grey, longhaired cat was curled up in the far corner beside a felt pillow. The pillow had a misshapen heart embroidered by a child's hand on it that said *I love my dad*. Each wall in this comfortable room, including the half wall below the double windows, was messily filled with shelves of books, framed photos, and knick-knacks. The photo that caught her eye was a black and white of Dr. Mahler as a handsome young man. It was a profile shot; he was wearing a black hippy hat, his hair in a long, dark braid. A couple of strands of beads were tangled around his neck. There was another photo of him, a few years older, with Mrs. Mahler, who had long blonde hair and the same beautiful smile she'd shown at the door. Each of them held a child. Intruding into Dr. Mahler's private life like this was already altering Avery's perceptions of him. After tonight, she wouldn't be able to forget the young man in the hat or the family man whose children lovingly embroidered pillows for him.

"Alright, Avery, I'm here." Dr. Mahler was dressed now, wearing his white shirt, sleeves rolled up, and his classic slacks with his clogs. He sat down in the armchair facing the couch, leaned forward, and folded his arms over his knees.

"I'm terribly sorry. I know this is really inappropriate, me just showing up at your house. I wouldn't even know where you lived

CHAPTER THIRTY-ONE

if you hadn't been so kind to me all those years ago. Thank you for inviting me in."

Dr. Mahler's face melted into a smile of forgiveness. Then his expression became more serious. "Avery, for a moment when I was standing at the door, I couldn't decide what was the right thing to do. But I know you very well by now, and I would say that if you have done something so extreme, there must be a good reason for it. I'm very, very glad that you made it through this dangerous storm. So please, tell me what's happened."

Avery told Dr. Mahler the whole story. The white haystacks of Dr. Mahler's eyebrows jumped several times, especially when Avery offered her unapologetic account of culling tools from the garden shed so she could break into her husband's desk. Maybe he considered himself lucky that she'd left her chisel and hammer at home.

Dr. Mahler was about to speak when they heard a knock at the door of the study. Mrs. Mahler entered silently with a tray bearing two mugs of hot chocolate and a plate of cookies and muffins. Thrown over her shoulder were a towel and a housecoat, clearly intended for the drenched and probably rather desperate-looking person that Avery presented. Without a word, Mrs. Mahler set down all of these items, smiled at Avery, and disappeared.

"Thank you so much, Mrs. Mahler," Avery called after her. She swept up her hair in the towel Mrs. Mahler must have just taken out of the dryer and put her arms into the sleeves of the housecoat, wearing it backwards to warm her. Then Avery stuffed half a muffin into her mouth and held the mug of hot chocolate to warm her hands.

Dr. Mahler smiled. "I'm happy to see you replenishing yourself."

Then he sat back in his chair and shook his head.

"I'm absolutely shocked Clare is Roland's daughter. *Oh my God!* It's unfathomable. And my feeling of shock? It must be a fraction of yours."

"And there's so much more I haven't even looked at yet." Avery pointed to the leather satchel beside her. "I just grabbed all the papers from his desk and ran out to the Jeep. I'm scared about what else I might find in Roland's crazy Ireland file. I just didn't want to do the rest on my own, and I couldn't think of anyone else … You're actually the only person in the world I can tell all of this."

Dr. Mahler furrowed his brow. "Yes, I do see what you mean. It's not just about the terrible shock: suddenly, you find yourself trapped in this web of secrets. And then there's Clare's privacy to contend with and all these completely unexpected connections. I do realize that I'm the one safe person you can talk to."

He hesitated before he continued to speak. "Quite honestly, I've never seen a situation like this before in my practice. Nothing even comes close."

Dr. Mahler leaned back in his chair and started to chuckle. "And we certainly don't have to worry about your assertiveness anymore, Avery. You demonstrated that at my front door just now."

Had he seen that movie with Bill Murray, too? It occurred to Avery that their shared sense of humour was an important element of their relationship over many years, a stress buster.

But now it was time to get down to business. Avery reached for the leather satchel and placed Roland's papers on the coffee table. She patted the seat beside her on the couch and looked at Dr. Mahler expectantly. He shook his head again as he raised himself up from the armchair and walked across the room to sit down.

"Alright, Avery, how do we do this?"

"I don't know … I guess I pull a paper out of the pile for us to look at together." *And then you'll see why I'm such a pissed off person. And a sad person, too*, she recalled thinking when Clare had said these words to her.

Dr. Mahler bent over the birth certificate.

"So, Clare Meghan Thomas is definitely your Clare's full name and that's the correct date of birth, right?"

CHAPTER THIRTY-ONE

"Yes. This is the same birth certificate she brought in her *Bio-Dad* file. Her adoptive parents must have added their last name to hers, *Lane*. She now goes by Clare Meghan Thomas Lane."

"And she was born in a hospital closer to L.A., it looks like. Chloé's her mother, but what's strange is that Roland didn't identify himself on the birth record or ... I guess another possibility is that Chloé chose not to record his name on that paperwork they give to the new mothers in the hospital. Perhaps we should consider both possibilities?"

"I guess that's true."

"But let's pause for a moment, Avery, and just focus on you." Dr. Mahler turned on the couch to face her. "I'm here for you first, and I wouldn't like to see your feelings being lost in these logistics of what has happened. Of course, your feelings for yourself are all mixed up with your caring as a psychologist for your client Clare. But now it's your turn to be heard," Dr. Mahler said softly.

Avery felt her eyes welling up. A wave of relief washed over her for being given permission to loosen her grip on the responsibility she felt for Clare's situation in all of this, as well as the absolute horror and shame she felt about her husband's behaviour and the pain it inflicted on her young client. Yes, she needed to put all of this to the side for a moment and just be there for herself. She inhaled deeply and then allowed that painfully contained breath to flutter unhurriedly over her lips.

"I feel like I've been stabbed in the heart. I'm so hurt that Roland didn't tell me he'd been so in love with someone else. Even if he didn't want to tell me the rest of the story, at least he could have told me this part so that I could ... know him. He wore her necklace every day and every night we were together; we didn't stand a chance with Chloé still around his neck. But what hurts me the most is that he had *his girls* before he even met me, and so I never had a clean ... fresh, honest opportunity to start a family with Roland. And I didn't even know it at the time, wasn't even in a position to decide about it. And, as you know, I *almost* did start a family with Roland, but … but I think Roland was relieved about the miscarriage. That's so hard for me to say out loud, Dr. Mahler …"

Avery could feel Dr. Mahler nodding beside her. She took another deep breath before she was able to continue. "And that's really painful, too. Here I was, in the worst pain, all that terrible disappointment to have lost my baby, and he was probably feeling relieved. I came to him that night of the miscarriage after I woke up alone in the bed, and I went downstairs to find him. I wanted him to console me and for us to grieve together. Now I know that the first thing he did after I fell asleep was to come back down to his office and look at the photo of his girls, his real girls. How absolutely naïve I was. You know, I think that night he realized that he couldn't go through trying to have a baby with me ever again."

Dr. Mahler reached over to the coffee table and handed Avery one of the cheerful yellow paper napkins Mrs. Mahler had delivered with their snacks. Avery blew her nose.

"How hurtful that photo must be for you and, as you say, that he had what you wanted the most and couldn't, or wouldn't, give this to you." Dr. Mahler pulled the black and white photo from among the papers and placed it on the coffee table between them. Avery's eyes darted to Dr. Mahler's family picture on the bookshelf and then back to the photo of Roland's girls.

"Yes, I can see all that love in the photo. More importantly though, I can feel your pain sitting here beside me looking at it," Dr. Mahler said. "It's a good thing, I think, to allow yourself to look at this photo now from your own perspective. To make that shift from seeing the loving mother that Clare lost, to realizing the huge loss it is for you to have just discovered all of this about Roland's past life."

Avery nodded, imagining Roland lying beside Chloé and little Clare. She allowed the sadness to wash over her until it softened.

CHAPTER THIRTY-ONE

"Thank you, Dr. Mahler. I needed to take that minute for me just now. I think I'm ready to carry on. I know it's so late at night already ..."

"Ok, Avery: let's see if there are more pieces of the puzzle in that file."

She found another official-looking form. *DDC DNA Diagnostic Center DNA Test Report, Date Collected December 21, 1995.* The form was organized into three columns of numbers, one labelled *Mother: Chloé Thomas,* another for *Child: Clare Thomas,* and one for *Alleged Father: Roland Frontiera.* She heard herself gasping, a strange guttural sound that startled Dr. Mahler. The numbers telling the story of matching genetic material made her feel sick.

"I've seen this kind of a form before. It's all so cold, isn't it, with these numbers coming from cheek swabs? It says here at the bottom: *The probability of paternity of the alleged father is ninety-nine point nine percent.* They should just say one hundred percent. This tells us for certain that Roland is Clare's father." Dr. Mahler's voice was gentle.

"So ... this DNA test happened just a week after Clare was born here in California. Why would he doubt Chloé? I mean, he really loved her—he loves her still—I am quite certain of that. Why did he put her through that?"

"Do you think you'll ever ask Roland this question?"

"I can't even imagine speaking to him at this point," Avery replied. "How am I even supposed to look him in the eyes again and not see Clare? And all her pain. And all my loss. Yet, I'm left with all these questions. Why didn't he make a go of it with Chloé and raise Clare together with her? How is it that Clare ended up with her mother and grandmother without Roland in the picture? Maybe one day we'll talk, but I can't see it now. He won't face the hard stuff."

"And I guess that was the final straw for you. When you were up in Canada this past weekend and found out about Chloé, you really wanted to talk to him about all this."

"But he just walked away from me. *Again*. He left me standing there in the middle of a busy sidewalk in a foreign city ... in my puddle of feelings and the questions I had a right to ask."

"Do you have a sense of why he walks away like that?"

"I'm not sure. He can be so nice and full of promises, so genuine, but when things get difficult, conflictual, threatening ... he just shuts down. It's like he doesn't even hear me anymore ..."

Avery felt nothing but anger again. "I will follow your lead, Dr. Mahler, and say *enough about Roland*, at least for now. I just need to get through the rest of this with you. For ... for me."

Dr. Mahler struggled to suppress a yawn.

"Look, there is something here written on parchment paper," Avery said. They bent over the letter like two detectives. It was handwritten in an old-fashioned cursive with a fountain pen and signed by *Sinéad Thomas*.

"Sinéad must be Clare's grandmother," Avery said, "Clare has patchy memories of her grandmother being sick and telling her it was time to look for her father."

The letter was addressed to Roland, and despite the unfamiliar handwriting and smudges, Avery was able to make out the most important fragments of this heartbreaking plea. *Do the right thing for your little girl Clare,* jumped out at her. Avery glanced at the black and white photo once again, the cherub-cheeked toddler lifted high in her mother's arms. *Her mother is gone*, Sinéad had written. Clare's memory came back to Avery now. She could almost see her little-girl legs swinging from the church pew where she sat with her grandmother at her mother's funeral service. *My health is failing*, Sinéad went on. The image of Clare on her fifth birthday came to mind, standing alone in the doorway screaming for help, her grandmother coughing up blood. *Roland, where are you in all of this?* Avery thought. She imagined the despair Sinéad must have felt while writing this letter. Dr. Mahler turned over the letter; there was an envelope stapled to it. *Roland Frontiera, meticulous at documenting*

CHAPTER THIRTY-ONE

heartbreak. The envelope was addressed to Roland at Frontiera & Sons, perhaps the only address Sinéad was able to unearth for her granddaughter's father. Avery touched the weathered stamp, *Eire 70*, and noticed the distinctly curved head-feathers of the national lapwing depicted on it.

"That's an Irish stamp; I've seen these before," Dr. Mahler said.

Avery inhaled sharply as she saw Clare, trying so hard to remember her passage from her grandmother's cottage to the home of her adoptive parents. She saw Clare again tracing hearts with her finger, unable to come up with the answer.

"Aer Lingus!" Avery announced. "Clare remembers that bright green shamrock logo of the Irish airline. A bunch of hearts joined at the center is exactly what that shamrock would look like to a child. She must have seen it on the side of the airplane. And that explains the gold bird pin on the green hat. That's the pill hat the Aer Lingus flight attendants wear. I noticed it myself on my trip to Ireland."

"Yes, I can picture all of that, Avery. Just how it would look through the innocent eyes of a young child. So at some point after Clare was born, she must have returned to Ireland with her mother and then the poor little girl stayed on with her grandmother after her mother Chloé died. What Clare went through, it's hard to imagine."

Avery felt the air go out of Dr. Mahler. His eyes darted across the room to his family photos and then back to Avery beside him. He took a long breath before he continued.

"Well, at least for as long as Sinéad could manage, it sounds like she did her best to care for her granddaughter. It must've been so very hard."

Avery nodded.

"And as far as we know, Sinéad didn't hear anything back from Roland?"

"Not that Clare knows of. But I do think this must've been around the time when Roland started to look into adoption for Clare here in California. It doesn't sound like Clare had other relatives in Ireland, or surely Sinéad would have called upon them. There was someone Clare called 'Aunt Aggie,' but she was just a kind neighbour. Clare has talked about her mother dying of breast cancer. There is no way she could have absorbed the nature of her mother's illness as a young child, so it makes me wonder if this piece of the medical history was passed on through the adoption agency. Maybe Sinéad or Roland wanted to make sure that Clare would come to hear about her mother's fatal illness when she was older. I mean, it's something she should know for her own health," Avery said.

"Ok, Dr. Mahler, this is starting to make some sense now. How ironic that Roland's meticulous nature—even his keeping the envelope with the Irish stamp on it—is helping us to piece things together. What Clare described really does resemble Irish countryside near the ocean, near Kilkee Beach, I guess. Oh yes, and her painting; when I remember it now, it really reminds me of Ireland. There's something about the hues of greens she used and the quality of the light, I remember that from my trip there last year ... with Roland."

"Yes, Avery. There you were at a conference in Ireland, thinking that Roland was using his days to revisit his favourite university haunts. But, of course, now for you the trip must have a different feeling to it."

Avery nodded, the brush of Dr. Mahler's empathy sweeping over her. She was ready to continue.

"Ok, so we were talking about how Clare came to be adopted by Molly and Jim. Clare recalls traveling with a woman, maybe someone like a liaison person for the adoption agency. But why wouldn't Roland just pick her up? How could he not accept his own flesh and blood? I'll never be able to wrap my mind around that."

Avery buried her face in her hands and cried. Every time she felt close to looking at this situation more logically, the emotions overwhelmed her. She cried for Clare, for Roland, for herself, for this unnecessary tragedy. As the tears slowed, she automatically

CHAPTER THIRTY-ONE

calculated the numbers in her head and realized that Chloé had died just a few years before she and Roland got serious.

Dr. Mahler waited until she finally looked up at it him. He was holding out the second of the cheerful yellow napkins. From the look on his face, it appeared he had done the same math.

"Hmm. Avery, something to think about here. Would you have chosen Roland if he were a single dad with a little girl when you met him? Would he even have been in school getting his Master's degree if he had Clare?"

She could see by the expression on his face that he couldn't fathom a man who would abandon his child under any circumstances. He, too, was searching for an explanation.

"I don't know how I would have felt about that. It would have been a lot to take on at the beginning of a relationship. But at least I … we could have made that decision, and it would've been an honest start. In fairness, I can't see that Roland's parents would have supported him in bringing his five-year-old daughter—if they even knew of Clare at all—into the family's life. Roland's father, he runs that family hard, and I certainly wouldn't describe him as supportive. There was a lot of conflict between Roland and his father, a lot of pressure for Roland to be like his older brother and become a part of the family business. That I do know. And his mother? She's still hard for me to read: kind of defeated, quiet and softer, but in the end, she definitely goes along with what her husband says. I know Roland told me once that he wished his mother had stood up for him more."

"You and I both know that these family dynamics are so important for understanding—not that they're an excuse."

Dr. Mahler reached for the last set of stapled documents and placed them on top of the pile.

"Ok, Avery. What we have here are the adoption papers for Clare. This line I'm reading is not a surprise for us, because it states the names of Molly and Jim Lane. The date of the adoption comes quite shortly after the grandmother's letter. So, I think it's safe to say, thank goodness, that at least little Clare was able to go right from her grandmother's care to Molly and Jim."

"Molly and Jim have been kind and consistent with Clare. She put them through the ringer, but she's coming to appreciate them now," Avery responded.

Dr. Mahler took off his glasses and rubbed his eyes.

"This is the last bit of it, Dr. Mahler."

"I would tell you that you've exceeded the fifty minute mark, Avery, but somehow, I think tonight is not the night to discuss the rules of psychotherapy," Dr. Mahler said with a playful smile. "So let's go through this last pile."

"I promise to never show up at your home like this ever again," Avery said. "You must be so tired. I am, too, but I feel that if I can at least know what everything is in this pile, I can …"

"You can what, Avery?"

"I can … even begin to process this. And then I can start working on acceptance; that'll be a long journey. Besides, I need to return these papers to Roland."

"Even though you can't agree with what Roland has done and his actions are an important part of your decision to end your marriage, these papers do belong to him." She could tell by how Dr. Mahler widened his eyes that he knew he'd made a therapeutic mistake.

"It's ok, Dr. Mahler; it's the middle of the night, you're tired, and we're going way over time. And it turns out, not surprisingly, that you're right. All that you've come to know about me over the years serves you well. I have indeed decided to end my marriage. I had the faintest hope in Victoria that we could talk to each other again. Even the secret of the Celtic knot, maybe we could've survived that. But it was when I needed to talk, to really talk, and he wouldn't, that was the end. And Roland knows it, too."

"I was worried that I'd over-reached."

They both nodded and directed their attention to the final stack.

CHAPTER THIRTY-ONE

"I believe you told me that when Clare turned twenty-one, she tried to contact her father. Look at this handwritten letter, Avery!"

"Yes, that's Clare's handwriting. It's quite distinctive. But she never showed me this letter. Maybe she didn't even keep a copy of it, or maybe she just decided to slam the folder shut before we got to that point," Avery said.

Dr. Mahler and Avery fell silent as they read Clare's letter.

Father,

This is Clare, your daughter. Remember me? I'm twenty-one today. Have you forgotten me completely? My mother Chloé, too?

I've no idea who you are or why you aren't in my life, like a father should be. Especially when your kid's mother died. I lost both my parents. My mom couldn't help it, but you could've stayed.

I bet you think you ruined me. That I'm some pathetic drug addict because you left us. Not the case. I'm smart. Strong, obviously much stronger than you. Feminist enough to make your head spin!!! I'm gonna be an artist. That's enough, that's all I'm telling you about me.

I want to know more about my mother. That's like 99% of the reason why I'm to writing you.

I can't promise anything, but I might give you a chance to explain yourself if you write back.

Clare

"Wow!" Dr. Mahler said, "that'd be a scary letter to read, especially if one is conflict-averse. But she's right in her anger, given what he did to her, I would say."

"Yes. All that anger, all that hurt," Avery said. "Clare's such a proud young woman. She hates admitting that she needs anything, anyone, but I can see she needed her father. I have to tell you, I'm not surprised that Roland just filed that letter away without responding."

"Do you know about the California Department of Public Health's Birth Index, Avery?"

Avery nodded.

"Oh my—look at this, Avery," Dr. Mahler said, as his finger traced the writing on the document before them. "I think this is the form that is sent to the biological parent by the Public Health Department—in this case, Roland—together with Clare's letter, and then he decides what he wants to do, whether he wants to accept the request of his child Clare to make contact … or not. It looks like he kept a copy of the form he sent back to the government. And this is the decision that would have come back to Clare in the mail …"

Avery looked where Dr. Mahler was pointing on the form. There was a check mark beside the option, *the recipient of the letter does not wish to reciprocate the contact.*

"I already knew from Clare that her father refused her request. She puts on this tough façade like she doesn't really care, but I also know she researched all of this and sent out her application on her twenty-first birthday," Avery said. "But now I know it was *Roland* who would have heard from the birth index, and I am picturing him checking off this box at his desk … less than two years ago, making a copy before putting it in the mail, locking up one more paper in that desk of his. Did he come upstairs after doing this, pour himself his Irish whiskey, and talk to me about his day? Who was I even married to?"

Dr. Mahler took a deep breath.

"I think you were married to a man who was deeply divided in his sense of himself. The good parts you felt were real and perhaps the best of him was able to grow in his time in Ireland, at least for a short time, but he was never able to face the darker parts, including his father, and all these mistakes that looked like they just kept building on themselves. Maybe he just couldn't see a way to turn back, make things right."

"I do have to admit there were many good things, and also these darker parts he couldn't or wouldn't face. A part of me always knew something was wrong, but I also chose not to see it. I'm absolutely exhausted, Dr. Mahler, but I'll survive. And I believe Clare will

CHAPTER THIRTY-ONE

thrive too in her own way, even without knowing all that we know. She's fierce."

"She is fierce. You *will* survive, Avery; you'll find your new path ... I must say, like you, I'm exhausted. Let's call it a night."

Dr. Mahler stood up and walked to the window. He checked his watch and turned around to face Avery.

"It's two seventeen in the morning. And it's still storming out there. I think it's best that you overnight here on the couch and make your trip home in the daylight tomorrow?"

Avery nodded, eyeing the cozy, crocheted blanket strewn across the back of the couch and the felt pillow she would have to share with the cat.

" Avery, I have an early morning tomorrow, so I'll ask that you just let yourself out. And I'll see you on Tuesday at two for ... follow-up."

She nodded again.

"To be clear: at my office from two until precisely two fifty," he added, with a mischievous smile.

THIRTY-TWO

In San Diego, May was the month of thick morning fogs, but for early commuters this seasonal annoyance came with a silver lining. Mid-afternoon the sun cracked open the thick grey cover and melted it into aquamarine skies that revealed the shoreline. The beach was in full swing now, Avery could see from her balcony, with ellipses of seagulls in flight, the varying shapes of families scattered on the sand and around the tidal pools, and dogs swimming out into the waters again and again to bring back sticks their owners just couldn't seem to hang on to.

April had been a month of transitions for Avery. Roland moved out, taking only his clothes and every single item in his so-called gentleman's room; she'd insisted on this. Avery hadn't seen him since his return from Victoria. Everything between them was reduced to the bare minimum of texts. Before he found an apartment somewhere in downtown San Diego, he'd stayed with his friend Matt and timed visits to pick up his belongings when he knew Avery would be at work. Roland's shame about his other life was reflected in this complete avoidance of her and in the generous offer sent by his lawyer. He wanted nothing of their La Jolla home or her office property, stating that Avery should keep these comforts of her daily life. It was the least he could do. His only wish was to preserve half of his retirement funds and half of their joint investments.

In this way, Roland had made things easy for her, and Avery was grateful to not have to struggle with selling their home and her beloved office suite. As much as she'd felt herself changing on the inside with all that had happened over these past months, she needed things on the outside to be still and didn't want to submit to the chaos of moving. Admittedly, the house felt empty, but it also felt swept clean. It had been about six weeks since Roland had cleared out his belongings, and Avery kept his office door shut. She planned to have this room renovated into something positive and life-affirming, like an at-home ballet space or art studio; a place to please her senses and wash away any residual ugliness.

The biggest hole in her practice was the absence of Clare. Clare had somehow become the centre of her practice; those never-ending surprises of show and tells, paintings and dreams, defiance and confrontation, interspersed with heartbreaking moments of emotion, recaptured personal history, and insight. Her absence left a question mark about where Clare would go with her life and the baby she was planning to put up for adoption.

May also marked the end of spring and the beginning of summer. Avery felt hopeful about the healing that the next season might bring. She now saw Dr. Mahler once every few weeks—at his office and not at his home—and she was still a regular at Madame Paloma's ballet studio. Avery planned to go there tonight for some personal time. Just last week, she'd invited a friend to her home for a glass of wine, putting out a simple board of cheeses and baguette that required little in the way of effort. She needed to fill her home with new connections and experiences. Nazz and Avery planned to visit each other in July; it'd been enough to explain to her best friend that the divorce was an inevitable final step in a long process of emotional separation and disappointments about not having a baby.

Dr. Mahler remained as the only person to know the full story of Avery, Roland and Clare, and this felt surprisingly comfortable to her. It was as if the jagged pieces of the puzzle had softened and fit together better in the safety of Dr. Mahler's hands, where she could see them, put them away for safekeeping, and find them again whenever she felt that need.

Avery inhaled the fresh ocean air and traced the path of one more seagull before she turned back into her office. She scooped up her ballet bag from the back of her desk chair, swinging it playfully as she walked across the room to open the door.

There he sat in the waiting room, his hands politely folded on his lap, still wearing his wedding band, a picture of patience and regrets. At the crack of the door opening, Roland looked up at her, and she saw the tops of his cheeks reddening above his beard. There seemed to be a few more lines around his eyes and a distinct sadness within their centers. Avery saw it now, the familiarity that occurred to her like a whisper when she first looked into Clare's eyes. She could also see the genetically distinct lines of his finely chiselled brow and nose that joined father and daughter. Clare's wild, curly hair and dimpled smile were all Chloé; their daughter had inherited the best of her parents' features. *I wonder what Clare's baby girl will look like?* Anger toward the man sitting in her waiting room washed over her.

"I needed to return the building key to you," he said, "and … and I wanted to talk to you … just one more time."

Avery hesitated, caught somewhere between surprise, concern and anger, but then her curiosity won.

"I have a few minutes, but then I'll need to leave," she said, setting down her ballet bag near the door. Avery stepped back into the room and lifted her hand to show him to the therapy couch. She saw his eyes hesitating on her bare hand before he lifted himself out of the armchair.

It'd been years since Roland set foot in this room. She remembered how excited he'd been about the purchase of the office suite, how eager he was to help her to set it up *exactly like you've seen it in your head ever since you started to dream about becoming a psychologist.*

CHAPTER THIRTY-TWO

There was no doubt he loved to see her happy, to throw himself into a project for her. She'd always loved that boyish part of him. It was the deeper things, her most important needs—and the needs of Clare and Chloé, it had turned out—where he fell short.

Roland sat down on the couch and Avery took her usual seat in her armchair. Suddenly, she felt like a traitor. Here was the man who'd injured Clare so profoundly, taking up this sacred space where his abandoned daughter had raged and despaired and struggled for months.

"So what is it that you want to talk about, Roland?"

"Before I ... I try to tell you what happened," Roland began, fear in his eyes, "I was wondering ... I was just wondering what you're telling people about what happened to us ... why we're getting divorced?"

"You're worried I'll tell them what you did?" Avery said, feeling anger rising in her chest. "You're worried that I'll tell them that you abandoned your own daughter when she was a little girl after her mother died. And that you hid all of this from me? Is that what you worry I'll tell them?"

She felt her cheeks burning. Avery was shocked by the uncharacteristic meanness she heard in her own words; the sound of someone spitting insult and injury. How ironic. Here she sat on her healing chair, brutally inflicting emotional lacerations. Roland looked down at his clenched hands, barely coping, about to lock down.

She softened. Maybe she should hear his story.

"Look, I'll be honest with you, Roland," she began again. "I'm not planning to tell people about Clare or even Chloé. It's just too ... too horrible, and also there are other people involved who could possibly be hurt ... I don't see how it would help things."

"I ... I'm grateful for that, Avery." The defeated old man who had once been her husband looked torn up but determined to tell his story.

"Chloé was my first love, Avery. All the other parts I did tell you about Ireland are still true. How carefree and innocent that time was for me, just being my own person and finally out from under my dad's thumb and all that family pressure." Roland's upper lip twisted at this thought of his father. "My parents thought it was a childish whim, going to university in the old country like that."

Avery nodded. Roland's love of Ireland was no secret, and she realized now how much of a reprieve it must have been for him to blossom there as his own person, far away from the reaches of his family. No wonder his first true love, maybe his only true love, came from that beautiful place. *What would it feel like to be someone's first and only true love?* No wonder she and Roland never really stood a chance. All these years, even at their wedding, had his family known about Chloé, about Clare? She had to know.

"Please be honest with me now, Roland. I have to understand and rebuild my own life too." Avery hated making herself even remotely vulnerable to Roland, but he nodded and waited for her to speak. She swallowed hard.

"Did your parents know about Chloé? Did they meet her? What the hell happened there? No one in your family has ever even mentioned Chloé to me."

"I hid Chloé from my family for quite a long time. I just wanted to live in my Irish bubble with her. But then I was close to graduating, and so was Chloé. She was a fine artist ..." Roland said, his eyes welling up.

Like mother, like daughter. What if Roland could see Clare's painting and how Chloé's artistry lived on in his daughter? He gruffly wiped away the tears with his sleeve before he continued speaking.

"She was getting a degree in Fine Arts. Something my father sees as a useless degree, by the way. And she was Irish, not American. She had strong opinions that she didn't mind voicing, she was a feminist, and she didn't much care about the establishment. Chloé was a strong, free person."

CHAPTER THIRTY-TWO

Unlike me, at that point in my life? But very much like her daughter Clare, Avery thought.

Roland held his Celtic pendant as he spoke of Chloé, but then he caught himself and put his hands back on his lap.

"And what about Clare? What happened there?" Avery asked. She was beginning to feel like she was an outsider observing this strange conversation between former husband and wife.

Roland's face darkened.

"Chloé got pregnant. We hadn't planned it, but we were really happy about it. It seemed very natural at the time …"

"I see," Avery said, "So there was a time in your life when you felt happy about having a baby?" Did he feel like he was on trial right now? Well, that was too bad for him, she thought childishly. She was off the clock, and she didn't mind casting judgment for once.

"Look, Ave … Avery, I'm trying to tell you what happened, how it happened. I didn't even know you then, but I can see now that the decisions I made, the mistakes I made, followed me into our marriage. I was just trying to make everyone happy, but in the end, really, no one is. You included."

"Me included. So tell me the rest of it. I can't sit here much longer," Avery said. The dark emotions were circling around her. She wanted to scream. *Your decisions, your mistakes, you not telling me all of this before I agreed marry you. And now it's too late. My time for having a baby is up.* But if she said this out loud, she knew she would never know the rest of the story.

"I persuaded Chloé to come to California with me. To meet my family. To have the baby here, so it …."

"*She*, the baby is *she*. Her name is Clare. I saw it on her birth certificate," Avery corrected him. Roland's face dropped in shame.

"Clare was born at a hospital just outside of L.A.," Roland said, his voice drifting to somewhere far away. The sun had set, and the room was slowly becoming darker. Avery felt paralyzed in her chair, unable to get up to turn on the lights or even reach for the table lamp. She was listening to a stranger telling her about a life in which she had no part. At this moment, she finally released from being Roland's wife, and it became easier to listen to the rest of the story. He was just another person telling her his darkest secret, his deepest regret, his constant pain.

"You see, we had to take some distance from San Diego. It wasn't going well. My father didn't like Chloé. She was too outspoken for him. He felt like she had *insinuated herself* into my life, those were his words, that she wanted to become an American, wanted the family's money; for him, there had to be some ulterior motive. It's true that she didn't have much of her own, growing up on a farm with just her mum. Her father passed when she was really young, and they had to make do. Chloé didn't really care about material things. But dad kept pounding away at me. He asked me how I even knew that the baby was mine."

"And finally your father got to you. He made you doubt yourself, the way he always has," Avery said softly into the shadowy room. She knew where the story was going next, but she was going to let him finish. Most likely, this would be the last time they would speak, and the only time he would ever tell anyone all of this.

"He just sucked the joy out of everything for me. Chloé was the first person I'd ever felt confident about. But being back home with my father, my mother who sat like a stone and said nothing to help, I didn't feel strong the way I did in Ireland. In Ireland I was like … Superman or something, sounds silly, I know … I felt so good about myself and Chloé and my life. Back home, I started to doubt myself. My father was like … kryptonite," Roland said. "Can you understand that, Avery?"

She nodded.

"So you asked her to do a DNA test right after Clare was born?"

"Yes; I guess you saw that paperwork. I did, and it was the biggest mistake of my life. You see, I was … I was Chloé's first—I mean, being Catholic and all, she didn't give herself easily. But she gave

CHAPTER THIRTY-TWO

herself completely to me, and I wrecked it." Nausea rose in Avery's gut. Although she already knew the basic facts, she felt like she had just discovered her husband in bed with another woman. Then again, she'd slept with Roland for years with Chloé's pendant around his neck.

"It must've really hurt her, being asked to prove that you were Clare's father."

"I'm so ashamed about it, even now. I didn't find out until later, but she was so upset about it that when she filled out the papers at the hospital for Clare's birth certificate, that she said she didn't know who the father was. Left my name off the form, just like that. She punished me, and I deserved it," Roland said. In the twilight she heard him crying softly.

"I went back to Ireland with her and Clare for a while. Chloé wanted nothing to do with my family, nothing to do with America. We had some good moments, the three of us …."

"Like when you took that photo at Kilkee Beach."

"Yes, that's the moment I've held on to all these years. She loved that photo, too. Chloé's mother encouraged us. She thought we should get married and make the best of it in Ireland, but …"

"But what?" Avery asked. How close had she come to never meeting Roland? To never going through this agony?

"We couldn't get the love back. Chloé couldn't get over what I did. And one day she told me to just go home, to go back where I came from. I remember her words exactly. *You're just not strong enough to be my husband, to be Clare's father. We can't depend on you. I've tried, but I just don't trust you anymore.* And so I left. She got so sick, and I didn't even know it until it was too late. She was right, of course, in what she said. You know she was right, Avery, because you couldn't depend on me, you can't trust me anymore either. I guess that's the end of the story, isn't it?"

So many conflicting emotions. *You're not strong enough to be my husband; you're not strong enough to be the father of my child.* But he was wrong. This wasn't the end of the story yet. Avery reached over to switch on the lamp on the side table. Roland looked surprised as he squinted into the light.

"It's part of the story, Roland. And it does feel better to hear what happened. I can see how you and Chloé couldn't stay together. But it's really not the end of it. What about Clare? You lost Chloé, but Clare lost her mother and her father and then her grandmother. Why didn't you go to her? How could you read that letter from her grandmother and then, later on, from Clare, the letters that you kept in that damned locked up file of yours, and decide not to be involved? I just don't understand how you could do that!" Avery knew she was raising her voice, but how could she not?

Roland had just been more honest about himself and his regrets than he had in thirteen years, but Avery knew that they had reached the end of that new frontier. His eyes darkened, and he was clenching his fists. Suddenly, he looked angry and defensive and put out by his ex-wife's incessant questions.

"It's not my fault that Chloé got that horrible breast cancer that killed her. You've no idea at all what I went through. I took care of Clare in my own way, and I still do. I picked the adoptive parents. Molly and Jim are their names, nice people, and I paid for her education. I made sure that she would hear about the breast cancer so she can protect her own health. And I let her grow up as a nice American girl who doesn't even need to know about Ireland or what happened there. Clare probably hasn't given me another thought!"

"You *read* Clare's letter, and you actually believe she hasn't thought about you? She wrote that letter the first day she could legally try to get in touch with you. And you declined. Weren't you at least a little curious about her?"

"There you go again, Avery. Poking and prodding, violating my privacy. You think you're such a clever psychologist, that you know everything. You're acting like you know Clare, and you don't know her at all. I closed that door, and it was best for everyone involved.

CHAPTER THIRTY-TWO

I knew I wasn't fit to be a father, so I let someone who could do the job. I don't like myself, Avery, in fact I hate myself for everything. Are you happy now?" Roland shouted. He stood up to pace around the room.

"I think it was best for *you*, Roland, convenient for you and your parents. I *do* actually know what people like Clare go through. Losing her mother at such a young age? That's a loss that stays with a person for the rest of her life. But at least you can fill that hole a little, soften its outlines, by knowing you were loved and that your parent was sick and didn't want to leave you. I imagine Clare knows this, wherever she is now. But that your other parent just didn't want you, didn't want to know you, there is no way of beginning to heal from that. Other than realizing that the parent who intentionally abandoned you was fatally flawed, lacked the character required for the job! Like you just said," Avery shouted.

She'd never seen such rage in Roland's face. She wondered whether his father's face twisted just like this when he had laid hands on Roland as a little boy. Roland raised his arms, then dropped them to his sides.

"This was a mistake, too, coming here. Just another mistake in a long line-up of mistakes—you being among them, Avery." He slammed the door so hard behind him that the figurines in her waiting room shuddered.

Avery's hands had stopped shaking and rested again on her lap. The only thing that was different about the door slamming this time was that she knew exactly how to close that door and how to change the locks. She was no longer that girl mired in her grieving family, when each slam of the door had shattered her soul all over again. Sebastian? He would love the strong woman that Avery had become.

THIRTY-THREE

*I*t had crept up on her. In this eighth month of pregnancy, Clare's body no longer felt like her own. All of a sudden, it seemed, there was so much to do, but she felt wiped out and not up to it. Clare sat on her balcony looking out over Fir Avenue's bustle of Sunday morning brunch-seekers in the popular Little Italy district. She'd been over to the café across the street minutes ago to order her usual coffee to go, except it was always a decaf now. She'd messed up on her order last week, requesting a full-on espresso after a bad night's sleep, and her baby had done a vigorous, happy dance in her belly that made Clare sweat and worry about an early arrival. Today she sipped on her decaf, her appointment book filled with to-do lists balanced on that "top shelf" of her gargantuan baby belly. Clare wasn't a to-do list type of person, but these days, she found herself losing track of details if she didn't write them down as soon as they occurred to her. She'd read about "baby brain," but found it insulting to women, even if it seemed annoyingly true based on her own experience. The week ahead was full. *Meet lawyer to sign paperwork. Print out final list of baby equipment and instructions. Finish painting.*

Clare came back inside her apartment and sat down on the stool facing her easel. Pinned to the unfinished painting was a photo of Jim holding Clare's hand as they were coming out of the lake onto the beach near her grandmother Martha's cottage. Clare, eight years old, was wearing a yellow bathing suit and a shy smile on her face.

CHAPTER THIRTY-THREE

Jim, too, was smiling, looking completely content to be where he was with his little girl. Molly had snapped this photo from where she sat on the picnic bench, waiting to give them lunch. Molly was surprised and *delighted*, she'd said, when Clare asked her to send a copy of the photo but to keep it secret from Jim.

Tacked to the left-hand side of her canvas was a snapshot of the Lane family coat of arms she'd researched to learn about Jim's proud Scottish ancestry. How fitting: the red lion at the center of the coat of arms meant courage, which was needed bigtime to take on a complicated little girl like her, Clare chuckled to herself. The whitish silver shield behind the lion symbolized peace and sincerity, which described Jim to a T. The black background of the emblem with green and orange leafed vines showed constancy. It was the realization of Jim's quiet and patient constancy in her life that brought tears to Clare's eyes; she was on the final tiny brushstrokes of transferring the coat of arms onto his knee-length swimming *trunks*, as he liked to call them. The rage she felt about Bio-Dad and that spilled into her relationships with men had blinded her to the humble goodness of Jim until she'd had a chance to go over all of that with Avery. Not all men are untrustworthy and unreliable, and Jim was proof positive of that.

Clare felt under her dress and ran the back of her hand lightly along the soft skin on her lower belly. There wasn't a hint of the many segments of the long scab that had formed over the wound she'd inflicted. When given a chance, without picking at oneself and reopening old wounds, the human body had a remarkable ability to heal itself. Clare needed to give herself that chance.

Clare took a photo of her finished painting and texted it to Molly, labeling it "top secret." Her phone rang immediately.

"Clare?" Molly said, "Your painting's gorgeous. It's just perfect with the coat of arms running up Jim's leg. The way you captured the movement of the fabric as he's walking up the beach with you makes the crest look almost like a flag in the wind. I just love it. Your painting's going to make him cry when you're home for his birthday. And you already made me cry, seeing your shy smile on the canvas. Beautiful memory. You're still coming for Jim's birthday, aren't you?"

Molly's voice suddenly sounded very vulnerable and Clare wasn't about to leave her hanging. "Of course, I'm coming, Molly. I booked my bus and I was hoping to stay for the couple of weeks in July with Jim's birthday in the middle," Clare said, "if it's ok to stay for that long?" It was Clare's turn for a shot of vulnerability.

"By all means. I'm thrilled to have time to catch up and for you to have a nice rest at the lake. The family will be so happy to see you when they come for Jim's birthday. You could come … right now if you wanted."

"I'm a bit busy in June, but I'm good to go in mid-July," Clare said. Understatement. A bit busy giving birth to her daughter and handing her off to Avery.

Clare's unshakeable confidence in Avery—that she would come to her senses and show up on the due date—shocked her at that moment. Then again, Clare had seen the moment of Avery holding the newborn in her arms in a recurrent dream. She felt the same sting of tears now that she did when she'd woken from that dream the first time.

"Yeah … I've got to finish my schoolwork and some other unfinished stuff," Clare stammered. It wasn't a lie; she was just leaving out details.

"I understand, dear. School comes first," Molly said, "but then we'll have a lovely time together. It's been a long time since you've been home for a good stretch of time."

"It's been a long time, Molly, too long. I'd better go, but I'll see you soon," Clare said.

All these hormones were turning her into a mush ball, she thought, as she brushed another tear from her cheek. Or would she just stay this way after the baby was born? Unthinkable. But maybe she was just going to stay a kinder person who allowed herself feelings other

CHAPTER THIRTY-THREE

than anger. That was Avery's influence on her. The thought of Avery set off another watershed. She missed Avery, but it wouldn't be long now until she saw her again. She just had to stay positive.

PART V:
Summer Finale

THIRTY-FOUR

The garden lanterns hugging the cobblestone path from the parking lot to the ballet studio were just starting to glow among the yellows, oranges, and pinks of Madame Paloma's fragrant wild roses. Avery walked through the reluctant dusk of the summer solstice. As the tall arches of the studio doors came into view, she reached for the nape of her neck, her skin warm and moist to the touch of her fingertips. She undid the clasp of her necklace, releasing the studio key into her hand; she felt its reassuring shape and weight, as she had countless times over the past months. The night breeze cooled her neck and sent a shiver down her spine.

A rush of memories rattled through her, marking all that happened since last year's summer solstice. She felt her hair softly brushing across the tops of her shoulders, realizing only then that her head was shaking slowly back and forth in disbelief. Just last summer, Avery still held hope to conceive a baby with Roland, or at least to adopt a child with him. This possibility was lost absolutely. For a long time after it had all been taken away from her, she had felt only that body-gripping anger, the disappointment, and the seemingly never-ending sadness; intense feelings that heated her to the core until finally that all-consuming fever broke and she could see new possibilities previously hidden from view.

She felt clarity about her new life; she could follow her instincts and make her plans without consideration for a stranger waiting at home. Roland lived in an apartment somewhere in downtown San

CHAPTER THIRTY-FOUR

Diego, and she was unlikely to hear from him again. Avery understood why Roland couldn't talk to her: he would drown in shame, regret, self-damnation. He'd never learned to cope with such uncomfortable feelings. Nor could Avery look at Roland without seeing him through Clare's eyes and all the pain that came with that. There was nothing to discuss and no good feelings left.

Clare had told her that June twenty-first was her due date when they last met, three months ago. During the last few therapy sessions, Avery had encouraged Clare to lean on a support person in preparation for the baby's arrival, but Clare was determined to go through the birth on her own and to select adoptive parents herself. *Especially now that my first choice of adoptive mother didn't come through for me,* Clare had finally said to shut down the topic. The words still stung. Avery had wished all along that Molly would be at Clare's side during labour, but she also understood that her headstrong young client wanted to make her decisions unfettered by others' emotional reactions.

After therapy had finished, Avery had heard nothing from Clare, nothing at all. During those final minutes, the expectant young woman's hands enfolded in hers, Avery wished Clare well as both of them fought back their tears. Avery had expected at least a few telephone messages or surprise appearances. This three-month silence since their last therapy session was strangely unnerving. It wasn't just that she missed Clare, or that anything had changed about the circumstances that prevented her from adopting Clare's baby, but that, somehow, it felt like the offer for Avery to adopt the baby was no longer on the table. She had no idea what Clare was thinking, whether there was an excited couple waiting for the baby girl's arrival or whether plans had changed altogether. The fact that Avery was no longer in the picture still disturbed her, like a story that had slipped away from her when it wasn't quite finished. Avery was grateful she hadn't discovered Roland's secret until after her therapy with Clare was finished, that she'd not had to hide the truth from her client.

Avery knew something was different at the ballet studio even before she pushed open the unlocked door. Madame Paloma stood with her back turned to Avery, one leg on the barre extended in the perfection and elegance only she could muster. White candles framed the perimeter of the room, their flames reflected in the mirrors and windows. Avery recognized the haunting melody of Swan Lake, its unmistakable depiction of human longing. The musical notes took Avery back to her childhood ballet lessons, when each young girl moved in unison and caught elusive glimpses of herself one day dancing the lead of this iconic ballet—as only a very few turned out to do, but Madame Paloma had been one of them, in Paris at the age of seventeen. Tonight, Madame Paloma's hair was knotted at the nape of her neck, and she was wearing a simple chalk-white ballet dress with old-world details of tiny pearls embroidered into a pattern around the waist. In the candlelight, she stood ageless in an era that was both uniquely her own and also a part of the collective unconscious shared by generations of dancers who had felt the same music, the same painfully beautiful sadness.

Did Madame Paloma wear the costume in which she danced her final performance the night before she defected from the Czech Republic? Was tonight a tribute to her parents and grandmother left behind, that she danced out each year on the night of the summer solstice? Suddenly, Avery felt awkward, especially because Madame Paloma surely must have heard the door opening, but still hadn't turned around to see who was standing there.

"It is fine, Ah-verry, you will come in now and warm up your muscles. I already know about the many things that 'appen in this room, and I always find new surprises. Tonight we will dance together for what we feel. You will follow along with me and experience a new ... *liberté*, it will help you and it's good for me, too. No words will be *necéssaire* ..." Madame Paloma effortlessly placed her other leg on the barre and began to slide it along the smooth wood until it could travel no farther, and it was time to bend at the waist and for her arms and head to extend toward the white ribbons on her toe shoe.

Avery shrugged her shoulders, her long, white cotton sweater sliding off to reveal the dancer's body she had resurrected over the past year. Avery dropped her canvas shoulder bag to the floor, along with any vestiges of self-consciousness and self-doubt remaining from her childhood as a ballet student. Her only purpose was to take her position at the barre beside Madame Paloma. Without a word, she followed her beloved teacher, and the teachers that had come before Madame Paloma, through the stretches, *pliés, rondes des jambes*—all of what was needed to limber the body and prepare the soul for what would happen next.

It could've been ten fifteen or midnight; Avery had no way of knowing, no idea at all, nor did this seem of any importance, when Madame Paloma invited Avery to the middle of the dance floor. By then, all ties with Avery's sense of time and place had been altered by the rhythm of the music and bodily movements. Madame Paloma arranged Avery into first position, softening her arms, neck, even her cheeks with breezy brushes of her fine hands. When she was satisfied, Madame Paloma raised her right index finger like a cross over her slightly smiling lips. Then she disappeared behind the stereo system. When she reappeared, her feet were bare like Avery's and the room was silent.

Avery could smell the scent of French perfume as Madame Paloma came to stand behind her, her arms gently encircling but not touching Avery's waist. They stood there silently, contentedly, until the music started again; it was still Swan Lake but a more lyrical version. Avery closed her eyes and felt each classical guitar note echo inside of her. The lightest touch of Madame Paloma hands over her arms told her it was time to surrender.

They wove and whirred through space and time over the dance floor, the room seeming to darken and the candlelight luminously pulsing to the music. When their arms extended upward and their hands hesitated over their faces, dark elegant shapes against candlelight, Avery no longer felt any separation from Madame Paloma. It was as if they were a unison of souls that met somewhere at the intersection of their painful memories and hopeful futures.

The crossed arms struck out to punctuate the beginning of a series of full-body swings extending from one corner of the room to its diagonal opposite. Avery's body had never moved more gracefully, more passionately, more deliberately, more effortlessly. The room was a blur of darkness and glimmering lights. As if possessed, Avery moved across the room to examine its expanse. She felt the white softness and movement of wings encompassing her, saving her before it all disappeared.

And then she saw *her*. The golden child was standing in the corner, her rose gold mottled face and body like a perfect portrait. The child's face was downcast, the shadows catching in the eyelashes of her averted eyes and reaching to accentuate her plump lips. She raised her little girl's arms toward Avery, beckoning her to come to her again. There was no fear, no trepidation, no considerations left to contemplate. When the golden child's face lifted and her grey-green eyes opened to declare her love for Avery, there was nothing left to do but to run to her.

Avery's eyelashes flickered, and she saw that sunlight was streaming over the wooden floor to where she lay in the ballet studio. She smelled Madame Paloma's perfume coming from the softness underneath her head. Had she slept here all night? She sat up to see the ballet studio in the beauty of the early morning light. There was no hint of the candles that she'd envisioned. Avery reached for the neatly folded cashmere ballet sweater, the scented pillow she knew belonged to Madame Paloma. The sheer *noncomprehensionada* of the moment baffled her: Avery had no idea whether she was awake, asleep, or dreaming, or whether that was even important. Yet there

CHAPTER THIRTY-FOUR

was still the hint of classical guitar notes pulsing softly through her body, like the gentle clarity of a rhythm that was meant to guide and encourage her, and at that moment, she knew that there was no question about what direction her life would take.

THIRTY-FIVE

"Yes, Dr. Frontiera." The receptionist at Sharp Hospital for Women and Newborns was only too eager to help the busy doctor on the telephone. "We have Clare Lane on Unit 12B in the recovery room. Let me just read the notes ... it was a C-section in the end, but new mum and baby girl are fine. How kind of you to check in on your patient on the weekend!"

"That's good news; thank you." Third time *was* a charm. With each call to one of San Diego's maternity hospitals, Avery had become more facile at exploiting her professional title to gain access to the patient registries.

BBC Siri, unflappable even this early in the morning, was speaking to her now. "Mind left and merge onto California Fifty-Two East. You'll arrive at your destination in twenty-three minutes." *A lot can happen in twenty-three minutes*, Avery thought, stepping hard on the gas.

The new adoptive parents Clare had chosen after Avery had declined could be arriving at the hospital. Clare could fall in love with her baby and not want to give her up. Avery could be stopped for speeding and reckless driving, she realized, as the driver of the car she had passed too aggressively leaned on his horn and gave her the finger. She slowed down to a mere twenty miles over the posted speed limit.

Minutes from her destination, the pretty, flying-kite logo of Rady Children's Hospital came into view. It was the place where, fourteen

CHAPTER THIRTY-FIVE

years since, she had spent her residency year. This was the hospital where she had discovered her passion for helping children during the same exciting year that marked her engagement to Roland. How ironic that this place had held all the possibilities of her future and stood next door to the women's hospital where Clare had just given birth to Roland's granddaughter.

"You have arrived at your destination." Avery didn't look back to lock her car doors as she rushed past the imposing white stork statue, a blue bag with white polka dots hanging from its beak. She was striding now through the sliding glass doors of the hospital's entrance. Hospital poster ads awash with babies and smiling new parents streamed past her as she ran through the lobby of the hospital.

Avery pressed the elevator button impatiently. She had to take a step back when the doors finally opened and a sea of blue scrubs poured out. Avery hit the button for the twelfth floor and took a deep breath. "Floor number four, piso numero cuatro." An unshaven, new-father type gripping a Starbucks unpeeled himself from the back wall of the elevator and exited much too slowly for Avery's liking.

She thought back to the last time she saw Clare, her hands, tiny splatters of turquoise paint on porcelain skin, resting on her pregnant belly. That was almost three months ago ..."Floor number twelve, Piso numero doce." Startled, she stepped out of the elevator.

The savvy expression on the face of "Nurse Kimberly" at the gates of Unit 12B told Avery that this was no place for imposters.

"Can I help you?" she asked, barely looking up from her computer screen.

"I'm here for Clare Thomas Lane. My name is Avery Frontiera," was all she could manage.

"Hmm ... Let me check the file."

Suddenly the expression on the nurse's face melted. She turned to Avery with a smile.

"Yes, of course, Avery. I see that Clare identified you as her next of kin when she was admitted yesterday morning. She said you might not be able to get here until today. Thanks for coming … She's been by herself until now."

"Next of kin?" Avery stumbled, "Yes, of course. May I see her?"

"Follow me," Nurse Kimberley said. "She's out of the recovery room now and back on the unit. She's a little mysterious, your Clare. Didn't want to say much about her family. She gave us some serious attitude, too, about her right to privacy when we inquired about family supports but, you know, during labour we forgive everything."

That's my Clare, Avery thought. She pictured her, even in the throes of labour, refusing to bend to the authorities. But how could Clare have been so certain that Avery would come, when Avery didn't even know it until she woke up in the ballet studio this morning? Or maybe Avery had always known. Clare naming Avery as her *next of kin* was dancing circles around her heart. That must be a good sign. Clare never stopped surprising her. She'd already challenged most everything Avery thought she knew about herself and now Clare was changing Avery's beliefs about how families are made.

THIRTY-SIX

*A*very hesitated in the doorway of Clare's hospital room. Clare was lying on her side, facing away from the door. The morning sunlight, filtering into the room through the palm fronds outside her window, cast a soft pattern of light spots on Clare's blanket. Clare's body was moving peacefully in the rhythm of sleep, her hair looking damp and sticky on the white pillow. A hospital bassinet was parked beside Clare's bed. Avery couldn't see inside from where she was standing. Her heart leaped into her throat with anticipation.

Avery tiptoed into the hospital room, grateful that it was a private and she wouldn't have to navigate strangers. She clasped her hands and pressed them hard against her chest in a desperate plea to contain herself. The rapid drumbeat from within was so palpable that for a split second, Avery considered that the sound of her heart would wake up the new mother.

Coming closer, she saw a sign inserted into the slot at the foot of the bassinet. *Baby Chloé.* She couldn't wait a second longer and stretched her neck forward to peer inside. Two tiny feet with creases around the ankles protruded from a soft peach jumper. Like Clare, baby Chloé was sleeping on her side, her little fist resting on pudgy cheek made of fine velvet skin, white with a touch of rose. A dollop of chocolate-coloured hair circled around the top of her head until it came to a fluffy peak. Mesmerized by the gentle movement of Chloé's breath, Avery leaned in a little closer. She closed her eyes and

CHAPTER THIRTY-SIX

inhaled the newborn scent, an intoxicating mix of fresh milk, spring rose, and almonds. She loved her already.

"You can pick her up, you know."

Avery looked up to see Clare reaching for the railing of her bed and slowly turning over to face in Avery's direction. She grimaced and placed her other hand to support her abdomen.

"Chloé is so incredibly beautiful. How are *you* feeling, Clare?"

"Well, I won't be doing any sit-ups today, I can tell you that much," Clare said, still grimacing, but then her face became serious.

"I want to see you picking her up. I've pictured it in my head for a really long time. So have you, I'm guessing ... Dr. Frontiera."

"Call me Avery. You're right. I feel like I'm stepping into my dream, but it's real, isn't it?"

Clare nodded and smiled.

Avery bent over the bassinette and carefully slid her hands and forearms under the tiny bundle. With tears filling her eyes, she carefully raised Chloé. It was true. She'd fantasized, hoped for, lost hope for, this moment. *I am a new mother too*, Avery thought, as she felt her lips curling into a smile.

"She looks good on you. Like I imagined it. I hope you're ok with Chloé for her name. It would mean a lot to me. You know ... in her memory," Clare said, her eyes filling with tears.

"Chloé is perfect. Now how do you feel about Sébastienne for a middle name?" The middle name had just sprung into her head. How nice it felt to be speaking freely to Clare. How nice it felt to be speaking from heart to mouth, without any deliberation or weighing of her words.

Clare looked surprised by the choice of middle name, but then her face brightened and she raised her index finger to make a point.

"Now I remember where I heard that name. It was this amazing woman I learned about. Her name was Sébastienne Guyot. She was a kick-ass engineer in France, like in the 1700s or something, and she designed a super aerodynamic airplane. She moved the winds in her own way, come to think of it," Clare said with a smirk. "It's all coming back to me now from when I took this course on *The First Feminists,*" she continued. "So, yes, I think it's perfect. But ... but what does the name mean to you ... Avery?"

Clare pressed the remote to lift up the head of the bed. She grimaced again as she levered herself into a more upright position.

"My brother's name was Sebastian. He ... died as a teenager. He meant everything to me growing up. Still does," Avery said. She surprised herself with her newfound candour, but she stopped short of spilling the heaviness of the full story into this moment of new life.

"Sucks that he died, then," Clare said.

Clare's eyes beheld a tenderness that Avery hadn't seen in her before and instantly made her feel cared for. Clare's cheeks reddened before she pressed on past the softness.

"So ... we've got two dead people we loved remembered in her name. I like that. Will her last name be Frontiera?"

Absolutely not, Avery thought, feeling her body tensing despite the soft loveliness in her arms. Baby Chloé yawned without opening her eyes, her little arm and fist tremoring along with the motion.

"Well, Clare, I'm getting divorced. So I'm going to go back to my maiden name ... Howard," Avery said, "So ... she would be called Chloé Sebastiénne Howard. To me that sounds strong and beautiful and honourable. What do you think?"

"I'm totally cool with it," Clare said. "So listen, we have stuff to talk about. Sit here," she added, pointing to the foot of her bed.

They did have a lot to talk about, but really, it turned out to be Clare who did most of the talking. Avery could tell that Clare had been planning all of this for a long time. Ok, *first things first,* the new mother said; she now had all the info she needed to fill out the government form to apply for Chloé's birth certificate. Once again, the bio-dad was *unidentified*—seems to run in the family, she said. But *not to worry,* there were only a handful of possibilities of potential fathers, and the young men she picked were always very

CHAPTER THIRTY-SIX

nice-looking and somewhat smart. Well, as far as men go, anyway. *Alright*, Clare went on, she'd give her adoption lawyer Avery's name and contact info, so all the tedious paperwork could be done. Avery dutifully texted her full name, address, and cell phone number to Clare for this purpose.

All previous boundaries between therapist and client were dissolving before their eyes like an Alka Seltzer tablet; once it hit the water, there was no going back. The lawyers' fees were easily covered by her trust fund, Clare continued; this was the one thing her bio-dad was good for and she may as well use his *guilt money*. Avery nodded. At that moment, she remembered Roland's face disappearing into the dusk, that evening he had shown up in her waiting room. He'd insisted that he'd cared for Clare in his own way. The trust fund must be a part of this.

"And … when were you thinking that I would bring Chloé home … to my house, Clare?" Avery asked, wondering how she would ever be able to let this little being out of her arms again, even for the shortest time.

"I thought about it a lot. I think you should take her today. I'm obviously not going to breastfeed and … and, although I want to be in Chloé's life a little bit, I don't want to get too attached. I want her to just bond with you as her mother," Clare continued, her lip quivering slightly. "The nurse has been helping me to start bottle-feeding, and she wrote down the name of the best kind of formula. I need to stay in the hospital for a couple of days, but Chloé is fine to be discharged by the end of the day. They're gonna give her one more really good look when the doctor comes by, like around three o'clock."

"Ok," was all that Avery could manage. She couldn't think of a moment in her entire life when she'd felt so overwhelmed, so dumbfounded, yet so utterly happy.

"Yeah, I know it's a lot, but I have complete faith in you … Dr. … I mean, Avery. I'll text you the basic list of things you need to go and buy today before you come back to pick her up. I've had more time to think about the details than you."

"Umm … Ok … Yes, that is completely true. So I'd better get hopping. Do you want to hold Chloé now?"

Clare hesitated. "Maybe just put her back in her crib. When Chloé wakes up, I'll get the nurse to bring a bottle. I'm going to catch a bit more sleep."

Avery lowered the precious bundle back into the bassinet. Was this really her *daughter?*

"Clare, thank you so much. I'll put my heart, my everything, into being a good mother. And I love that we'll stay in touch, that Chloé will know you. And that you and I'll stay connected."

Clare nodded, her eyes filling with tears. She waved Avery out of the room now, and turned her head away.

Avery let Nurse Kimberley know she'd be back to pick up Chloé.

"That sounds like a good plan. Clare told us it would happen like this. I wish every young woman we see here were as sensible as this one!"

As soon as Avery got back into her car, she instructed Siri to make a call.

"Nazz, you have to come a few days early. I … I have a baby girl!" How much simpler life becomes when you just ask for what you need. And how absolutely brilliant life is when you get what you always wanted, regardless of the long list of complications that would be certain to follow.

THIRTY-SEVEN

In one smooth motion, Roland slid out of the cool dark of Redfield's Sports Bar on to the crowded sidewalk of San Diego's Market Street. The midsummer sunlight so late in the afternoon caught him off guard, and he squinted before settling his Ray-Bans on the bridge of his nose. The details of the business deal nailed down just before lunch were stored on his iPad, inside the leather satchel slung over his shoulder. After lunch, he and his newly minted business partner tackled a long line-up of craft beers, tequila shots, and perfect Padre pitches broadcast over the large screen television. The lingering scent of lime emanated from his fingers as he massaged the fault lines of a headache.

He headed northeast on Market Street toward the Gaslamp District, his eyes hidden behind extra-dark lenses and his hands buried in empty pockets. Accustomed to walking home to his downtown bachelor pad, he told himself that he didn't miss driving his Jeep back out from the city to the La Jolla hills. *She* was probably sitting on the patio overlooking the La Jolla shoreline at this very moment, sipping a glass of chilled pinot grigio, ruminating about the deal-breaker secret he'd kept from her all these years. This image disturbed him; he massaged his temples and walked more swiftly to escape the impact of his thoughts.

Roland's quickened steps gave way to a full-out run, so that he almost missed his left turn onto Fifth Avenue. He caught himself just in time to zig-zag through traffic and land safely on the sidewalk.

CHAPTER THIRTY-SEVEN

Out of breath and nauseous from the heavy mix of emotions and hangover headache, he leaned over with hands placed above knees and took several deep breaths, his head lowered to catch the nauseating dizziness.

Roland unfolded himself gingerly and stood up to absorb his surroundings. He looked across the street at the high-arched glass doors and copper tiled patio of the familiar Seasurfers Restaurant. Two elegantly suited doormen bookended the entrance to welcome guests to the popular eatery. Still catching his breath, he observed those lucky enough to have secured a patio table. Before he could make sense of what he was seeing, a visceral shock emanated from his gut and shot down his suddenly elasticized legs.

Across the street, behind the wrought iron, half-fence of the patio, he saw her slight back, clad in her favourite black sweater, the shoulder-length waves of auburn hair unmistakably hers. She was sitting on a stool, intently leaning over something, maybe her purse or some shopping. With tenderness that was uniquely hers, she slowly returned to an upright position. But she didn't stop there. Her shoulders engaged and then her arms rose upward until, like a slow sun rising, a roundish orb of something floated over her head. He couldn't make out the sounds, but the softness of motion and gummy smile was enough to tell the love story of a mother and child.

She slowly pulled the baby downward and then in toward her chest until it disappeared from his view. Mesmerized by her swaying back, he felt a love for her deeper than at any time during their marriage. She was in her element now and, however she'd pulled this off, there was no role left for him to play in her life.

Just as he was about to turn away, his attention was caught by the flurry of a young woman with striking curls of ginger hair hurrying toward the door of the restaurant. She dismissed the doormen with the wave of her hand, leaving them open-mouthed as she disappeared into the restaurant. He thought about an expression he'd not heard for many years and had almost forgotten. This fine young lass was a true *windmaker*.

Automatically, his right hand emerged from his jacket pocket, moved upward to his throat, and enveloped the Celtic knot on his silver necklace. As he squeezed it tightly in his hand, he felt a slow procession of tears tracing his cheeks.

Just then, the windmaker came back into view, now swiftly moving through the tables closest to the front windows and striding out onto the patio. What the …? The lass stopped in front of *her* table, and the aloof face of the windmaker melted into a familiar, loving smile. The last thing he saw was the baby being passed into the windmaker's arms, and another round of kisses landed on the cherub's chubby cheeks. "*Slainté, mo chailín álainn,*" he whispered, his Irish spirit rising up for a final salute to his beautiful girls, good health to his beautiful girls. Without another word, he turned his back, once again, and walked in the opposite direction.

The End

Dedicated to the memory of

KERRY ANN DOYLE

JULY 30, 1958 – DECEMBER 8, 2019

MARION EHRENBERG is a Canadian psychologist, professor, and writer.

Marion has been practicing psychotherapy for over twenty-five years. She earned a Ph.D. in Clinical Psychology from Simon Fraser University and served as Director of Clinical Training at the University of Victoria. She has published extensively on her research on diverse families.

Marion has cultivated her lifelong love of literature into a creative writing practice through a certificate program, workshops, and mentorship. Her experiences as a psychologist uniquely inform her fictional depictions of the human psyche, mental health, and suicide. For more information, please visit www.marionehrenberg.com.